FALL FROM EARTH

a novel by
Matthew Johnson

 Bundoran Press
Publishing House

This is a work of fiction. The characters, incidents, and dialogues are products of the author's imagination and are not to be construed as real. Any resemblance to actual events or persons, living or dead, is entirely coincidental.

Cover Illustration: L.W. Perkins

Published in Canada by
Bundoran Press
4378 1st Ave
Prince George, BC Canada
V2M 1C9
www.bundoranpress.com
Printed in Canada

Johnson, Matthew, 1972-
Fall From Earth / Matthew Johnson;
cover illustration by L.W. Perkins

ISBN 978-0-9782052-4-9

I. Title

PS8631.E7336F34 2009   jC813'.6   C2009-904091-3

This book is for Megan, of course.

CHAPTER ONE

"Planetfall in ninety seconds," the computer said.

The falling pod hit atmosphere, shook violently as the air pushed back against it. Any items the convicts had left unsecured bounced from wall to wall in smaller and smaller pieces; the pod itself seemed nearly as fragile, groaning from the stress. There was no guessing how old it was, part of a dropship probably built for the Corp Wars almost two double-dozen years ago. Of course, things aged more slowly in space, as Shi Jin knew. Her Nine Dragons, the ships she and Griffin had salvaged and used to start their rebellion, had been as old as this. She had studied enough poetry at the Academy to know irony when she saw it.

Jin closed her eyes, tried to relax before the landing thrusters kicked in. At thirty, her body was not quite as compliant as it once had been, but going limp was something it could still do. She tensed and relaxed her muscles from head to feet. Her grey hempen coveralls marked her for a convict, the black badge pinned to them for a traitor, and with the next ship not due for five years there was no chance of escape.

For as long as anyone could remember, most criminals had been conscripted into the Fleet, given the hardvack or Nospace jobs that warped genes and minds. She had changed all that. Most of the Fleet people who had sided with her during the rebellion had been just those draftees, people who had seen the Borderless Empire's failings firsthand, and now it was not considered safe to let convicts serve on Fleet ships. Instead they were used to prepare planets for colonization, clearing land and building roads, houses and sewers. If things had been different she might have come here ten or twenty years later, a Fleet officer given a grant of land at the end of a distinguished career. But things had not been different, and it was her inability to pretend they were that had made her rebel, led her here. Despite everything, she did not think she would want to trade places with any version of herself that had made a different choice.

The roar of the landing thrusters was so loud Jin couldn't hear the other convicts screaming. Minutes later, the pod touched down with a shock, throwing her against her restraints. There was another rumble as the pod lurched a few degrees to the side, then silence.

"Planetfall achieved," the computer said at last. The restraints opened with a click and Jin and her cellmates rose unsteadily to meet their future.

In the ship above Griffin sighed, remembering his last conversation with Jin before the ship made orbit. "You don't have to do this," he had said, just before she boarded the pod. "If you stay, no one will be able to do anything about it."

He could not come with her, of course: having lived his whole life in zero-gee, he would probably not even survive the landing if he tried. But there was nothing keeping her from staying on the ship.

Jin turned away. "I know. But we're a month away from any other Empire world here. I can make new plans, find a way off this rock—"

He reached out to hold her shoulders. "Jin, it's over. If they thought there was anything more we could do, they wouldn't have let us live."

"They didn't think I could do anything the first time, either. This could be exactly the right place for me to be."

He shook his head, his shaggy brown hair and beard trailing slowly behind without gravity to keep them in line. "I wouldn't count on the other convicts lining up to join you. Most of these people are dissidents and petty crooks, not revolutionaries."

"You've never given up on me before. Don't start now."

The landing pod's airlock had opened then, the countdown to release begun. She had turned to look at him again and kissed him lightly on the cheek. "I'll be in touch. The pods have comm units so..."

He had nodded, pushed himself away, the reaction pushing her gently into the pod. She was right. Fool that he was, he was caught in her orbit. "Take care, plyemyanik."

Jin stood up, felt her legs fail beneath her, victims of more than a month at zero-gee. Steadying herself against the wall she moved slowly out of the room, leaving her three cellmates to find their planet legs and clean themselves off. She headed for the airlock, impatient to see her new prison. A few of the other convicts were already out of their cells, hunger and gravity conspiring to make their steps slow and unsteady. She ignored them, stepped into the 'lock and waited for it to cycle. A sour, rotten smell reached her as the outer door hissed open, overwhelming the stale recycled air.

They had landed in a long, broad valley bordered by hills on one side and a wide river on the other. All around were jagged blades of a stiff brown grass, and as the ground rose to the hills on the horizon it was covered with hundreds of identical, stunted trees. The rotten smell was almost overpowering now, the sky above a sickly yellow.

Turning her head, Jin saw the other three pods scattered across the valley. She set off for the closest of them, about a li away, a few minutes' walk. The grass, as sharp and stiff as it looked, tore through the legs of her coveralls and drew blood. Halfway between the pods she began to feel dizzy, and sucked more air in. Her vision was starting to blur, her lungs to burn; she stumbled and felt the grass slice through the skin of her knee. How far was it to the pod—a hundred paces?

She tried to control her breathing, forced herself to keep going. Up ahead the pod's airlock was opening. She had no breath to spare but had to warn them to stay inside. No sound came out when she opened her mouth, and before she could do anything else the world went grey and slapped her, hard.

Jin opened her eyes, fought to focus on the figure standing over her. It was an older man, in his late fifties or early sixties, with very short white-blond hair. As he leaned closer, she saw where shreds of plaskin had eroded around his right eye, revealing a shiny metal socket and camera lens.

"Are you hurt?" he asked.

Jin fought for breath to speak. "Air…airlocks, close…not enough oxygen…"

"Yes, I know," the older man said. He sat down next to her, helped her sit up. "We've let all the pods know to stay sealed." He paused, leaned closer. "My name is Father Theou, by the way. Heresy."

She pointed to the black badge pinned to her coveralls: "Shi Jin. Treason." There had been no question of hiding her badge; she needed it to get her food rations, and her grey hempen coveralls had no pockets in which to keep it. It wasn't really necessary to have badges to mark them as convicts—with the next ship not due for five years, there was no chance of escape—but then, the real purpose of the badges was not to let others know they were criminals. It was to make sure they knew.

Father Theou nodded. At this distance, Jin could see his implant clearly enough to see the tiny character *Ti'en*, heaven, stamped on it; his mark, she supposed. "I thought as much—you look rather like the actor who played you in your trial."

"I didn't see it. How was yours?"

"Very informative. I confess I wasn't going to watch, but I wanted to know how they'd come up with a recantation for me." He smiled. "At any rate, we have more important things to discuss."

Jin stood, slowly. "The atmosphere. We can't—"

"It's not quite so bad as that," Father Theou said. He was keeping his voice low and level, trying to calm her. "I suspect your collapse had as much to do with your being hungry and unused to gravity as with the lack of oxygen. A few other people have been outside exploring since you arrived. The air is thin, and there's something in it our bodies don't like—probably whatever it is that makes it stink so much—but we should adapt in time."

"We'll need to generate more oxygen to get that far," Jin said. "And there's no way we can terraform this place. They just sent us with basic construction equipment, not oxygenators."

"Perhaps there was a gwai in the first survey team's data, giving the Colonization Office the wrong information. We'll know soon enough."

"What do you mean?"

"Didn't I tell you? The Colonial Magistrate is on his way. He should have answers to some of your questions."

"I hope so," Jin said, wondering what kind of incompetent a civil servant would have had to be to land this assignment. Being sent to a place like this was almost as much of a punishment for the Magistrate as it was for the convicts.

She turned to the airlock, looked out through its porthole. Outside,

10

a young man wearing the blue and gold silk robes of the Soft Church was helping an old man walk over to the pod. Each was carrying a pen-sized breather they brought to their mouths every few minutes, like the one Father Theou had taken from the pod's kitbox to rescue her. The younger man stopped regularly to swear at the sharp grass tearing at his legs. The older man was wearing standard convict-grey coveralls but did not have a badge showing his crime. Instead, he wore the stylized bowl of the Colonization Office pinned to his chest. It was silver, marking him for a Magistrate.

Jin leaned against the porthole, trying to get a better look at the old man. As he came nearer to the airlock, she saw his face.

"Thank you for coming," Father Theou said, helping the older man inside and giving him a new air puffer. "Magistrate Linden, welcome. And your name, Brother—?"

"Bennett. Sims, Brother Bennett Sims," the young man said awkwardly. He was tall, with light brown hair cut close to his skull; his face was red from exertion, and the dozen small cuts on his legs were dripping blood on the carpet.

Father Theou nodded and smiled at the young adelfos. The creed they had each been taught told them to embrace the similar: best to do that now, and hope Bennett might see past the white heresy badge that separated them. After all, the way Theou saw it, the Church had split from him, not the other way around. "You've no doubt noticed, this world is not what we expected," Father Theou said.

Bennett nodded, and turned to Linden. "Magistrate, what do you—that is, what can we do to meet our new terraforming needs?"

For a moment Linden said nothing. It seemed to Father Theou as though the Magistrate was not fully there. Something about Linden, he could see, had made Jin furious: she was shooting him daggers and avoiding his glance by turns, but to all evidence Linden saw none of this, staring blankly ahead as though seeing ghosts.

"I don't know," Linden finally said.

"I think Magistrate Linden is saying—" the young adelfos, Bennett, began haltingly.

"Don't use that title," Linden said. "Call me just Ande. Please."

No one spoke for a moment. Father Theou knew magistrates could never admit to not being in full command of any situation, and were trained in particular words, postures and vocal tricks that made people instinctively grant them authority. Linden was using none of those, and Theou could see that it puzzled Jin as much as it did him.

After a moment she spoke into the silence. "There's a Traveller— a Spacer, still up on the ship, who's a friend of mine," Jin said. "They know some ways of generating oxygen without dedicated equipment. If I can contact him—"

"There are two message rockets on the ship," Bennett said, to Ande. "If we tell the Colonization Office about the situation, they'll send someone to help us."

Jin turned to face Ande, finally looking at him directly. "Sir," she said, clearly choking on the word. "We can't wait that long. It will be at least a golden month before any help can come. We need a new source of oxygen right now. You have to authorize it."

"I can't," Ande said after a pause.

"Will you authorize sending the rockets?" Bennett asked.

"No. I won't—do what you need to do." He closed his eyes, took off his silver bowl pendant and put it in the pocket of his coverall.

Father Theou looked from Bennett to Jin, saw each of them unsure of what to do next. He could not know why Ande had refused his charge, but it was clear this was his best chance to earn a place for his followers on this world. "At any rate, we must stand together," he said before either of the others could speak. "With what we are learning about this world, disunion could be fatal."

"I'm not sure—" Bennett began.

"I hope you're good at holding your breath," Jin said. She shrugged and turned away. "I'm going to use the communicator. If any of you want to help get an oxygenator going, you're welcome to."

"I need to—we have to send that message," Bennett said to Ande. "We can't let her—" He turned to Theou beseechingly.

Father Theou could see the younger man's face darken as his glance fell on Theou's Heresy badge. "We are more alike than different," Theou said.

Bennett paused for a moment, and then shook his head. He turned back to Ande. "I'm sorry," he said, and then turned to go back into the pod.

Bennett could feel his eyes glazing over as he stared at his datapad screen. This was not going well. He rubbed his eyes with his hands and turned away from the screen. The featureless white walls of the pod's maintenance room offered little in the way of relief from the screen's glare.

He closed his eyes and remembered the look of the planet outside, tried to reconcile it to what he had seen on the briefing vid. It was impossible. Life on that planet would have been hard, yes, but he hadn't asked for an easy assignment. With only light terraforming to be done, he could have helped the convicts become a community—and perhaps, once they no longer felt like outsiders, he could have convinced them that they could again become Compatible within the Church. There is more glory in ministering to the lost, they said, than in giving Enosis to the Lonely One, the Emperor herself.

This planet, though, seemed almost beyond hope. It looked like the very first thing they would have to do to survive would be to disobey orders, making their own oxygen. He was here to minister to the convicts, not get involved in politics, but still—to be Compatible meant all of humanity sharing one same culture, the same beliefs, and the authority of the Magistracy was central among those. If enough started listening to Jin, this whole planet might be lost to the Void.

The sky was the hardest thing to accept. All the worlds in the Borderless Empire, even the marginal ones like Jutland or Setebos, had blue skies, or else blue-tinted domes. That was what the blue on his robe stood for, that shared link with all humanity and Connection with the Allsoul. Could this be a sign that he had been wrong—that he had not been called here after all?

A voice came from the door. "Brother Sims?" she asked.

"Yes?" Bennett said, turning in his chair to face her. He started at the sight of the red murder badge on the young, terribly thin woman's chest, and then reminded himself this was why he was here.

"I heard that you had come with us, to minister to us," she said. "It has been a very long time since I have been to a Service. Would I be permitted back?"

He made himself smile, uneasy. "Of course. That's why the Church is Soft; everyone who sincerely wants to can become Compatible."

"And if my crimes are too great?"

"Nothing you could have done is so bad it can't be forgiven."

She was silent for a moment. "But what if they are? What if the Enemy has claimed my soul?"

"There is no Enemy. There is only the Allsoul and the Void." Bennett studied the girl's face, looking for some hint of what she was thinking. He wondered where she had gotten her ideas; the last of the Tartarids were supposed to have been excommunicated dozens of years ago. He supposed every heresy lived on in pockets here and there around All-the-Stars.

"Of course," she said. "Thank you, Brother Bennett."

He rose from his chair as she turned to leave. "Is there anything else I can help you with?"

"No. Thank you."

It was only after she was gone and he had settled back down in chair, thinking that his time studying in the House hadn't prepared him for this, that he realized he had never learned her name.

Griffin was floating in front of a viewport, watching the planet turn below him. He thought about what Jin had told him about it, wondered how many of the convicts would have accepted this option if they had known what to expect. Almost all, probably. His people were living proof that life would survive anywhere it had even the slimmest chance.

Drifting aimlessly about the ship for a few hours now, he'd only just realized how much he'd become accustomed to the noise of the engines. The ship sounded very quiet with them stilled. The air recycling system, on the other hand, was starting to grumble menacingly. It was old, and not meant to be used for such long periods—well, he could probably patch it to last at least a few more years. As it was, he was hardly straining it, all by himself. He was used to stale air, had never known any other kind, and only occasionally dreamed of flushing all the sweat, gas and garbage smells out into vacuum and pumping in a tank of fresh air.

The vidscreen on the wall nearby pinged and displayed the characters MESSAGE WAITING. Griffin hit the OPEN CHANNEL key and Jin appeared.

"Griffin, we've got to get started. Will it be easier to build it up there, or send the parts down in the boat?"

"I'll send it down," he said. "I'm going to have to figure out exactly what we need."

"Okay. Listen. I could use something else: a list of anyone here that has any background in xenoscience. It should be in convict records—let me know when you have it, all right?"

The image blinked out, replaced by a camera feed of the planet outside, and Griffin was alone. He sighed. She had snared him right away when they first met, pulled him from his people and into her orbit. Together they had, perhaps, done a little good; but that was over. Now it was time to remember where he had come from.

Jin put the last piece in place, sat down on her bunk. She could never feel at home until she had set up her chess set. Even if the pieces were just scavenged spare parts, the board carved into the surface of a desk, the game was always the same. It was the one she and Lieutenant Wiesen had left unfinished, that she had carried in her head wherever she went. So long as she kept it set up, she knew someday she would win.

Other than Lieutenant Wiesen, the only person who had ever beaten her was Ande Linden. During her rebellion, she had outplayed every other Fleet Magistrate they had sent against her, but he had always been one move ahead of her.

She picked up one of the white bishops, diagrammed its options. She sometimes wondered if the gambit she had planned would really have worked, or if it had been part of a trap laid by Lieutenant Wiesen. In all the years since she had never been able to find one, but that did not mean it was not there. She wondered now if Ande's strange behaviour, his refusal to take command or even wear his uniform, had a trap hidden in it.

She picked up her datapad, keyed it on. That was the one good thing about having Bennett on board: they had all been given datapads so they could receive Enosis, be joined with the community, Church and Allsoul. Jin was not too proud to take one for its more secular functions. Later she would use it to learn all the names of the other convicts, memorize their faces, but for now she had to find someone who could help with the oxygenator.

The list Griffin had compiled for her had only one name on it. Not surprising—xenologists, who studied the life native to extraterrestrial planets, were some of the most valued workers in All-the-Stars. She leaned back on her cot, called up the file. The datapad's screen showed an image of a copper-skinned woman with streaks of gold running through her black hair. A Core Worlder, then, from a family with enough pull to give her cosmetic genework.

"KAUR, RUCHIKA," the entry read. "Born on Gemini colony, Year 7 Monkey, made Meritorious Citizen at birth. Graduated Xenological Institute (Mars) Top Honours 9 Fox, granted Imperial Citizenship. [Redacted]. Arrested 9 Rabbit, convicted 10 Rooster of [Redacted]. Sentenced to merciful death; sentence commuted to life in exile as per Colonization Office request, assigned to mission to Colony Planet 10 Horse One. Assigned bunk B, Cell 9, Pod Two."

Jin closed the datapad, wondering what a xenologist could have done to earn a death sentence. She took a few more deep breaths, prepared herself for the trip over to Pod Two. *Exile for life*, she thought to herself. Maybe by the end of it she'd be used to the smell.

Bennett cleared his throat, peered inside the open door. "Magistrate Linden?" he called, straining to see inside the dark room. He heard movement, saw a flash of white hair.

"Please, come in," he heard the old man say. His voice was shaky, held into his chest so that it came out almost a whisper. It reminded Bennett of Father Philo, his Doctrine instructor at the House, whose lungs had been burned by the air on Jutland. The lights rose to half and Bennett could see the older man sitting on his bunk.

"I'm sorry, I—did I wake you?"

"No. I was awake. Come in, please. Brother...Sims, isn't it?" Beneath the shakiness, the old man's voice was deep, reassuring.

"Yes, zi Linden." Bennett stepped inside, gave him a half-bow. He waited for the old man to say something. After a few moments, it became clear that if they were going to talk he was going to have to do most of the work.

"Please, zi Linden, you can't just resign this commission," he said. "This colony needs your leadership. These people, they aren't ordinary colonists, you know that. We can't let people think this mission is just a chance for them to repeat their mistakes."

"Surely you can give them the guidance they need?" Ande said.

"I can't get involved in politics."

Ande stood, started to make his bed. "And I can? Tell me, Brother Sims, what would you say if I told you I'm not fit to lead? That I am the last person here who should risk repeating his mistakes?"

Bennett watched him carefully. Was he being tested? "You were given this commission by the Magistracy. It's not for us to question our duty."

"No?" Ande turned to face the young man again. "Tell me, Brother Sims, why have you not taken your new name yet?"

"I'm not a full member of the Order. This is my initiating mission. But you haven't—"

"Five years is a long time, isn't it? Aren't most initiations only six months?"

"Yes. I requested this mission because it was so long—I thought no one else would want it."

"And were you right?"

A pause. "Yes."

"So. You are doing something difficult—staying for five years among criminals, heretics, those the rest of the world considers beyond redemption—so that a better end may be achieved." The shakiness in the voice was almost gone, Bennett noticed, replaced by a reassuring warmness. He could feel himself nodding, agreeing almost as much with Ande's voice as with his words.

"Yes. And that's what I'm asking you to—"

"I am doing something difficult as well. I was born, raised and schooled to do what you are asking. I spent more years than you have lived doing it. Now I must not do it—to achieve a better end. Do you understand?"

Bennett stood unsteadily, put his hand to his temple. "I—I still don't…"

"No, you don't understand, but you still agree. They all would— that is why I can't help you. In this life, on this world, we can't afford to agree with things for reasons we don't understand, nor can we afford to make the same mistakes twice. Now, you can stay if you like, but I must tell you I won't be saying anything more of any importance—

and you, I expect, are a very busy young man."

"Well—thank you," Bennett said, turning to leave. He paused. "Why did—why did you take this commission, if you didn't intend to serve?"

"I'm a criminal, just like everyone else here; the only difference was I got to keep my rank. But make no mistake, this planet was meant to be my prison."

Ruchika shook off her field jacket, a cloak of stiff green rubberized cotton. She had just remembered something else she'd need, her sample scraper, and had to find room for it in one of the pockets of her vest.

"Shouldn't you be unpacking?" someone asked from the doorway.

"I'm not staying," Ruchika answered, not turning to look. She had had enough waiting, enough delays. "I have to work."

"The work is here, zi Kaur. There's nowhere to go, and we need your help to build that oxygenator."

Ruchika sighed, put down the scraper. It was a woman talking to her, in her thirties, with straight black hair. "Shi Jin, yes? Sorry, zi Shi, but I'm not a terraformer. You want one of those big hairy people with tremendous lung capacity." She pulled the UV penlight out of another pocket, put it down and replaced it with the scraper.

Jin stepped in her path. "You must know there's not enough oxygen out there. You can't go."

"There was a survey team here, ten years ago. They would have built a research station somewhere out towards the mountains, and it'll have its own oxygenator. All I need is enough oxygen in puffers to get there, and I can get back to work."

Jin looked at her as if she had sprouted wings. "It doesn't matter. You can't go now. You're the only one who can help us build the oxygenator. If people hear you wouldn't help—"

"What does it matter what they think?"

"It matters because this is a ship full of dangerous people, and they won't much like it if they hear you refused to help them."

"Are you threatening me? You're not in charge, you know. Nobody is in charge here. We're on our own."

"You're right. There's nobody who can tell two hundred angry

criminals to ignore the fact that you wouldn't help them survive."
This time Jin caught her eye. There was something there—some look,
something in her voice—that made Ruchika stop and listen. "You
might wish there was, though."

She crossed her arms. "If I help you with this, will you let me go?
You won't draft me into any more terraforming?"

"If you really want to go—"

"I do. Now, what do you need me to do?"

I study hard during the cold nights
And my sleeves are wet with tears.
Yet future rewards are in my mind
Like the blue sky on the horizon.

Bennett put down his datapad. So far he had been working for an
hour and had gotten no further than choosing the correct poem to in-
troduce his report. Fleet ships could move between the stars, but there
was no way of sending information across that distance except for the
two TSARINA-equipped rockets. That meant his message had to be
perfect: he had heard of minor clerks junking memos just because
they had an irregular meter, or used the characters in the Lonely One's
name.

He looked around the room for inspiration. There was little to be
found in the spartan bunkroom, just the linens and meagre personal
effects of himself and his bunkmate. He closed his eyes, hoping the
internal landscape would be more fruitful. All he could see was the
scene outside, the sky yellow like a rotten fruit and the grass bloody
where he'd walked on it.

"How goes our message in a bottle?" came a voice from behind
him.

Bennett opened his eyes, startled. "What? I mean, I'm sorry?"

Father Theou was standing at the doorway. Something in his posture
made him look as if he were still wearing his robes, instead of a grey
coverall with the white badge that marked him for a heretic.

"The message, about our situation, how is it going?" Father Theou
prompted.

"Oh, that," Bennett said. "I didn't know what you meant, about a
bottle."

"An old story from the time before the Borderless Empire. Hanzi is mostly water you see, though ironically they called it Earth then, and people were often lost at sea. Some of them would write down who and where they were, and put it into a glass bottle that they would throw into the water, hoping the bottle would be carried to land and they would be saved."

Bennett nodded, hit the SAVE key on his 'pad. At the rate he was going, he couldn't afford to lose even what he had—especially since he still had to convert it from SoftScript into good calligraphy. "And were they ever? Rescued, I mean?"

The older man considered for a moment. "No," he said sadly. "I don't suppose they ever were."

Feeling uncomfortably like he was back in his first days at the House, Bennett stood. It was no use. He was only an adelfos, a missionary, while the older man was a pateros; even though the priest and his whole congregation had been excommunicated, Bennett had been conditioned to defer to him. "Well, I think we have a better chance than they did," he said. "We know where it's going, and who'll receive it. And they know where we are."

A small smile appeared on the priest's face. He was back at the House all right, Bennett thought. That was the only other place where they laughed at you when you were trying to be serious.

"They also know *who* we are, Brother Sims. The Borderless Empire runs on two things: time and energy. How much of either do you think they will waste on two hundred criminals?"

"You can't say that. They won't just—" Bennett stopped and looked at the datapad in his hand—looked at the space on the screen waiting for his words, words that would explain what had happened without implying that the Colonization Office had been wrong to send them there. "Do you really think it's no use?" he asked.

Father Theou sat down on the bunk opposite. "I'm a priest, Brother. If I didn't believe in calling out to a higher power, where would I be?"

"But you aren't—"

"I still have faith, and so should you."

"What you said, though, about the bottle. If I don't think they'll send help, how can I do anything?" Bennett stared at Father Theou, feeling that he had again fallen into one of the logic traps that Sister

Stagires used to set for him.

Father Theou gestured to Bennett's bunk. "Sit. Take a load off your feet. Now take a load off your shoulders. You aren't responsible for the physical wellbeing of these people—you mustn't confuse faith with hope. Hope is based on circumstance, and it isn't our business. Hope won't make that message heard. But you can have *faith* that your mission here can succeed. You can give faith to others. Anyone could write that message—you have a job here that no one else can do."

Bennett held up his hands. "I know. I came to give Enosis, but it's too soon. They don't want it."

"It may very soon be too late. If your message isn't heard, if Jin's machine doesn't work, we'll have two hundred men and women in danger of dying Incompatible, their souls forever lost to the Void. Perhaps more importantly, if this colony is to succeed, it must be a community—and we are the ones who can make it one."

Bennett turned his datapad off, making sure to give thanks to the adelfoi who had laboured for months in the computoria to make the 'pads for his mission, painstakingly copying and soldering circuit boards from the original plan. "We'd need to set up a network. We don't have power to run it, not for long."

"If there's power to run the oxygen machine, there's power for the network. I've run them on low-energy grids before."

Bennett watched Father Theou as the pateros waited for his answer. "You have, haven't you?" he asked. "That's why you have that white badge." He turned partly away from Father Theou, turning his 'pad back on. "I'll have to think about it."

Father Theou stood stiffly. "This isn't a time to be doctrinaire, Brother Bennett," he said. "I am your only ally. And we are the only ones who can save these people for the Allsoul. Think about that." He paused for a second longer, then turned and walked away in silence.

Ruchika looked up to see the ship-to-surface boat coming down. All she could see was its landing thrusters, glowing white as it struggled to slow its descent, and occasionally the flash of the attitude jets keeping it pointed up and on target. It thundered as it hit the upper atmosphere and started to grow even brighter with re-entry heat. A few seconds later she could see the shape of the boat itself, a long, eight-sided cone, and a second after that a thin plasteel parachute opened out of the nose. It began to fall more slowly, and seconds later the main thrusters cut out as a fine rain began to fall. Another thunderclap, a real one, rang out as the rain increased and the boat touched down, hard, at the side of the river.

"As soon as you feel short of air, use your puffers," Jin was saying. "You can run out of oxygen very quickly, so it's better to go back in to refill if you have to. Yell out if you notice anything strange."

The sky had darkened and was filled with brownish-orange clouds. Every few seconds, a flash of lightning on the horizon made everything look bright yellow. The others stepped gingerly, wary of the sharp grass, but as Ruchika had expected it curled up into tight loops at the rain's touch. Jin gave her a quick look, frowning, and then started to walk toward the riverbank, gesturing to the others to follow.

"Don't run," Jin said. "Uses too much oxygen. Steady steps."

The rain was getting worse now, coming down in fat round drops that stung where they hit skin. They reached a long muddy bank at the side of the river where the boat sat at a cocked angle.

"It's sinking," one of the other convicts said, a young man with a Petty Crime badge.

"If we let it sink it won't be able to lift off again," Jin said. She hit the OPEN key on the boat's hatch and quickly drew her hand back from the still-hot metal. The hatch hissed open. "Ruchika, do you know which ones are most important?"

Ruchika shook her head, not bothering to look inside the hatch. She wasn't about to give this farce any more of her time and attention than she absolutely had to.

Jin paused for a second and then nodded. "Teams of two. You—go inside and keep filling up the spare puffers. Ruchika and I will get the parts out of the boat. You and you, carry from the boat to the pod."

Jin stepped into the boat and began pulling equipment out. Ruchika sighed and joined her. The pieces looked like each had been taken from a different source, and all of them looked old.

"This planet stinks," Ruchika observed, trying to budge some ancient machine where it had wedged in the hatchway.

"What do you think it is?" Jin asked.

"Maybe part of a hydrocarbon. It has that rotting smell," Ruchika said, knocking the machine free with her shoulder. She held her mouth open, waiting to receive a puff of oxygen. ,

Stepping back inside the boat, Jin and Ruchika each gathered up another armful. The boat lurched and began to sink more quickly.

"We're almost out of time," Jin said. "Do we have everything we need?"

"I think so," Ruchika answered, glancing around the boat.

Jin hit two keys on the small control console next to the hatch, stepped outside the boat. Its bottom had sunk nearly a bar into the mud.

"We'd better get back to the pod," Jin said. She began to walk quickly away from the boat.

Ruchika followed close behind, taking a hit of oxygen from her puffer when she started to feel light-headed. "I thought you said not to run—is that thing dangerous when it takes off?"

"Not normally, but with the mud…"

The boat's main thrusters went off, pushing it up and the ground down with equal force. A shockwave of mud flew toward them, knocking them to the ground and soaking them with stinking water. The boat was in the air.

Ruchika struggled to her feet and spat a mouthful of mud onto the ground. *It will be worth it,* she promised herself.

Jin's feet sank into the mud as she stepped out of the pod. The others had all been anxious to get back inside once the equipment had been brought in, but as soon as she'd seen the rain was letting up she had decided to explore. She looked around. The grass was still curled up—now that she'd felt the stinging, acidic rain, she understood why—and the river was running much higher than it had been. She'd have to find a place for the oxygenator where it would not be at risk of getting washed away.

Remembering that she had seen a small island just offshore, she started to walk toward the riverbank. After a few paces she glanced back at the pod and stopped, moving to examine the small pits she saw all over its hull. She ran her hand over its surface, could feel small cracks below the surface as well as the ones already visible. She took another puff of oxygen and set off for the nearest pod, to see if it was in similar shape.

Pod Four was the furthest of the pods from the river, probably less than a li from where the stunted trees began. It had landed on uneven ground, and Jin noticed that there was a small overhang where the rim of the pod bridged a depression in the soil. Finding it, she peered underneath, ran her hand along the underside, which had been sheltered from the storm. It was smooth, intact. It was the rain, then, and not the air that was corroding the pods. She frowned. If it was corrosive, it might not be possible to electrolyse the water without it destroying the oxygenator. For that matter, the river water might not even be drinkable.

Jin straightened up, felt a pain in her lower back, gravity getting back at her for having been away so long. She stretched, and then froze as she saw movement at the edge of her vision. Turning her head she saw something moving just inside the tree cover—something large, more than half her height. She rose slowly, took a step toward the trees. Whatever she had seen, it was gone now. Shaking her head, she peered into the darkness between the closely spaced trees. She took another step forward, looked into the forest for another few seconds then turned back towards the pod, stepping gingerly on the slowly unfurling blades of grass.

Ruchika paused to swipe her bangs away from her eyes as she tried to pry the power converter open with a screwdriver. She was lying on her stomach in the pod's machine room, craning her neck to see the underside of the machine she and the Traveller had cobbled together. Her hair fell back in front of her face and the screwdriver slipped from her fingers, landing in a spot where it would be nearly impossible to retrieve.

"Vack it!" she shouted.

"Problems?" Griffin's asked, over the speaker.

"No, it's all right," she said. This whole project was an annoyance. She should have been out of the pod hours ago.

"You want to take a break?"

"I'm nearly done."

"Still. Calm your nerves."

She scowled, but pulled herself out from under the machine and sat up. "Easy for you to say. All you do is sit up there and give orders."

"When you ought to be giving orders to me, is that it?"

She said nothing for a moment, wondered if he was really annoyed or just joking. She had never been good at reading things like that, even face-to-face. "I didn't mean—"

"I'm not offended. It's natural that a xenologist wouldn't expect to take orders from a Traveller—or a rebel." He paused. "Of course, not many xenologists end up in places like this. You never did tell me..."

She sighed. He had been fishing for her story since had they started work. Was he just a busybody, she wondered, or did he—or Jin—suspect why she was there? "There's not much to tell," she said. "I published some unpopular findings."

"Which were?"

"I was part of the survey team on a recently discovered planet that had some odd features. After weighing all the evidence, I realized the only possible conclusion was that the planet had been altered by an alien intelligence." She expected that would be near enough the truth to be convincing.

"That's a crime?" Griffin asked.

"Sure. One of the early emperors—David the Second, I think—made looking for aliens illegal. He said the Borderless Empire had the mandate of Heaven to rule over all those that were part of the Soul, and anyone who wasn't part of the Soul couldn't possibly be intelligent."

"So if you knew it was illegal, why did you publish?" Griffin asked.

Ruchika shrugged. "I was right. I'm a xenologist. What could I do?" She twisted a piece of copper wire round her bangs and then crawled back under the machine, seeking the screwdriver by touch.

"Why were you so sure?"

"Xenology stuff. Hard to explain." She had said too much, made him curious. It had been so long, though, since she could tell anyone what she knew, what she had discovered. The temptation to tell everything was strong.

Well. She could wait a little longer, if she had to; and when the time came, she would have a lot more to tell.

"Are you sure of this?" Father Theou asked.

Shi Jin's eyes flashed with anger. "I'm sure that I saw something. And yes, I know the survey didn't find any animal life of any size. We know how reliable the survey's been."

"Yes. Still, with the environment so harsh…" Father Theou trailed off.

He had to handle this carefully. Jin would be an ally of convenience, if that, but it was vital that he maintain the balance between her and Bennett: it would only be by keeping them both convinced that they needed his support that he might be able to keep his faith alive here. It was ironic, he thought, that while this planet was the last place in All-the-Stars where the Apomekanid heresy still existed, its main tenet—that the network that joined them in worship could itself have a soul—was meaningless here. It would be years, perhaps decades before his new network was sufficiently sophisticated for anyone to worry about whether or not it had a soul.

"The grass survives. So do the trees."

"Plants, yes. But I've served the Church on a dozen different worlds, and I can tell you how few had any animal life that we didn't bring there." He held his hands out in a calming gesture. "A lot of colonists—very bright, educated people—have had fantasies about encountering aliens. In an unfamiliar place, especially one so strange and exotic as this, it's only natural."

Jin frowned. "I didn't say I talked to anything, just that I saw something. Some planets do have animals."

"But you don't believe that's what it is." Father Theou sighed. He knew her type—for all that she had been a rebel, Jin was Fleet through and through: an argument to theology would be useless. "I'm trying to be empirical, Shi Jin. You could start a panic just by jumping to conclusions. People use up a lot of oxygen when they panic, you know."

"So what should I do?" she asked. "Tell everyone I just imagined it?"

"You've told people?"

"They deserve to get the truth for once," she said, eyes narrowing.

"What truth? That you saw something that may have been moving, that may have been alive? That they have one more reason to be afraid?"

"Fear is healthy if it makes you more careful. If what I saw is dangerous, we have to learn more about it."

"And if it isn't dangerous? If people get lost in the woods looking for it, and pass out?" Father Theou shook his head. "No. We'll investigate, but just a few of us. If there is something out there, it's avoiding us so far. For now, we have to get your oxygen machine running. Then we can decide on our next step."

"Okay," Jin said after a moment. "But I'm not going to tell people I was—" She stopped. "What is it?"

"Oh—nothing," he said. "I thought I heard someone outside in the corridor, but there's no one there. There, you see how easy it is to imagine things? None of us is immune."

Ruchika stood nervously in the airlock, waiting for the air to cycle. She calmed herself by doing the exo-check she had learned at the Institute: tapping her puffers to hear if they were full, patting all of the pockets on her vest to make sure each held the tool that belonged there. Finally the inside door sealed shut and the outer door began to open. She realized that she had been hyperventilating. She took a puff of oxygen and tried to calm down.

The outer door opened and she stepped outside. The sulphurous smell assaulted her, stronger than she remembered it, but she suppressed her gag reflex and told herself she'd have to learn to like it. This was the chance she had been waiting for all her life. She hoped the oxygenator in the station was still working.

Looking around, she found the edge of the valley beyond Pod Four. She drew her datapad from her vest and called up the first survey team's notes, trying to compare their map to the topography in front of her. She started to head up the rise, toward the forest. Fifty paces out she decided she'd drawn the right conclusion from what she'd overheard: Jin didn't know anything, and the realities of life here would keep her from investigating any more for a while. Smiling, she went up out of the valley and into the stinking forest beyond.

"Ruchika?"

Jin looked around the maintenance room for any hint at where the xenologist might have gone. She saw the assortment of parts that she assumed was the oxygenator and stepped over to examine it.

"Perhaps she's taken a break," Father Theou suggested, hanging back in the doorway.

"I don't think so," Jin said, looking closely at the machine. It was very fragile for something all of their lives depended on. "She said that she wanted to leave as soon as she was done. She could have—"

Noticing the vidscreen on the wall, Jin walked over to hit and hit the OPEN CHANNEL key. "Griffin? Hey, Griffin," she called.

"Yes?" came the voice from the speaker. "Jin? How're things?"

"Do you know where Ruchika is? Did she finish building the machine?"

"Yes—yes, she did, she was going to find you. Didn't she?"

"No. But the machine is working?"

"I think so. She said she ran a few litres through it and it worked. Listen, what's going on down there?"

"I'm sorry, Griffin, I'll call you back, all right?" Jin hit the CLOSE CHANNEL key and turned to Father Theou. "We'll have to test the river water, see if it's as corrosive as the rain."

She stepped past Father Theou into the corridor and the two began walking toward the airlock. The hallway was full of people clustered around the viewports, trying to see if they could spot whatever it was Jin had seen. Several of them stopped her as she walked by, but she told them she had nothing more to say.

"And if it is corrosive?" Father Theou asked, following closely.

"Then we'd better hope that Brother Bennett is right, and the Magistracy won't just let us die here."

They turned a corner and saw Bennett coming toward them. "Brother Sims, you must come with us," Father Theou said pleasantly, to forestall conflict between the other two. "We are on a fact-finding mission."

Bennett got in step with the others, a bit behind to speak quietly to Father Theou. "Father, I've thought about—"

"That should wait until we can address the group," the pateros said, shaking his head slowly.

When they reached the airlock, Jin stabbed at the OPEN button, glaring at Bennett. "I won't think any less of you if you'd rather stay here," she said.

Bennett stepped into the 'lock as the inner door opened. "I was going to say the same thing. You may have already used more than your share of oxygen."

"We can all go," Father Theou said. "If the machine does not work, two more puffers aren't going to make a difference."

The outer door slid open and they all recoiled from the smell of the air outside. Jin stepped out of the airlock, started toward the river. The other two stepped out more cautiously, the older man taking a puff of oxygen. Jin kept up her pace, only occasionally looking back. Father Theou was making slow progress, trying to step on the grass without cutting himself, while Bennett had stopped to examine the pod's pockmarked outer hull.

Passing Pod One, Jin saw faces at the portholes watching her. She wondered how much communication was passing between the pods. Did they know about the rain, about what she had seen? She stopped at the edge of the river, where the bank was made up of thickly clumped black sand. The water was shallow here, where it reached out to meet a small, sandy island ten or so paces offshore. She crouched by the water, holding her hand over its surface. *There is no other way to know*, she thought, remembering how her skin had reddened and blistered where the rain had hit it.

She tried to blank her mind then thrust her hand into the water, waiting for pain. It felt cold, but that was all. She looked over her shoulder to see Father Theou and Bennett approaching.

"It's clean!" she shouted to them. She cupped her hand, brought water to her mouth and drank deeply. "It's good," she said, swallowing. "It's water. We have water."

Seized by an impulse she had not felt in a dozen years, she pushed her whole face in the running water, blew bubbles up to the surface. She knew the priest and the missionary were watching her, probably amusing themselves at her expense. Well, let them; she knew what the Travellers said, that water was life. She drank as much water as she could hold, feeling like she had gone years without either.

Liz Szalwinski pushed her way to the front of the circle. Most of the convicts were taller than her, and she had to give a few good shoves near enough to see what was going on. She was surprised at what she saw: the Magistrate was nowhere to be seen, and instead

Brother Bennett, the Soft Church missionary, was standing next to two convicts whose badges marked them as a rebel and a heretic.

"Most of you have heard that the oxygen machine is now working," Bennett said. "You may also have heard some rumours going around. I've called this meeting to make sure everyone knows the truth."

His words were drowned out by the crowd's response. Liz had heard at least a dozen different rumours in the last few hours: that the old survey team was still here, that a group of raiders had their camp here, that there were alien ruins here.

"There's something alive out there!" Jin shouted, briefly quieting the crowd. She held her hand parallel to the ground, about at waist-height. "It was about a bar and a half tall, and it moved—quickly. We need to protect ourselves. We have the equipment to build an electric fence around the pods, to scare off any animals that come near."

"Fortifications are a direct violation of colony law," Liz said, re-alizing only after she closed her mouth that she had spoken aloud. This was insane. They had a perfectly good Magistrate to run the set-tlement; he had no right to refuse to do it. As it was, everyone was panicking, yelling and wasting their oxygen arguing with a traitor.

"We need protection!" Jin shouted back at her. "Who knows what's out there?"

"The survey said no animal life. This is just an excuse to build you a little base where you can pretend you're still fighting your rebellion."

Liz didn't wait for Shi's answer but turned and started back to her pod. Just by being part of this argument, she was giving it credibility, admitting that the convicts could break the rules if they all agreed to. None of the others knew the kind of damage rebels did. They were lis-tening to Jin as if they had all the right in the universe to decide things for themselves. Well, she had thought that herself, once—and she hoped that learning better would hurt them every bit as much as it had her.

"We can build a barrier without breaking the rules," Malcolm Smith said, bringing his voice up from way down in his stomach to be heard over the crowd. "I was a farm foreman back on Hesiod. If we just make it out of wire and keep the voltage low, the Equitable

Marketing System permits it."

That law, which held the Borderless Empire together by making all the worlds dependent on each other, was one he knew well: he had studied it carefully, looking for a loophole that would let him hold back enough crops to feed himself and his family. There was no such loophole, of course. That was why he was here.

"There's another issue," Bennett said. "Our power supply is limited. If we build the fence, we might not have enough power left for the network."

"We have to have priorities," Jin protested.

"I know my priorities," Bennett said. "If I didn't value your souls above my physical safety, I wouldn't be here."

That won him a few points with the crowd, Malcolm thought. He had to admire Sims for volunteering for this job, though he'd never exactly been a devout believer, sometimes going a month or more without Enosis. Out here, though, he could see the appeal—a community that didn't judge you, accepted you without question. He missed a lot of people from back home—after his arrest for holding back food his wife, his friends, his children had all been sent to different labour camps. A lot of the others must feel the same way, he knew. For a lot of them, being part of something might just turn out to be more important than survival.

"We've got power—a whole ship's worth of power," someone was saying. *Peter Huyt*, Jin thought, *that was it*. He had been a City Magistrate on Palimpsest who had been conned by a passing Traveller into infiltrating a non-existent spy ring and gotten a Treason charge for his trouble.

"Griffin has to stay up there," Jin said, knowing that standing up for the Traveller wouldn't help her standing with the convicts. Oh, well—even in this game, there were some pieces she refused to sacrifice.

Weren't there?

"He got the same sentence the rest of us did," the man said.

"Why should he stay up there when we have to deal with stinking air and Soul-knows-what kinds of animals are out there?" Huyt asked.

"He can't take the gravity—" Jin began, but it was too late. Huyt had found the perfect lightning rod for all the anger and frustration that had been building up in the convicts since the ship had left the detention centre on Xerxes.

"Why should he g-get the whole ship to himself?" Another convict, a thin man with blotchy skin and a red Murder badge, moved to stand next to Huyt. "I have to share a b-bunkroom—he thinks he's too good to touch the ground."

"How do we know he won't just take the ship and go?" Huyt asked.

"You can't trust Spacers around equipment. They'll take things they don't even need," Nick Leung said. He was one of the few convicts Jin already knew: a former Fleet Pilot who, like most of them, detested Travellers on principle.

"The TSARINA's been disabled—he can't go anywhere." Jin protested. She scanned the crowd, looking for anyone she might get support from. Someone was watching her, she realized—a wire-thin woman with straight black hair and a red Murder badge. She was looking right at Jin, ignoring the commotion.

"We must have compassion," Father Theou said from behind her. She had begun to wonder if the priest was going to say anything or just stand there like a statue. "Don't you agree, Brother Sims?"

Bennett looked overwhelmed by the anarchy of the debate. He had never encountered anything like it before, just as most of these people likely never had; most people could go their whole lives without ever being asked to decide anything for themselves. Now it was all coming out like a flood.

"Yes, yes," Bennett said weakly. "We can't—we must do no harm. But communications, we can conserve power if we limit those, and that will let us run the network."

Jin looked from face to face in the crowd, wondering how they would take Bennett's proposal. Some of them seemed disappointed they weren't going to see any blood, but his Soft Church robes and a lifetime of conditioning kept them from arguing. As the crowd started to break up, she stepped over to him, hoping to make him pay at least a little for what had happened.

"Tell me, Brother Bennett," she said in a carefully controlled voice. "You weren't going to let them bring Griffin down—you were going to speak up if Father Theou didn't—weren't you?"

Xiang Kao moved to where Jin was sitting on the grass, her eyes closed. "Excuse me," she said.

"Can I help you?" Jin answered, not opening her eyes. She was so fragile, so vulnerable: Kao had imagined that, having survived so much, Jin might be more solid than all the rest, but she was not.

"I think that you are right," Kao said. As always, it was difficult for her to put words together in the right order. "They are wrong. I think they are wrong. I believe Tartaris the Enemy moved them."

Shi rose to her feet. Kao noticed she had cut her hands on the grass while pushing herself up. "I always heard there wasn't any Enemy. Murderer and heretic isn't a very common combination."

"There is an Enemy. I am his child."

Kao saw Jin looking at her carefully. "What's your name?" Jin asked.

"I am Xiang Kao," she said. She could see the disbelief on Jin's face.

"I didn't know," the other woman said after a moment.

"No. Nobody does until too late." The habit of hiding, of being invisible, was so ingrained that Kao could hardly believe she had told the woman her name. She had to, though, before she did what she had to do.

"Thank you for saying you agree with me," Jin said. "But why didn't you speak at the meeting?"

"If I spoke out, people would learn who I am. They would not want the Enemy's child among them."

"That's not true," Shi said.

"They would be correct. I am a child of Tartaris; killing is all I am able to do." Kao said, not wasting any energy arguing. "For many years I was only able to do wrong things because of my curse. Now I think I can do a right thing with it."

"What do you mean?"

"I will kill Brother Sims for you."

Jin was speechless. Could it possibly be true this woman was Xiang Kao, the assassin? Stories about her, the terror of Palimpsest, had spread for more than a dozen years; Jin had never known whether or not to think Xiang Kao actually existed. The woman watched her, her face impassive, as she tried to think of what to say. Better not to show she doubted her.

"No. No, Sims is the only thing keeping a lot of these people in line, right now. I hate to admit it, but we need him."

"You must take command," Xiang Kao said. "It will be easier if he is dead."

"If he dies, he'll become a martyr. There are enough people here who still have an investment in the system—they'll take his place if he's gone." She paused, watching Kao's expressionless face. "Thank you for your offer. But it's—it just isn't what we need right now."

"Of course," Xiang Kao said. "I see." She turned slowly and walked back toward her pod.

Jin watched her carefully as she left, saw the barely perceptible slump in her shoulders as she entered the airlock. She wondered if she would regret not taking Kao up on her offer.

CHAPTER TWO

Bennett rarely slept for more than a few hours each night. Throughout his years at the House, in training to be a missionary, he had been kept in a constant state of sleep deprivation and the habit had stuck. On this night even that little rest was denied him: Jin's words had been eating at his mind all night. Would he have spoken out to protect the Spacer? The question pursued him even as he finally fell into a fitful sleep. Had he so easily forgotten his vow to have compassion for every being that arose from the Soul? Now the servants of Tartaris (there is no Tartaris, his conscious mind said uselessly) tortured him with swords made of burning stars. Their leader was the woman with the Murder badge, whose skin had fallen off and was now revealed to be a demon of pain, urging the others on. As they tortured him for all his crimes they joined forces, burning their way into his head through a single point on his cheek. He lay there, helpless, as he realized in the way one does in dreams that their next step would be to climb inside his mind and use his body as an agent for evil. He called out to the Allsoul for help, but it was as cold and distant as the stars above. He was on his own.

Waking with a start, Bennett put his hand to his cheek. It was sore, the area around it wet. He felt a drop of water hit the back of his hand and rose, carefully avoiding the ceiling just above his bunk. He turned on a light and looked for where the drip had come from. He found a section of ceiling almost a fingertip width corroded away with a steady drip of burning water falling from it. There would also, he realized suddenly, be a loss of oxygen to the outside. The pressure was about the same inside and out, so it would be a slow diffusion, but it would not be long before their air reserve was gone.

He checked his watch, which he had reset the night before from golden time to the planet's blue hours. Sunrise was still hours away. There was not anything he could do until then, he supposed. He turned out the light and lay down, covering his face with his blanket.

The harsh light of the morning sun assaulted Father Theou's eyes as he stepped out of the airlock. He could see Jin and Bennett nearby, examining the side of the pod, already arguing. *Only the young*, he thought, *could get into a fight this early*.

Father Theou closed his left eye and glanced around with his implant, looking for heat sources. He had been keeping watch for the creature Jin had reported seeing, but had not yet detected anything. Turning the implant back to camera mode he opened his eye again, walked over to Jin and Bennett. Up close, he could see that neither of them was any more rested than he was, each carrying dark pouches under their eyes. He supposed that they had gotten up early to try to be outside before the other, whereas he had had to wait for both of them to come out—as he knew they would.

"...can't say oxygen isn't the most important thing now," Jin said bitterly. She was smarting from last night's defeat. Father Theou regretted having let the crowd turn against the Spacer, but he couldn't compromise on having the network constructed. He had been surprised Bennett had not said anything sooner until he had remembered what being an adelfos was like, convinced by the missionary's zeal that every upgrade the Church Council approved was the key to making the galaxy Compatible. Novices did not have to be taught that the end justified the means—it was unspoken in every one of their lessons, and Bennett had learned his well. *Maybe too well*, Father Theou thought, wondering if he had listened equally well when told to stay out of politics.

"I'm not going to let you start a panic," Bennett replied. "There's no reason we can't fix these. It's just a matter of how."

"Good morning, Brother. Shi Jin," Father Theou said cheerily. "We have, I see, a common problem."

"How many people know?" Bennett asked, concerned.

"Not many. Few are yet awake, and the holes are few and far enough between that not everyone will see them."

"They will," Jin said darkly. "They'll notice the air getting thin, for one thing."

"The question then is, what are we to do about it?" Father Theou tapped his implant twice for emphasis, watching as the others tried to hide their unease. Bennett, especially, was disturbed every time he called attention to that graphic reminder of his heresy.

"We have to repair the holes, obviously," Bennett said. "The patching strips—"

"Won't work," Jin interrupted. "They're no stronger than the original hull. They'd only last us until the next storm. And sooner or later the pods will fall apart."

"Life abides," Father Theou said. Dealing with these two was like working with first-year Novices, constantly having to separate them to keep the peace. "It has abided on this planet. Perhaps it has lessons to teach us."

Father Theou saw Jin look at him with annoyance and then turn away, considering. "Those trees do okay," she said slowly. "If we could build with them—use the patching strips on the inside, make them airtight…"

Jin and Father Theou waited for Bennett's objection. Bennett paused, watching them, and then nodded. "It's worth a chance. We have to learn more about the local ecology anyway, if we're going to meet our five-year plan—don't you think, Shi Jin?"

Father Theou closed his eyes, counted to ten. If he made it through the day without killing someone, he thought, it would be a miracle.

Jin had not realized how steep and rocky the rise at the edge of the valley was. Father Theou had decided to set off past Pod Four into the treed area where Jin had made her sighting; whether he hoped to prove or disprove her story she didn't know. The one advantage of the rocky terrain was that the grass was more sparse, so that they only had to be careful to avoid tripping, not cutting themselves. She stopped, took a puff of air and looked back at the clearing. The damage done to the four pods was invisible from this distance, and from here they looked like four perfect brown balls scattered haphazardly on a lawn. *A giant's game*, Jin thought, though she could not imagine what the point of it might be.

The sulphurous smell had been getting stronger as they rose higher. She wrinkled her nose but refused to cover it. She would, she reminded herself, just have to get used to it.

"Look—blood," Father Theou said, stopping. He crouched down

and pointed out a blade of grass with a thin coating of dried blood along its edge.

"This must be the way Sister Kaur went," Bennett said.

"I think you're right," Jin said. "What I saw was at home here. It wouldn't cut itself."

"The station must be nearby, then," Father Theou concluded. "We should keep an eye out. I don't imagine it's safe for her to be here alone."

"If she is alone."

Father Theou shot a warning glance at Jin, took a puff of oxygen and continued forward, the others following behind.

The three walked on in silence until they reached the point where the trees began. They were sparse there, but further ahead they became more dense and it was impossible to see further. The trees were only two hands around and six bars tall, just twice an average man's height, so that even Jin had to duck to avoid being scraped by their lower branches. They had broad, flat, hand-sized leaves with sharp edges like those on the grass, and each tree bore dozens of egg-shaped fruit with waxy, dark orange skins. More of the fruit lay on the ground, many of them split open and rotting, each one containing thousands of seeds. The smell was strongest here, coming from the fruit.

Jin put her hand on the trunk of the nearest tree, pulled it toward her. It bent at her touch, hardly giving any resistance. She pulled harder and it snapped, the top section falling toward her.

"That answers that," she said sadly. "No way we could build anything with this wood."

Father Theou took another pull from his puffer. "The air is thinner here," he said. Jin looked at him for a moment—he looked like he was about to say more—but he remained silent, breathing shallowly.

"It's not just the air," Bennett said. "The smell comes from the fruit, I think."

"Maybe we can use them for something," Jin suggested, reaching to pick up one of the intact fruit from the ground. It burst when she touched it, covering her hand and the ground with seeds and stinking pulp. She recoiled and tried to wipe her hand on her coverall. "Never mind," she said.

"They do survive the rain, though," Bennett said, examining one of the trees. "We could use the leaves to—"

"Quiet," Father Theou said suddenly. "Hold still."

Jin tried to stay as quiet as they waited to see whatever it was Father Theou had reacted to. She took a careful step back, into the shade of the nearest tree, and Bennett did the same. Father Theou held his finger to his lips then pointed to where the forest darkened. Unable to see anything at first, Jin became aware of a skittering movement within the dark area. A second later something moving emerged into the light.

It was the size of a small dog, walking on six triple-jointed, stick-like legs. A hard, brownish-green shell covered its segmented body that ended in a head that had six eyes, in two rows of three, a delicate pair of mandibles and two long, twitching antennae. It was moving toward them cautiously.

Jin tried to control her panic, keeping her back to the tree. She had never seen an extraterrestrial animal before, and precious few terrestrial ones: none had ever been brought to Garamond, her home planet, and those few that remained on Hanzi were kept in parks and zoos, far from the Academy. Judging from Bennett's expression, his experience had been much the same: only Father Theou was standing in the open, looking directly at the creature and opening and closing his left eye— switching from normal to implant vision, Jin realized. The creature continued forward. It was waving its antennae at the fallen fruit, occasionally picking one up with its mandibles and swallowing it. It had not noticed them.

The creature continued toward them, its head down, until it found the fruit that Jin had accidentally broken open. Its antennae waved around that in a frenzy, after which it raised its head and turned it from side to side, twirling its antennae in wide circles. It finally noticed Father Theou and stepped over to him.

The priest stood absolutely still, not moving except to hold out his right hand, palm upward. Jin could see he was shaking, but he held his ground. The creature waved its antennae wildly around Father Theou's hand, as it had done with the burst fruit. She could see the priest flinch as they occasionally brushed against him. The creature took a step back and stood still for a few seconds, then turned awkwardly around and started back the way it had come.

Jin, Bennett and Father Theou all stayed still for minutes after that, waiting to make sure the creature was gone. Finally Father Theou brought his puffer to his mouth and inhaled deeply. The others did the same and Jin and Bennett stepped forward to support the priest, who was on the verge of fainting.

"How did you see it so early?" Jin asked Father Theou. The priest had sat down and had his left eye closed. Activity lights were flashing on either side of his implant.

"The infrared," Father Theou said quietly. "It was very faint—I wasn't sure it was there at first."

"We have to assume it's dangerous," Jin said.

"We had to walk a half-hour just to see one," Bennett argued. "They may not be interested in us at all. That one didn't bother us."

Jin shook her head. "What if it's just a scout? What if they decide we smell tasty?"

"Even so, it couldn't do us much harm," Bennett said. "That one startled us, but it couldn't have hurt us much."

"Unless there are bigger ones."

"Bigger—?" Bennett paled. "No. Even that size, it shouldn't be possible—"

"So bigger is possible, too. So they may be dangerous."

Bennett turned to Father Theou. "Father—what do you think?"

The priest looked up at them, opened his left eye. "They're intelligent," he said simply.

Jin and Bennett exchanged glances. "With all respect, Father, I think…" Bennett began.

"What are you talking about? How do you know?" Jin interrupted, less diplomatically.

"I don't know. That is, I don't know how I know. But I do know," Father Theou said. "I know what you're thinking. An Apomekanid sees souls everywhere. But…" He paused and looked around him. "They're farming these trees. The fruits fall straight down and we haven't seen any birds. It must be them."

"There are some animals that do that. Insects, even. And we don't know if this is organized farming at all," Bennett pointed out.

"I know. You're right, but I still feel…I can't prove it to you, not yet. But I know they're intelligent."

"Father Theou," Jin said carefully. "You told me lots of people—intelligent people is what you said—have thought there was sentient life on new planets. They were all wrong. You said that."

"You have a very inconvenient memory, Shi Jin," the priest said sadly. "You were only watching, though. I was the one who was inspected by that creature, and I am utterly certain there is an intelligence there."

"So," Jin said, "does that mean they're dangerous, or not?"

Father Theou looked thoughtful. "Perhaps. We know they're there now. They know we're here. We should definitely keep building the fence until we get new information."

"And where will we get any new information?" Bennett asked. "That one wasn't very talkative."

"No, it didn't," Father Theou said. "That's why I'm going to find their nest."

It was twilight, and people from all four pods were coming out to stand in the grass, datapads in hand. A half-dozen had implants like Father Theou's, each of them with a thin cable running from the implant to their datapads. *The last of the Apomekanids*, Jin thought, *those few who had survived the assault on Jutland*. Like the Magistracy, the Church did not hold with dissident voices.

The convicts that had come to the Service were standing in rough rows, with Bennett at the front. He was holding the master pad that was used to administer Enosis. It occurred to Jin that this was probably the first time he had ever done this, bringing a group into connection with the Church and the Allsoul itself. Luckily for him, the crowd was not a hostile one. They were watching Bennett carefully, waiting for him to begin—hoping to hear news about the animals that had been seen, Jin thought, but also needing something, anything familiar to tell them they were not so far from home.

"Brothers and sisters," Bennett began, holding two fingers across his forehead in the sign of Gefyri, the bridge. "I welcome you to this Service. I welcome you to the Church, the thread that holds all of human life together. For we are not a Church of one people, of one planet, of rich or of poor. We are a Church of the Soul that joins us and sustains us. When we touch this Soul, the differences between us disappear, and we can communicate as we did in the time before words."

His voice, Jin noticed, had deepened when he began preaching. His bearing became more relaxed, as if he was in his element at last.

"But to touch this Soul we must forget our differences. We must forget we are on a nameless world at the edge of space, forget who we are and what we have done. We must be as one: we must be Compatible with all of others who touch this Soul. We must ourselves be souls, not bodies, not individuals, that we may remember the time when we were part of the Allsoul, as we will be again. And so I give you Enosis."

Bennett unobtrusively touched a key on the master pad and a note rang out from his 'pad. It was a long, low rumble, and some of the worshippers began to echo it—Jin could hear Malcolm Smith's deep bass off to her right. As the tone slowly climbed more and more people joined in, wherever they were most comfortable, until everyone's voices were joined.

Bennett touched another key and text began to appear on each of the worshippers' pads. Taking their cue, the worshippers turned their voices to words, began to sing the Song to the Allsoul. They sang in the languages of their childhood, rather than in Earthlang, and though there were many in the crowd who had weak or hoarse voices the whole thing came together somehow—the way the Allsoul was said to be the sum of all humanity, the well from which living souls were drawn and then returned. Jin noticed Ande Linden standing at the back of the crowd, unnoticed, singing along with the same look of bliss as all the others. Telling herself she needed the convicts to see she was one of them, Jin connected her 'pad to the network, saw the text appear on the screen. She could not remember the last time she had been to a Service—probably before she left Hanzi—but she remembered the words she had sung so many times at home on Garamond:

> The Soul of the song is my soul
> The heart of the song is my heart
> My brothers and sisters, sing my song with me
> The Soul is my song and I sing my part

Jin felt her voice crack as she sang the last line, remembered how it had always made her cry, even as a little girl. It was no wonder nearly all of the convicts had come—they needed that sense of belonging more than anything else, here at the edge of the universe.

The Apomekanids, Jin noticed, were not singing. Their eyes were closed and the lights on their implants were flashing in unison. They were, she had been told, 'singing' over the network, singing to the network. If Bennett saw the heresy going on in front of him, he made no sign of it.

The song ended slowly, dissolving back into pure sound and fading out as the singers' voices grew tired. There was a moment's pause, filled with the sound of convicts sucking air from their puffers, and then the crowd went silent as Bennett spoke again.

"The way of the Soul is the way of peace," he began. "The Soul is the part of us that is not of this world, and when things in this world are difficult, or seem unjust, we have the peace of the Soul to turn to. There are times, however, when we have to face things in this world, in service to the Soul."

Bennett paused, taking a pull of oxygen from his puffer. Jin remembered Father Philipes' weak words of comfort when the food ships had not come to Garamond, and with them her reason for hating the Church. It held the heart of All-the-Stars but preached peace, not change; love, not justice. Even its rebels were philosophers, wasting their time on hair-splitting arguments about whether the Allsoul had an Enemy and whether or not computers had souls.

"There was once a man who loved and admired his horse, and wanted to communicate this to the animal," Bennett continued. Jin thought she had once read this story in the Book of Parables, but could not recall ever hearing it told at a Service before. "For this reason he gave it only the best of straw for its stall and the best oats for its dinner. He used a silver shovel to take away its dung and a jade urn to catch its urine. All night he would sit by the horse's side and sing songs of love to it, all in the hope that it would understand how much it meant to him.

"One day the man happened to see a fly landing upon his precious horse's hindquarters. Without a thought he swatted the offending insect, but in doing so he startled the horse and it kicked in alarm, killing him.

"The man had done everything he could to tell the horse how much he loved it, but no matter what he did, the horse was still a horse."

The message was not lost on Jin, or on the crowd. The story of their encounter with the creatures—and of Father Theou's beliefs regarding them—had not taken long to spread through the camp. The lights on Father Theou's implant and those of his followers flashed in unison, their faces inhuman in the half-dark. Father Theou opened his eyes, stepped forward to face Bennett.

"Once a turtle was walking down the road," the pateros began.

Bennett opened his mouth as if to interrupt, then closed it.

Father Theou went on. "Tired and thirsty, it stopped by a well. In that well was a frog that, seeing the turtle was tired, invited it to stay the night.

"'Do join me,' he said. 'I have everything I need here—flies to eat, cracks in the stones to sleep in, and cool water and mud at the bottom for hot days.'

"'I could not fit in your well,' the turtle said. 'My home is the ocean, and it is a hundred thousand times bigger than your well is.'

"'Impossible!' said the frog. 'There can be no such place. You're just making it up because you're jealous of my well!'"

This parable was an old favourite, with the frog usually representing someone who refused to accept the Allsoul, and many in the crowd had started laughing even before they heard the last line. Father Theou paused for a second, then asked: "Brother Sims—are you sitting in a well?"

Jin could not help but smile as Bennett struggled to answer. Father Theou's telling had been masterful—she began to understand how he had recruited so many to his cause despite the risks. Bennett was no doubt searching his memory for another parable that would answer Father Theou's, but after a few seconds gave up.

"Only we have souls," Bennett said bluntly. "All others are beasts."

Father Theou turned to the crowd. He had chosen his spot carefully, so that he was standing with his back to the setting sun, its last rays lighting him with a golden aura. "Are you so sure of those answers? Here on this planet where the rain burns and the sky is yellow, are you sure that all the old answers hold true?"

"Father Theou's right," Mariela said. She was a pretty girl with olive skin and wide eyes, whom Jin had seen following Father Theou around. She did not have an implant as he did; only priests had the technical and medical skills to install them. "If the ants are farming the trees, they might be intelligent. We have to bring them the word."

"B-bring them the word? They probably want t-to eat us," answered Daniel Wood. "We should b-burn those trees down, so we'll s-see them coming."

"Murderer!" Mariela shouted out. "What have they done to you? Or do you just get your kicks out of killing innocent people?"

Wood's face hand moved to cover the badge on his chest that showed he was, in fact, a murderer. "Y-you shut up," he said, shaking.

"Brothers, please—" Bennett said, trying to be heard over the crowd.

"Why are we letting those heretics join our Service?" Peter Huyt asked. "Using their implants right in front of us?"

"The implant gives us a purer Enosis. There's nothing evil in it," Father Theou said, as calmly as he could in face of the angry crowd. "The Church is simply afraid of change, as people were when the Church was first founded…"

Father Theou's protest went unheard as the crowd broke up into loud squabbling. Bennett, too, was trying to quiet the convicts, without success. Jin wondered if he had ever expected his first Service to turn into a free-for-all.

"Hey!" she shouted. It was the first thing she had said all evening, and many of the convicts turned to listen. "Someone has to find out more about these things. Father Theou will go whether we let him or not—unless you want to lock him up. We know we need the fence, now, too. Can we afford to have two people doing this job, with everything we need to do?"

"Do we really need that fence?" Mariela asked.

"We don't know—" Bennett began.

"I'll bet they had insects where you come from—did you ever see just one?" Jin said. "There are more. If they decide they don't like us…"

"So why talk to them?" Huyt said. "I say get rid of them, before they decide we're on their territory."

"Murderer!"

"We don't know how many there are—or if any are bigger," Jin said. "The first one I saw was at least twice as big as the one we saw today. We have to learn more about them." She looked around. The crowd had become quieter, watching her. "I think Father Theou is the best choice. He can record what he sees with his implant, and if they are intelligent, he might be able to find a way to talk to them."

Many people in the crowd were nodding at Jin's words, but far from all. Roughly a third of the convicts had clustered around Bennett and were muttering in low voices, casting glances over at Father Theou and his followers.

At the head of the remaining group, Malcolm Smith turned to Bennett sheepishly and said, "She's right. We need to know more, and we need that fence."

Bennett stared hard at him for a second, and then turned to Father Theou. "It seems I cannot stop you," he said.

"Nor should you, though you think otherwise," Father Theou said.

Bennett's hands had balled into fists. The convicts in the group between Bennett and Father Theou were looking nervously back and forth between them, unsure of what would come next. "This project will, of course, take most of your time," Bennett said.

"Yes," Father Theou answered.

"Good." Bennett turned around and walked back to his pod. Most of the convicts stood around a few more moments, waiting to see if anything more was going to happen, then began to wander off. Jin smiled grimly, thinking of the long road that awaited her tomorrow.

Jin paused, catching her breath. She had not slept well the night before. Her dreams had been of defeat, not victory—back in her flagship orbiting Tallinn, watching as Ande detonated ships she'd thought she'd captured, in just moments destroying the fleet she'd spent years salvaging, and all she could do was howl in frustration…

She shook her head, trying to dispel the memory. There was work to be done. She leaned against one of the trees and felt it bending under her weight. Further into the forest she found one thicker than the others, but just as rubbery; she paused for a second, considering, then slowly pulled the top of the tree down to her knee level, so that it was almost bent double. She stood gingerly on its thickest branch, allowed the tree to spring back with her on it.

The tree snapped back up and she slipped off it, landing on her rear. She got up and tried again, holding on with both hands and feet. This time she followed the tree's movement and was able to get her head a bar above the forest canopy before falling back down. With the trees nearly all the same height, from that altitude it was easy for her to spot the old xenologists' station, a half-dozen domed white huts perhaps ten li away. Thankful that she had brought a full complement of puffers she picked herself up off the ground, headed off in its direction.

Just over an hour later, she finally reached the station. When she had first seen the huts, they had looked new, but up close they showed signs of having been abandoned: the airlocks on most were burst, in some cases even missing. There were eight huts, strung in two groups of four along a path that had once been smooth concrete but was broken into shards where the bladegrass had pushed through. Peering inside one of the huts, she could see some of the xenologists' gear still there, lying discarded on the floor. In some spots the rain had burned through the roof of the hut and then the floor. The next hut she looked into had half its roof missing and three of the spindly trees growing in it. In the next, oddly, were the remains of a fire. She took a careful step inside and poked the ashes with her feet, uncovering a thin tube, about a bar long and nearly transparent. After a moment she realized it was a segment of one of the creatures' legs, hollowed by fire and decay.

Jin shivered. She'd never put much stock in talk of *gwais,* souls that had been Incompatible at death and denied return to the Allsoul, but felt sure that if they did exist this was the sort of place they would be. Haunted. She backed out of the hut and moved down the path, heard a low machine hum coming from the next-to-last hut on the right side. Its airlock seal was unbroken and patches of woven bladegrass covered the roof. She hit the signal button, waited. She took a puff of oxygen and rapped her knuckles on the 'lock, hoping Ruchika was not feeling paranoid after her time alone.

After a few seconds the 'lock hissed open, and Jin stepped inside. Moments later the inner door opened and she stepped into the hut. It was small and filled to bursting with computers and survey equipment. Monitor screens covered the walls, the largest of which showed the opening to a large tunnel dug in the earth at the base of a hill. The only concessions to comfort were a wall-mounted mattress and a small cabinet that Jin assumed was the bathroom. A small oxygenator chugged away next to it, cables trailing to the hut's battery, and an empty hydroponics box was in the corner. The air smelled like a Traveller ship, saturated with body odour and stale smells. Jin supposed that either the hut did not have a shower, not even a sonic one like the pods had, or else Ruchika had simply been too busy to use it.

Ruchika was sitting at a console by the wall, on the only chair in the hut, whose base ran in a groove along the console. Her back was to Jin as she manipulated the camera that was pointed at the tunnel entrance. She was wearing her basic duty singlet, her geneworked black-and-gold hair hanging in thick, greasy strands. "What is it?" she asked.

Jin took a breath. "You knew," she said.

CHAPTER THREE

"Brother Sims! You have to come quickly."

Bennett sat up, hitting his head on the ceiling as he did every morning. A young man with long black hair had appeared at the door to Bennett's bunkroom and was shouting him awake. Bennett checked his watch: it was only a few minutes before sunrise, a time when few people were normally awake. The planet had a rotation time of only twenty-two golden hours, which meant that more of the day had to be given over to sleep.

"What is the matter, brother...?" Bennett asked sleepily. He tried to recall the young man's name from his file—he was a restaurant worker from Avalon who had been arrested for selling narcotics—but it didn't come.

"Kenneth. And you have to come see." He turned and ran out into the hall without waiting for him.

Bennett shook his head and wearily climbed out of his bunk. The distribution of food was never entirely equitable in each pod—probably Kenneth had had his breakfast stolen and expected him to settle the situation. After last night, he thought, he could not afford to waste any goodwill, and after pulling on his coverall he headed out after the young man.

As he neared the mess room he started to notice a strong smell. He wondered if the air from outside was beginning to seep in enough to be noticeable, but realized this was not the same. This was more pungent, rancid. When he reached the food dispenser where Kenneth was waiting he saw the source: a package of sweet soymeat dumplings whose seal had been broken at some point in the trip. It was completely rotten, turned to mush in the ship's vacuum hold.

"Just a bad one. You can have mine, I'm not hungry," Bennett lied. He removed the Soft Church insignia from his coverall—the dispenser was programmed to recognize it as it did the convicts' badges—and pressed it to the sensor pad. The light above flashed green and a few moments later a second bag of dumplings popped out of the chute. It too was a tray full of grey mush and smelled even worse than the first. Bennett pressed his face carefully against the chute entrance and immediately drew back, gagging from the intensity of the smell.

"Are they all bad?" Kenneth asked, worry visible on his face. Bennett noticed that there were a few small bites missing from one of the dumplings on the first tray, a testimony to the power of the young man's hunger.

"We'll see," Bennett said, avoiding Kenneth's gaze. There was only one way to find out, and only one person who could help him. Hating the very thought of it, he went out to find Father Theou.

"Yes," Ruchika said. "I knew."

Jin felt disappointed. She had been half hoping for a denial or at least an angry refutation, but Ruchika simply did not care about what she had done. "Why didn't you tell us about the ants? Someone could have been hurt."

"Only stupid people would have been hurt." Ruchika swivelled her chair around fully. "Stupid people shouldn't be on this planet. In fact, people shouldn't be here at all. They're just repeating their mistakes."

Jin frowned, unsure how to pursue this. She had been trained to lead, to take control of each situation, but all of those techniques seemed to pass right over Ruchika's head. "Okay, forget why," she said. "How did you know about the ants?"

Ruchika shrugged. "This is the kind of planet they like."

Jin nodded. "They were on another planet, weren't they? A planet you surveyed. That's why you were arrested."

"Yes. The probes found X1 and X2 just over twenty years ago. We renamed X1 'Formicary' after we had been there awhile. It's from an old language only xenologists still use—it means ant house. We're on X2."

"So are they really ants?"

Ruchika shook her head. "No. They're not even insects like the ones on Earth. They have an endoskeleton inside—a regular skeleton, like we have—and then the exoskeleton you've seen. They're warm blooded, and they communicate with one another, though we never figured out exactly how."

She was becoming more excited now, Jin noticed, starting to lecture. That was the key to getting answers out of her. "So why has nobody heard of them before?" Jin asked.

"The Magistracy destroyed them," Ruchika said. "They called us back as soon as we sent our first report, and wiped out the whole planet—plants, animals, everything."

"Why? Are they dangerous?"

"No. There were things about them, things in my report, that were...awkward for the Magistracy. Then when we got the first results from this planet..." Ruchika paused, bit her lip. "That's all you really need to know."

Jin took a breath. As she'd feared, steering the conversation back to practical matters had reminded Ruchika she had secrets to keep. "So they're not dangerous?" she asked.

Ruchika shrugged. "Well, they could be, I suppose. Each one has a job to do and they do it. Don't get in their way and you'll be fine." Ruchika turned back to her console and started to refocus the monitor.

"How do we know where their way is?"

"They tend to stick to the hills."

Jin stood still for a minute, watching as Ruchika zoomed in on one of the ants coming out of the tunnel. It waved its antennae in a circle in front of it and started to awkwardly turn to the left. "Do you think they're intelligent?" Jin asked.

Ruchika paused. "No," she said slowly. "No, they're...organized, they interact, but I don't think they're intelligent. Not the way we are."

"Father Theou thinks they have souls."

"That's his business," Ruchika said offhandedly.

"Maybe—but a lot of the other convicts seem to care about it. They'd be keen to hear what you think about it."

"No. Absolutely not," Ruchika said. "I need privacy here—I don't want people tramping around the forest, disturbing my observations."

"Well," Jin began, weighing her words carefully. "Nobody but me knows where this place is. Only a few other people even know it exists."

Ruchika raised an eyebrow. "Is this another deal?" she asked.

"Just a request. Keep me informed about the ants—let me know if you find out anything that might be helpful."

"To the group, or to you?"

Jin let that go. "One other thing—Father Theou's determined to go exploring, try to find a way to talk to them. With these cameras, you should be able to get a decent idea of what he's doing. I'd like to know about it."

Ruchika sighed. "All right. If it'll make you leave me alone."

"It will," Jin reassured her. "I'll let you get back to your work right now. I'm a little short of oxygen, can I—?"

Ruchika nodded, pointed to the oxygenator. Jin attached her first puffer to the nozzle and watched the indicator needle rise.

"By the way," Ruchika asked as Jin started filling another puffer. "Suppose I find out the ants are a threat to you. What will you do then?"

"I don't know. Why do you ask?"

"Just don't expect me to help you if anything goes wrong."

"What?" Jin asked. "Why wouldn't you—?"

"I have research to do here. I don't want you mucking it up."

Not knowing how to respond, Jin filled the rest of her puffers in silence. She still had a long walk home ahead of her, and the day was not even half done.

Bennett stood in the doorway to Father Theou's room, looking warily at the mess inside. Like Bennett, Father Theou had his own bunkroom—though in the priest's case it was because other convicts, his followers, had doubled up elsewhere to make room. It looked like a miniature computorium: the empty bunks, and much of the floor, were littered with tools and equipment scavenged from the ship and elsewhere in the pod, sorted into neat piles.

"I'm not here to ask you a favour," Bennett said warningly. "This has to do with the survival of the community. It's in your own interest to help."

"What is it?" Father Theou asked carefully.

Bennett looked away, exhaled in frustration. "It's the food—I think the storage may be corrupted. I have to find out how much is still good."

"Why do you need me?"

"I can't open the storage holds, but I thought with your…technical knowledge…"

Father Theou stood up haughtily. "The Church has never much valued my technical knowledge before," he said.

Bennett bit his lip. "Will you help or not?" he asked.

Father Theou paused. "Lead on," he said at last.

The two men walked in silence along the corridors to the mess hall. A crowd of people was there, looking expectantly at them. A dozen packages of soymeat dumplings were sitting in the corner, quietly reeking.

The crowd parted to let Bennett and Father Theou through and the older man kneeled down in front of the sensor pad. Bennett watched as the pateros used a minitool to open the plate of his implant, then extended a contact from it and inserted it in a small jack just below the sensor pad.

"Well? Can you do it?" Bennett asked.

Father Theou sighed and closed his left eye. After an interminable few minutes, the light above the sensor pad turned green, three long flashes, and they could hear the click as the access door unlocked.

Bennett pulled it open and was knocked back by the smell of decay that came forth. He held his breath, looked inside and saw that the vast majority of the meals were unsealed and rotten. Maybe ten percent, he guessed, were still edible. "We have to check the other pods," he said. "Now."

Father Theou looked up, his composure shaken for once. "Should we try to keep this a secret?" he asked nervously. "To prevent a panic?"

Bennett dropped his head, more tired than he could remember ever having been. "I think it's too late for that," he said. By the time they got to the next pod, everyone would know. He could only hope the other pods were better off, or the convicts would be justified in panicking.

Jin had been trying to find her way back to the valley for several hours. She knew the basic direction to go but kept getting turned around, her head spinning from all Ruchika had told her. She did not even realize she was near the edge of the forest until she heard the groaning nearby.

"Who is it?" she called, wondering if Father Theou or Bennett had come after her and gotten in trouble. She heard a yelp of pain in response and ran toward the source, ignoring the blades of grass cutting at her legs. Kenneth Fujitu was doubled over in pain, clutching at his stomach, groaning loudly and crying. Mariela was standing behind him looking frightened.

"What happened?" Jin asked her.

"The food's gone—we were so hungry." Mariela said.

"He ate one of the fruits?"

She looked down at her friend. "Just a few bites…we didn't know what else to do."

"He has to throw it up. Soul only knows what it'll do to him."

She nodded, leaned over her friend and carefully pushed her fingers down his throat. Jin wondered why she had not asked him to do it himself, then noticed Kenneth's hands were spasming uncontrollably. He choked loudly then vomited yellow-orange pulp onto the ground. Mariela helped him back to his feet.

"What's this about no food?" Jin asked them. "We should have enough for five years."

Kenneth shook his head angrily. "It's all rotten. We came up here to see if these things were okay to eat—you said the ants eat them."

"They live here. We're just passing through. Can you walk?"

Kenneth rose to his feet, with Mariela gripping his right arm tightly. "I'm all right," he said.

"Good," Jin said, starting off at full speed. "You two help him back to the pods. I have to check this out."

Spotting the pods in the distance, Jin started down the slope toward them. As she came near, pausing to take a puff of oxygen, she noticed a crowd had formed in the clearing. She could just hear Bennett's voice, hoarse from shouting.

"Please—there's nothing we can do right now. Please go back to your bunks and try to conserve energy," Bennett was saying.

Jason Barr nodded as he heard this. Once a big man, he had shrunk in every way since Anna died. To shrink to nothing, now, seemed fitting to him, almost worthy of addition to the Classic of Poetic Irony.

Another one of the convicts spoke up, the sandy-haired woman who had stormed out of the last meeting—Liz Szalwinski, that was her name, Jason remembered. He had always valued his memory for words.

"This is our punishment," she said, looking for challenges. "You don't believe it, but it's true. Every one of your crimes will be paid for."

An agon, then; a two-voice poem. Jason had written his share of those, knew the form. The first voice would answer, giving counterpoint to the second.

"Sister, you know that's not so," Bennett said. "Punishment in this world only comes from the Lonely One, and she has shown us mercy."

"What kind of mercy?" asked Jenny Gao, a short woman with long black hair. "To leave us here to starve?"

"It was a mechanical failure—" Bennett was saying, but Jason was no longer listening. He already knew the form, knew how the poem ended.

"Brother Bennett's right," Nick Leung said, moving to stand next to the harried adelfos. Jin was not surprised to see him backing Bennett up: Fleet culture was all about hierarchy, and without a Magistrate to follow the pilot needed another leader. "Nobody did this on purpose. I had to live off those meals for a year once, and by the end a lot of them had gone bad, just like these."

"So you're saying they gave us a hold full of expired food? What are we supposed to do with it?" Peter Huyt asked.

"What I did—we ration it," Nick said, staring him down.

"How much do we have?" asked a pale, stooped woman with grey-brown hair and a Sedition badge.

"A little over a year's worth, at one meal a day," Bennett said. He gave a nod to Nick. "The rescue ship will be here with the right oxygen machines in a few months. We have nothing to worry about so long as we don't panic."

"We wouldn't have to ration it if we only fed the right people," Huyt shouted. "Why are you even letting those heretics stay, Brother Bennett? Didn't the Church condemn them to death?"

"Their sentences were commuted," Bennett protested.

"That's the crime we're paying for!" Liz Szalwinski said. "They're why the food is rotten. They're what's rotten."

Here we go, Jin thought. Some of the angrier convicts were gathering around Huyt and Szalwinski.

"Nobody is going to be denied food. We do not have that authority," Bennett said firmly.

"Well, you don't have the authority to stop us, either," Huyt said, taking a challenging step forward.

Nick aimed a quick kick at Huyt's right leg and hooked his foot around the knee, sending the big man sprawling to the ground when he drew it back. Szalwinski sprang forward and tackled Leung, who tried to kick back but was unable to connect with any force.

Sighing, Jin moved towards the fight. She gave Huyt a precautionary kick in the ribs as she reached around Szalwinski's neck, pulling her arm close in a sleeper hold. After a few moments' struggle, Szalwinski went limp, rolled off to lie on the ground beside Leung.

"Everyone, calm down," Bennett said. He knelt down and offered Nick a hand but he refused it, pulling himself up by his elbows to a sitting position.

"Brother Bennett will send the second message rocket, letting them know about the food situation," Jin said.

Bennett nodded, held his hands out in a calming gesture. "There is no more to say about this for now. This has been a stressful day for all of us—I suggest everyone return to their rooms and rest."

Some of the crowd grumbled at Bennett's order, but many looked ashamed or uncomfortable at what had just happened—few of the crimes they were here for were violent ones. Jin herself had begun to regret what she had had to do. The illusion that the Magistracy still had authority here was all that had been keeping them in line, she thought, and her use of force had just undermined it. She had had to protect Bennett, of course—better he be in charge than someone like Huyt—but it had come down to force much sooner than she had expected. She glanced over at Huyt, who was walking off with his arms around the shoulders of a few admirers, and found herself wondering if Xiang Kao still took commissions. Forcing the thought from her mind, she turned to Bennett.

"So was that the truth?" she asked. "Do we have enough for a year?"

Bennett paused. "Maybe half that. But if the food ship comes on time—"

"If?" Jin asked. "Don't you mean when?"

He looked at her for a second, smiled ruefully. "I tried to send the second message rocket as soon as I knew what had happened." He paused. "Somebody already launched it."

Jin's eyes went wide. "So…"

"So if you're right, and the rescue ship isn't going to come," Bennett said, nodding, "We have no way of contacting anyone. And if we don't find something we can eat on this planet, we're all going to starve."

Jin closed her eyes, remembering the young man choking on stinkfruit. She had a feeling others were going to make the same mistake, despite her warnings, as the food grew more scarce. "Isn't this where you tell me the ship will come?" she said.

"As someone else said, I'm here to provide faith, not hope," Bennett said. "All we can do is wait."

"Funny, that's what my father said," Jin said. "And a ship came all right, but it wasn't the food ship. It was an escaped rebel."

"Is that how you became a rebel?" Bennett asked.

"No," she said. "I didn't even know what he was until much later. All I knew was his ship had food on it, and he could teach me things that let me go to the Imperial Academy."

"What happened, then?"

"One year when I was away at the Academy the food ships were late, again. My father waited, again—but this time no ships came at all. I found out later that he tried to grow algae for food in the mines, the way the Travellers do on their ships. It kept people from starving, but when the food ships finally came they reported it to the Fleet. All the leading citizens were executed for violating Equitable Marketing System rules, including my father.

"That's how I became a rebel."

Father Theou drew a short breath of oxygen out of his puffer and tried to remember how many remained in his bag. He had gone into the forest that morning as soon as he and Bennett had discovered the state of the food supplies. If there was any hope of them surviving here, they would need to find a way to learn from its inhabitants. The stinkfruits were poison, it was true, but he suspected the ants did not eat them either—he had noticed that the one they had seen did not so much eat the fruit as chew it up and store it in a small bladder under its mouth. It was possible that they brought the fruit paste back to the nest to process, like bees turning nectar into honey.

The ant he had been following was taking a path that seemed entirely random. It was the same size as the one he had seen before, though a darker green, and was collecting stinkfruit and storing the pulp in its mouth sac. Finally, when the sac was stretched to almost the size of the creature's head the ant stopped picking stinkfruit and began retracing its steps. Throughout its journey, it waved its antennae along the ground, as if sweeping the dirt ahead of it. Father Theou never saw any sign that it was making use of its six eyes, or that it had made any notice of him.

He could not say why he was so sure the ants had souls. He simply knew, the way he had known when he had glimpsed the soul in the network back on Avalon. At first he had assumed it was a gwai; one of the ways Soft Church pateroi served their communities was to drive gwais out of the people and machines they had possessed. What he had found, though, was quite different—not the poor, tattered shreds of ego that attached themselves to computers to stave off oblivion, but a living, healthy soul. The difference had been as clear as that between a corpse and a newborn child.

He had not accepted this revelation right away, of course. People had said that it was his implant that made him see souls where others didn't, but it was just the opposite—the implant was an instrument of his scepticism, his need to examine what he was seeing more closely before he would openly speak heresy. It had only confirmed what he had already known, and he had a duty to the Allsoul not to keep silent.

The ant led Father Theou to where the ground became too rocky for the trees to grow. The pitch was steep there—this was one of the high hills they could see from the valley—and the opening of a wide tunnel was dug out of the dirt and rock. The ant was heading directly for the tunnel entrance. Father Theou closed his eye, switched his implant over to light-intensifier and went after it. As he stepped under the ledge he realized another ant, this one the size of a large dog, was standing just inside the tunnel mouth. Its shell was a different colour than the other's, a green so dark it was almost black. It waved its antennae over the other ant's face, after which the smaller ant continued into the tunnel. Father Theou, holding his breath, stepped forward and allowed the large ant to do the same to him. To his surprise, the guardian ant gave him only a cursory examination then turned away. Father Theou hurried deeper into the smaller and smaller tunnel, which soon became too small for the ant outside to pass. Its walls were made of an odd, rough substance, like a coarse plaster. He crabwalked forward, wincing at the pain in his knees, until it became so dark that his implant's light intensifier became useless and he had to risk activating its guidelight.

The small cone of illumination it cast showed him that the tunnel was about to widen again. Taking heart from this he pressed on until he came to the mouth of a small cavern. Looking around he saw that it was a meeting point for a half-dozen other tunnels of the same size. Across from him was a tunnel larger than the others, sloping upward like the one he had come from. The floor of the cavern was covered with small pits containing some dark paste or liquid each surrounded by ants of the type he had seen outside a well as another variety, larger and with darker shells. They were holding branches from the trees on the ground and pulling the bark off with their mandibles, then stuffing it into their mouths and chewing it. They then seemed to kiss the smaller ants, passing the chewed bark into their mouth sacs. The small ants then regurgitated the mixed pulp and bark, mouthful by mouthful, and after chewing it energetically they spat it into the pits.

Keeping a close eye on the ants, Father Theou walked up to one of the pits. Again the ants ignored him, carrying out their tasks as though he was not even there. Staying clear of the expectorating ants, he crouched at the edge of one of the pits and put his index finger in the paste. When he drew his hand to his mouth, the paste had hardened on his finger. Closing his eyes he gingerly put his tongue to it, and was rewarded with a taste more disgusting than anything he had ever encountered. The intense urge to vomit that accompanied it convinced him that the process made the fruit, if anything, more toxic. He tried to scrape the dried paste off his finger with his thumbnail but discovered it was rock-hard—he could no longer bend his finger where the paste covered the joint. He rapped his finger against the cavern wall to no effect.

Resigning himself to his trapped finger for the moment, Father Theou slowly made his way around the cavern wall to reach the large tunnel opening. Two more of the large ants stood within, one on either side. Trying his best to appear unthreatening he made a two-fingered Bridge of blessing on his forehead, and waited while they examined him. This time they were much more interested and waved their antennae all over his right arm, touching the shell of hardened pulp on his finger several times.

He forced himself to remain still, reminding himself that the Allsoul would not have let him come this far only to fail. The two large ants turned their heads to face one another, waved their antennae around one another's mouths, deciding what to do with him.

Finally the ants moved aside awkwardly, their antennae still waving in an agitated way. He waited for a few seconds to make sure they were finished with him and then exhaled and took a few nervous steps forward. With the guardian ants behind him he stopped, leaned against the wall and drew a breath from one of his puffers. As he did so he realized the wall was made of the same material that was on his finger. One thing was certain: the ants had a very definite hierarchy, and that likely meant a chain of command. There were undoubtedly other types of ants, some he might be able to communicate with.

He took a few more quick breaths and pushed himself onto his feet, starting up the slope of the tunnel. After a few minutes he was surprised not to see daylight, and wondered how far the tunnel extended. Instead of opening to the surface, the tunnel levelled out and continued onward. Its shape was less organic here, its sides more smooth, the walls and ceiling lighter in colour. He activated his implant's infrared sensor and saw that the walls were being warmed from the outside: he was no longer in a tunnel but a structure on the surface, one made of the material that the ants had been mixing in the vats.

Father Theou followed the tunnel to a T-junction and turned left. He set his implant to record, so that he could retrace his steps if he needed to, and followed the darker walls. These were the inner ones, without the light of the sun behind them, and the ants in authority were most likely at the innermost point of the nest. As he walked along the corridors he saw a number of ants headed in various directions, the small fruit-gatherer types and a few of the bark-chewers. There was also a type he hadn't seen before, cat-sized and bright green, with a bloated yellow mouth-sac that extended all the way along the underside of its body. None of them paid him any attention.

Following the inside walls, he found a broad passage that was headed to the core of the nest, where one of the large ants was standing guard. With a better sense of what to expect he was able to step up to the ant calmly, but this time it did not step aside after it had finished inspecting him. He tried to step past it but it blocked him with surprising speed. It was not aggressive, for which he thanked the Allsoul—its mandibles could probably kill him in a single blow—but was nevertheless determined that he would not pass it.

Undaunted, he went back up the corridor and tried to find another way into the heart of the nest. After a few minutes of tracing the darker, colder walls, he found another broad tunnel with a guardian ant standing in it. He was about to turn back when he saw movement further down the tunnel, pushed his light intensifier up to maximum. He saw another ant, of a type he hadn't seen, where the passage ended in a T-junction. This ant was smaller than the guardians but had a different posture than the others, its head and thorax elevated above the rest of its body. It had a double set of mandibles, a pair of small ones tucked inside the larger ones, and its shell was almost pure black with a pattern of gold blotches down its back. It caught sight of Father Theou and turned its head toward him, the first time he had seen one of them use its eyes.

The ant turned, much more easily than the other types, and moved toward him. Rather than inspect him, the gold ant brushed its antennae along the mouth of the guardian ant for a few seconds and then, satisfied, turned back down the tunnel.

Seeing it turn away, Father Theou willed himself to act. "Hello!" he shouted at it, knowing it was useless. He had seen no evidence they even had a sense of hearing. Trying to get the golden ant's attention, he turned his implant's guidelight back on, waved its beam down the tunnel. It made a weak circle of yellow light at the end of the passage, and the ant stopped, waving its head toward the circle with what Father Theou guessed was surprise. He shook his head, making the light wobble, but after a few seconds the ant turned and continued down the tunnel.

Father Theou stood there for a few minutes after the golden ant had gone, then shone his guidelight on the wall nearest the guardian ant. It turned its head for a moment and then turned away again. He turned off the guidelight and scratched his head, trying to sort out all that he had seen; after a few moments he decided he had seen as much as he could hope to assimilate in one day. Turning around, he began to follow the lighter, warmer walls, hoping to find a way back outside.

As he followed the curving passages he noticed that the walls were getting thinner and thinner, his infrared sensor detecting more and more heat coming through. Soon he reached a corridor where the wall was nearly translucent, though still steel-hard, and he could feel the warmth of the sun on it with his hand. After a few more minutes he reached a tunnel where he saw daylight for the first time in hours. The tunnel was very small—too small for the guardian ants, he noted—but he was beginning to feel claustrophobic and did not want to wait for a larger one.

He lay down on his belly and began to inch forward along the passage. As he did the substance of the floor beneath him changed from the strange fruit-pulp substance to smooth rock. He struggled to squeeze his shoulders through before finally freeing himself, and found himself on a rocky plateau with the forest and valley visible below. Pits had been cut into the rock, each one half full of rainwater. He could see, now, the outside of the nest: it looked like an enormous sand castle made of the yellowy-brown fruit concrete, built at the top of the rocky hill they had carved all their tunnels into. He estimated that the structure was at least the size of the ship he had arrived on, and he could not guess how many ants it might contain.

Father Theou sat down on the rock, saw the sun low in the yellow sky. He wondered suddenly if this planet had seasons: the survey report had said it was temperate all year, but it had been wrong in so much...

He emptied his puffer and stood up, stretched painfully and started down the hill. He did not have time to worry about things that weren't a problem yet—no need to borrow trouble when you already have a cupful, as his mother had said, back when he was a child on Colicos. It was a lesson he had never learned, of course. 'Borrowing trouble' was what she had called it when he had told her about the new ideas he had been learning at the seminary on Avalon; he was sure she'd thought the same, though she'd said nothing, when he began to preach

Apomekanid doctrine. He was almost glad she had died before things went bad. She would have been sent here with him, or at least had her citizenship downgraded for giving birth to an infamous heretic, and he knew that her pride would have made it impossible for her to live with either punishment.

Still, though he knew it was impossible, he hoped some bit of her was still her, and not just part of the Allsoul, so that she could see what he was going to do. If you do borrow trouble, she had said to him once, sooner or later the world is going to want it back—so you'd better be sure you're ready to give it to them. With what he had found, what he was sure he would soon find, he was ready to give it all back and then some.

Jin took a step back to see how Kenneth Fujitu and Malcolm Smith were doing plastering the fence. Since returning from the ants' nest the week before, Father Theou had found a way to reproduce their fruit-pulp concrete by boiling it in rainwater. It seemed to be the perfect building material for this planet, impervious to the rain and able to make an airtight seal; they used that to hold the posts together and anchor them to the wire.

She had sketched out the fence to leave as much room as she could for later construction, suspecting that it would not be long before some of the convicts wanted to live outside the pods. For one thing there would probably soon be new families: Population Control rules were normally very strict on new colonies, but with the food rationing she suspected they might not be getting a full dose of antifertility drugs. She wondered how they were going to deal with the inevitable arrival of children, especially if they were unable to solve the food shortage. *Just what we need,* she thought, *another thing for people to fight over.*

"Good work," she said to Kenneth, whose face was shiny with sweat. She ran her hand over the smooth pulpcrete, felt its reassuring solidity.

"Hot work," Malcolm said, and Kenneth nodded.

"Message received. Go and tell Jason Barr it's his shift."

Before the others were more than a few steps away, a shout stopped them in their tracks. Jin vaulted to the top of the fence, looking for its source: one of the large black ants, one like the first she had seen, had come down from the forest. It was walking in a strange way, in short tangents and half-circles, but was definitely headed for the compound.

Jin looked along the length of the fence, trying to see who had screamed, and saw Kenneth's girlfriend Mariela. She had been at the base of the fence, plastering the boards with pulpcrete, and the ant had come near her, waving its antennae in her direction. She stood still, unable to move, watching as the ant advanced on her slowly.

"Don't worry," Jin said softly. She carefully sidestepped along the narrow fence to within five paces from the ant, watching it carefully. She tried to remember everything Father Theou had said about his experiences with the creatures. "They haven't hurt anyone so far. Just stay calm and wait 'til it moves."

Mariela's back was to the wall, with no way to escape that would not bring her in reach of the ant's mandibles. Kenneth had climbed up the fence and was hanging down from it with one hand, lowering the other to her, but she was unable or unwilling to take it. The ant was very close to her now, waving its antennae over the bucket of pulpcrete she was carrying and the trowel she had been using to apply it to the wall. As the antennae brushed her hand she gave a small cry but swallowed it, holding her breath.

"Mariela, come on. Come up now," Kenneth was saying. He was hanging as far down the fence as he could, and reached down to touch her shoulder.

Mariela dropped the bucket and trowel in surprise, spilling the paste all over the ground in front of her and on the ant. The ant started waving its head from side to side, its antennae moving frantically, loudly snapping its mandibles open and closed.

Kenneth let go of his rope and jumped on the ant with a shout. The ant reared back, tossing him to the ground, and turned toward him. It advanced as he lay stunned and bleeding from the grass. Mariela picked up the bucket and trowel, threw them at the creature ineffectually.

Jin's mind was racing. She had learned a lot about how to fight over the years, but had no idea how to attack something like this. People within the compound had heard the commotion, were running to see what had happened. She ran to where Kenneth was lying and grabbed under his shoulders, trying to pull him away from the ant. It was still disoriented, moving toward them with its antennae flailing. Three of the convicts that had tried to rush Bennett at the Service—Peter Huyt, Liz Szalwinski, and one Jin didn't recognize—had arrived and were picking up stinktree branches used to build the fence. They started to poke at the ant with the sticks, getting it to turn around, but were unable to injure it. The ant, enraged, seized one of the sticks in its jaws and backed the convicts to the wall.

A larger crowd had gathered and was standing back, waiting to see what was going to happen. Some of them were throwing branches that bounced off the creature's dark green shell. Some were running back to the pods, probably to find heavier objects to throw.

Jin noticed Xiang Kao in the crowd: she was slowly moving to the front, carrying a stick a pace long. Jin saw that it was a branch from a stinktree that had been sharpened and dipped in the pulpcrete to harden it.

"Please stand back," Kao said quietly, stepping inside the range of the ant's jaws.

The three frightened convicts looked at her in panic. Expressionless, she raised her stick and stabbed it, in a movement so quick Jin could hardly follow, into one of the ant's six eyes. It shook its head from side to side, dripped a blob of thick goo from its mouth onto the ground, filling the air with a harsh smell.

"Get away now," Kao said to the others as the ant turned toward her.

They made a break for the pods and the rest of the crowd scattered as the ant snapped its mandibles together loudly. The ant moved toward Kao who, retreating, fell on her back.

Jin took a step forward. Before she could do anything Kao held her stick up as the ant stepped over her legs, plunged it into a point on the creature's underside. The ant's jaws opened and closed spasmodically as Kao slowly turned the stick around. Finally, with a small grunt of effort, she used the stick to lever the ant onto its back. It lay there for a few minutes, legs twitching, while Xiang Kao sat beside it in the grass, cleaning her stick.

The remaining crowd started talking quietly among themselves as Jin walked over to Xiang Kao, offered to help her up. Kao looked up at her blankly, took her hand and stood.

"Thank you," Kao said.

Jin didn't know what to say. "I thought you had fallen," she said finally. "How…how did you know what to do?" she asked.

Kao tucked her spear into a belt she had made from cargoweb. "It is my curse. Killing is not an effort for me. Not killing is." She was not looking at Jin, but watching the crowd as they edged away from her. "If I were to kill you now I would strike you in the fifth vertebra, to immobilize you, then stab you in the brain through your eye. I can see myself doing it, as I look at you."

Jin took an involuntary step back. "But you must have learned that. You couldn't have known, with the ant—"

"I did not know." She paused then turned to face Jin. "They all hate me now. People hate what they fear."

"I'm sorry."

"Do not be. They would have learned what I was sooner or later, and I think I may have done a right thing."

Jin looked at the corpse of the ant. "Maybe. Yes, you did. I was hoping they weren't dangerous but…"

Kao poked the creature with her foot. "We do not know that they are. This one may be as I am, one that cannot live in society."

"That isn't true."

"It is. Father Theou said these creatures are a part of the Allsoul. Perhaps some are children of Tartaris, as I am. The rest may be harmless, as you are."

"I'm not harmless," Jin said, fighting back a flash of annoyance.

Kao nodded. "I apologize. It was not an insult—I meant to say that you only do harm when you choose to."

"Oh," Jin said. "You—you did the right thing, here. It needed to be done." She paused, trying to read Kao's face. "What are you going to do now?"

Kao looked around. "I believe I am going to fasten this creature to the fence, as a warning to the others. If they have any intelligence, it should teach them to fear us."

"No, I mean, are you going back to your pod?"

"Yes. They will not be satisfied if I leave before they eject me. They might feel a need to express their frustration through violence, and I have no desire to kill any of them." She started to get a grip on the dead ant's body. "Thank you for speaking with me, Shi Jin. You are the only person who has ever listened to me for this long. I think

I have enjoyed it."

Jin's eyes widened. This was not the way she preferred to make friends. "That's good. I mean, you're welcome, of course. I'm...going to go back to the pod for a bit."

"Of course. I will see you later, Shi Jin."

Jin backed nervously away; then, not wanting to look afraid, she turned and walked back to the pod. Before she opened the 'lock she looked over her shoulder and saw Kao lifting the corpse, nearly as big as she was, and shoving it over the fence.

By morning it was gone.

Chapter Four

Solitude was new to Griffin. To a Traveller, being alone could only mean that you were the last one alive—and indeed the ship felt like a ghost vessel now, its outer ring no longer cradling the cargo pods, the command core no longer full of clumsy landsiders.

It never failed to amaze Griffin how they viewed ships as nothing more than machines built to get from place to place. To Travellers ships were life, alive with their own quirks and personalities. Going from one ship to another was like a landsider moving to a new planet: each had its own customs and taboos. The large ones, especially those that had the TSARINA, were like cities, acting as meeting and trading points for the ships that were stuck in real space. To all the ships, though, big or small, the rules of clan and family meant everything. The first stories a Traveller ever heard were parables about children or adults who had turned their backs on their families and who had died, airless and alone, because no one was there to help them. And now here he was, alone.

The INCOMING SIGNAL chime sounded three or four times before he recognized it. He pulled his legs up to his chest, planted his feet on the viewport he had been looking out of, and pushed himself backwards to the console. He saw that it was a full audio-video transmission, activated the screen. Jin's face appeared, looking excited.

"Jin, what's going on? How are things down there?" he asked.

She filled him in quickly on the ants, the food supply, the near-fight between orthodox and heretic worshippers and what Ruchika had told her. He had to ask her to slow down several times so he could follow all the news.

"Sorry," she said, out of breath. "I thought I could sneak in this transmission while they're all outside. Father Theou found a way to make a plaster that will stand up to the rain—it's how the ants build their nests. They're out now patching the pods, and some of Theou's people are talking about building huts so they don't have to share bunks with the others. But listen, what's important is what Ruchika told me. What it means."

"That there were ants on Formicary, right? Do other people know yet?"

"No, I haven't told them. I wanted to check with you, see if you think I'm right. Ruchika said she knew there would be ants as soon as she saw the planet. If that's true, the Colonization Office probably would've known too. That means we weren't sent here to terraform. We were sent to find the ants."

Griffin looked sceptical. "Why send a ship full of convicts?" he asked. "They'd send scientists, xenologists—"

"Maybe the rest of us are just a cover. Ruchika said her team was called back once they reported what they'd found. Maybe the Fleet doesn't want any one else—the Church, other parts of the Magistracy, the Emperor even—to know about the ants."

"Why not? Why would it be so important to keep the ants a secret?"

"In case they really are intelligent, like Theou said. The Fleet is entirely directed against mutinies and rebellions. So long as we're the only intelligent species in the universe, there's no outside threat to make the Borderless Empire seem vulnerable." She paused, catching her breath.

Griffin thought for a moment. "It seems to make sense," he said at last. "I can't imagine those things would be much of a threat to the Fleet, though."

"It's not them—it's the possibility, the danger that something else might be out there." Jin said. "If there was other intelligent life we'd know there were other ways of doing things, other ways of defining right and wrong, than what the Magistracy says. That's what they won't allow. But that's not all."

Griffin saw Jin smile as she said that and knew she had one more surprise up her sleeve. It was the smile he'd first seen twelve years ago, when she'd explained to him why they were risking a blind Nospace shot to go to what should have been empty space. "What is it?" he asked.

"The ship's TSARINA was supposed to deactivate once we got here, so we couldn't leave. But if they actually have something invested in this project, it must still be operable. We could be mobile again."

Griffin looked over to the console that held the TSARINA controls. Like those on every other ship, it was soldered shut and bore a warning in the strange snaky lettering the Engineers used. Translated, it read:

TOP SECRET ANTI-RELATIVISTIC INTERSTELLAR NAVI-GATION APPARATUS

ALL REPAIRS, MODIFICATIONS AND UPGRADES MUST BE PERFORMED BY A CERTIFIED QUANTUM DYNAMICS ENGINEER

WARNING: TAMPERING WITH THIS UNIT WILL CAUSE IT TO AUTO DESTRUCT.

"Even if it's still working, there's no guarantee I can get it started." Griffin said. The rule on the sign wasn't absolute: back in the old days, aboard his nameship, he had been famous for knowing how to keep a TSARINA going without ever crossing the line into tampering, and in his time with Jin he had pushed that line even further. Still, he had grown up hearing too many stories of Travellers whose ships were stranded at sublight, or who passed into Nospace and never returned. He shook his head and decided to change the subject. "There's something else, though. You said they wiped out everything on Formicary to kill the ants. Do you think they'd bother to evacuate us if they decide to do the same here?"

"That makes it even more important that we restart the TSA-RINA," Jin said. "We may have to get out of here in a hurry."

"What about the others? The boat couldn't carry more than a dozen at a time."

She exhaled softly. "You're right. We need…some other plan. But keep the boat ready, just in case."

Griffin nodded slowly. "All right. Let me know how it goes."

"Okay. Listen—I hear people coming back in. I'd better go. I will keep in touch, though. I promise."

"Sure."

Griffin touched the CLOSE TRANSMISSION key then pushed away from the bulkhead, so that he began to spin slowly in place. Jin always worried him when she got like this, bouncing from idea to idea like a three-body orbit. Even he had not really believed her plan would work, not even when the Fleet arrived at Tallinn and he saw the ships moving into orbital positions for a textbook blockade just as Jin had said they would. It was not until her scavenged ships had come screaming out of the asteroid belt and attacked that he could really believe it. The Fleet ships had been slowed the planet's gravity well, unable to move to battle position in time, and more than two-thirds of them had been disabled or destroyed in minutes.

It had been a brilliant plan, but a tremendously risky one—they had to take out that many enemy ships right away to have any hope of success. A single miscalculated variable and the whole thing would have fallen apart.

Griffin closed his eyes and smiled. That was a game among Travellers, a dance: spinning, hands joined, adding body after body until the system became chaotic. He hoped Jin's guesses were as good this time around, hoped what he had done would not be the variable that made her system chaotic. She had done that to him when they had first met, all those years before, the first time he had gone to the Hanzi waystation.

It had taken him kilhours to convince Elena and Vasili, the Eldest, to leave their usual route and visit the Core. There, he had heard, there were thousands of landsiders that lived in space for months at a time, building ships and crewing defence stations and that would actually talk to a Traveller. It was the promise of profit, of hundreds of students and civil servants willing to pay anything to send souvenirs to their parents and get familiar goods to alleviate their homesickness, that had finally convinced the Eldest to make this journey.

Waiting impatiently for the negotiations to finally end, Griffin let himself drift briefly while the landsiders were conferring amongst themselves. He had watched through the viewport for as long as he could as the ship approached Hanzi, a green-blue planet whose night side was covered with long strings of light in a web pattern, and moved to dock with its waystation. The waystation was a flat disk with an enclosed centre, an asymmetrical lattice of docking spaces spreading out from it.

He had been acting as interpreter for five hours now, during the negotiations with the satellite manager for permission to dock, with the Physical Plant supervisor for oxygen and water refills, with the local merchants for their outgoing cargo, new vids and games, and then with some black-marketers for illegal copies of repair manuals to sell to workers on Distant World colonies.

Vasili had come to the negotiations, for the sake of formality, but was letting Elena do most of the talking. It had been some days since Griffin had seen the Eldest and he was looking much worse. His grey hair, already sparse, was almost gone, the lines on his forehead deepened and his small, thin frame curved in a way rarely seen among his people. Travellers, spared the effects of gravity on their bodies, lived longer than landsiders in the rare cases where they avoided accidents. Vasili was at least a hundred and fifty kilhours older than Elena, and his genes had simply reached the end of their trip. Though he was clearly in a great deal of pain these days, he looked at peace just then—in fact, Griffin realized as he heard him softly snoring, he was asleep.

Finally the negotiations were over; the landsiders, three short, nervous men in the two-piece woven-paper suits fashionable among civil servants on Hanzi, produced the data wafer that was to be their side of the trade. Elena inserted it in her datapad, quickly checked then contents, and then nodded.

Griffin turned to Elena. "Can I go now?"

She looked up from the screen of her datapad, mulled it over a minute. "Yes," she said at last. "But keep track of where you go. We can't afford to come looking for you."

Griffin curled himself up, his back to the 'lock, and shot himself down the hallway. Unlike the maze of scaffolding that made up the docking area, the core consisted of a series of rings, each one higher and broader than his entire ship; after a few moments he emerged in a commercial zone, in the outermost ring, where hundreds of people were milling around, shopping for souvenirs at the various colourful stalls that filled the space. Commerce was not permitted in the Distant Worlds, but here in the Core the rules were more loose. Entrepreneurs were allowed to sell anything which they or their family members had made, which had led to many shop owners adopting or marrying promising cooks and artists. Every store sold icons of all the Emperors, bar-high holosculptures surrounded by auras of light. Floating over the stubbornly horizontal crowd Griffin marvelled at the selection of video art from Gemini, adventure vids from Xerxes, and the latest styles in clothing from Hanzi below. There were dozens of food vendors as well, promising cooking from a hundred different cultures, and they were all vaporizing bits of their meals so that the smell would expand in a cloud of mist, leading patrons to them by the nose.

Griffin saw one of the vendors advertising "Spacer Food" and nudged himself over to get a smell of it. It was highly fanciful, flaming balls of battered meat and free-fall spheres of pastry that were nothing like the ampoules of red algae borsch he had eaten since he was a child, or the powdered-egg puffs Elena made for him on special occasions.

People were staring at him: he levered himself 'down' to the crowd's level and tried to get his feet to adhere to the fuzzy floor surface. He felt conspicuous in his one-piece coverall and briefly thought about buying a simple paper suit to help him fit in. He decided against it when he saw that the landsiders were not bartering for their goods but transferring data from their 'pads to the store computers. Vasili had told him that in pre-Imperial times, before the Equitable Marketing System, people had bought everything by exchanging tokens, but that after the Corp Wars it had been outlawed everywhere but some of the Core Worlds. Even here there were strict controls to make sure most of its value ended up back in the Magistracy's pockets.

Looking at goods he was unable to buy soon palled and Griffin thought about going back to the ship, but realized he could not leave without having seen the Zero-Gravity Gardens. He had heard so many stories about them, how beautiful they were; they had actually been designed by a Traveller hired to improve on some mythical garden from Earth's past.

He found a station map and propelled himself down the corridors until he came to an airlock labelled FLOATING GARDENS. He cycled the 'lock and felt moisture in the air within. The airlock opened on the outer wall of an enormous sphere, with 'locks dotting all of its sides. The room—easily a li around—was full of clumps of earth, bound with webbing, and tanks of green water. Growing out of these were plants of all kinds, trees and flowers and vines that grew in all directions. There were four large lights on the walls which were at a low setting. The entire wall, where there were no lights or 'locks, was covered in a soft green moss. Some of the larger patches of earth had rope ladders leading from one to the other, so that someone unfamiliar with zero-gee could do the tour of the entire room hanging onto them. The air was full of intense smells he could not identify, some sweet and some heavily organic, like fermenting algae halfway to being voidfire.

He turned to face the wall and pushed himself at the nearest clump of dirt, covered with turf. He collided with it gently and let his momentum carry him into the long grass and the soft earth it grew from. He rose to a crouch and pushed himself further into the room; at its centre was a huge tree whose limbs grew outward in all directions.

He had never seen a real tree before, except in vids, and wondered what it would feel like. He caught onto the nearest limb and ran his hand over its bark, surprised at how hard it was and yet so different in texture from metal or plastic. He looked around, trying to absorb every detail and burn it to his memory.

"Are you a Spacer?"

He let go of the tree in surprise, turning to face whoever had spoken to him. He had not realized anyone else was there, but he could now see a young woman with her legs wrapped around one of the tree's lower branches. He reached out to grab the branch and pushed himself toward the base of the tree.

"We're called Travellers," he said. "Why do you want to know?" She looked slightly younger than him but much shorter, as landsiders tended to be, with straight black hair, cut short, and wearing a light-grey paper suit. She gave him a fierce look, as if daring him not to take her seriously.

"I need to do business with a…Traveller," she said. "I was told this is where you come when you visit here, because they do not have plants on their ships." She was speaking very carefully, occasionally stumbling over her pronunciation of words. Earthlang appeared to be her second language, as it was his.

"Yes, I am," he said, catching hold of the tree with his foot. "Are you selling holoscenes? I brought some vids to barter…"

"No. I need passage to Garamond."

He looked at her curiously. "There are passenger ships—are you in the Academy?"

She nodded. "Yes. I'm about to graduate. We're supposed to go home first, for a last visit before we receive our first assignments. But there are no ships going to Garamond."

"I'm sorry," he said, scratching his beard. "I don't know if I can help you, uh…"

"Senior Scholar Shi Jin."

"I'm Griffin." It was Traveller custom never to give their true names to landsiders, only the names of their ships. "I don't think I can help you, Shi Jin. Our ship's pretty small, and we don't take passengers anyway—it's really not allowed."

"I can pay. I have technical files that would be worth a lot in the Distant Worlds."

"Look, I can't really make this kind of decision."

"Can I ask your superior?"

He sighed quietly. "I really don't think—"

"I understand," she said, closing her eyes. "I can't ask you to break the rules for me. You don't owe me anything."

"Well, it'll be all right if you're late, right? There'll be some ships going that way soon enough."

She shook her head. "There are no ships to Garamond," she said.

"Why is it so important to you?"

She closed her eyes. "My father is the Colonial Magistrate there. I haven't had any word from him in over a year, and now they've suspended all travel there."

"Suspended? They'll arrest you if you go."

"I'll take that chance," she said. There was an intensity in her eyes that was hard to look at directly. "Spacers—Travellers are guaranteed freedom of movement by the Magistracy. You are the only way I can reach my father."

He considered her offer, knowing he shouldn't. He knew the Eldest would say that the landsiders' sentimentality was their weakness, but he could not help feeling sympathy for her. More than that, she seemed unlike any landsiders he had ever encountered; the only one he had ever thought was actually listening to him.

"Listen," he said, his heart beating quickly at the thought of what he was doing, "it won't be a luxury trip - there's hardly room for us as it is—"

"It'll be fine. Can we go now?" She was all business now. Listening to her voice, though, he realized how hard she was trying to conceal her joy and relief, how hard she had been trying all along to hide her anxiety.

Griffin checked his watch. "Not yet," he said. "If we get there just before they're about to leave they won't argue so much. Meet me at Dock Three at ten station time."

She nodded and clumsily disentangled herself from the tree, then pushed away with her arms and slowly drifted toward the nearest airlock. He waited until she was halfway across to follow, turned to take one last look at the Garden. He knew he was being irresponsible; he felt guilt but no remorse. What good did it do to cross the universe, after all, if you couldn't meet new people, do some good?

Griffin laughed, his mind back in the present. She had snared him right away, turned him from a comet to a moon in her orbit. Well, he had met new people—maybe, even, done a little good; but that was over. Now it was time to remember where he had come from.

Bennett found Ande Linden just outside the ditch where the fence was to be raised, building a small hut out of stinktree wood and pulpcrete. Unlike many of the huts rising inside the compound, this one was built according to a plan, with the spindly trees piled in a cone for more stability than the pulpcrete alone would provide. It was also much smaller than the others, large enough for only one or two people inside. Ande had been working for several hours in the heat, and the yellow sky made his sweat look gold on his newly tanned face. Seeing him struggle with a large plank, Bennett took an end and helped the older man lift it into place. Ande stepped back to look over his work.

"What do you think?" he asked Bennett, smiling.

"It looks very solid."

Ande nodded. "It should be. Back on Cicero we had this habit— a ritual you might call it—we had to spend our whole thirteenth year out in the wild. No gear, no food but what we picked or caught, just a knife and a field bag. Of course, that didn't mean your parents couldn't spend the year before teaching you what to do—and that's the kind of shelter they taught me to make."

Bennett tried to imagine this immaculate old man living like a Traveller for a year. Somehow he just couldn't see him getting dirty. "Respectfully, you should be teaching the others what you learned, zi Linden. Most of them have never built a shelter before."

"No. The Magistracy encourages specialization of skills—if I showed them how to do it, I would become the shelter-building expert, or one of them would, and none of the rest would bother to learn. And then who'll teach their children how to do it?"

"You were taught."

"So I was. But my parents weren't there to help me. I was the one who had to make it sturdy enough to keep the heat in and the wild animals out."

"Speaking of wild animals—"

Ande held up a hand. "Yes, I know. I hoped we could prolong the small talk a few more minutes; it's always been the part of conversation I enjoy most. But you want to talk about the ants, and what to do with them, or to them, and so small talk is over, yes?"

Bennett wondered if he had hurt the old man's feelings somehow. It was always hard to tell if he was joking or not. "I'm sorry—I know you didn't want to be involved—"

"You're right, I don't. I hope I'm showing that by building my home outside of the fence—I want to give nothing and owe nothing." As Bennett opened his mouth to speak Ande put a hand up, stopping him. "It's not really possible, I know, but it's the best I can do."

"Well, I thought, with all your experience, you might have some suggestions."

"My experience is all worthless. This is a new world, Brother Sims. All the rules and regulations I knew are light-years behind us. When you realize that, you'll stop asking me for help."

"This is still an Imperial Colony. We have a beast out there that may want to wipe us out and we have to decide what to do, if you could just…"

Ande shaded his eyes with his hand, looked over to the hills. "I suppose I owe you something for helping build my house. Well—I wrote a book once, do you know that? It was for my Magistrate of War thesis. I studied every war, rebellion, raid and coup since the days of the Organization of Colonized Worlds, to create the final word on keeping the Borderless Empire together. The first rule I figured out was that you must know at all times if you're at war. War can start a long time before the fighting starts, of course. If you aren't, don't think about it—let people enjoy peace and they won't want to mess it up. But if you are at war, don't think about anything else until your enemy is dead, buried and their name forgotten." He smiled, letting his teeth show. "Meaner than I look, aren't I? The original book is still in the Academy Library, you know. I bound it in olive green leather; I can still remember the smell."

Bennett studied Ande's face carefully before speaking. "Do you have a copy? Could I—could I read it?"

The older man was about to speak, then stopped for a second. "No. No, I don't. You'll have to make do with what I told you. Now, if you'll excuse me, I have only an hour of daylight left and a house to build."

Bennett thanked the old man and walked back to the compound, lost in thought. He had never seen things so clearly. Whether or not the ants were intelligent, whether or not they had souls, was not important. What mattered was that they were at war. Heretics had souls, and traitors, and no one ever questioned fighting against them. You were supposed to forgive them, of course, if they asked for it—but only a fool would let them walk all over you. Ande was right. It was time for him to stop waiting for the fighting to begin, and to start to wage the war.

$$\cancel{2}$$

Peering carefully through the closely spaced trees, Jin wished she had been able to bring a more effective weapon. Ever since the ant attack the forest had felt menacing. There was no way to talk to Ruchika without going there in person, though, and she needed answers. What remained to be seen was whether she had the right questions.

She caught sight of the old station to her left, started toward it. There was a sudden movement above her and she froze. She looked up nervously and saw a small animal struggling in the sharp leaves—a bird of some kind.

"Now, what are you?" she asked, reaching up to help it and making a small cut in her right hand in the process. One of the first things she had noticed about this world was that its yellow skies had no life in them. There had been some birds in the briefing vid, but she had assumed they were as much gwai-glimmer as the gentle meadow and abundant oxygen it had also promised.

The bird lay limp in her hands, its chest rising and falling rapidly. On closer examination, 'bird' was a rough description for the creature. It was shaped roughly like an Earth bird, but instead of feathers, it had broad, stiff overlapping scales. Its head was covered in knobby skin, like a turtle's, and it had a powerful beak. It was black and metallic red and about two hands long.

Jin held her puffer to the bird's beak and gave it a blast of oxygen. It revived and stretched, causing its scales to interlock in a single stiffened wing, but then seemed to change its mind and fell back into her palm.

"Another mystery," Jin said, cradling the bird carefully in her hands and heading off again. "I hope nobody minds you sucking a little of our oxygen."

She came to the xenology station and found bright red triangles stuck to the outside wall of Ruchika's hut. The outer door opened when she banged on the airlock and she stepped inside.

"You're back sooner than I expected," Ruchika said. She was sitting facing the entrance; most of the monitors on the wall were showing views of the area around the hut, and Jin could see the path she had just taken. One of them showed a wide view of the compound and another, a view of just the sky. The hut was, somehow, even more full of equipment than before, with much of it piled up in front of the airlock. The hydroponics box was now full of green leaves. Next to it, half a dozen stinkfruit lay rotting, giving the air the same sulphur stink as the atmosphere outside. There was another smell as well, one she could not identify.

"I have better questions this time." She stepped gingerly over the pile of gear. "Have you seen one of these before?"

"No. Where did you get it?"

The bird gave a small cry, stretched and folded its wings. The hut's oxygen-rich environment was making it more energetic, and it began to make experimental flaps.

"Just outside of here." It tried to bite her, gave her a sweet look.

"Look at those wings," Ruchika said. "They lock to make a better airfoil for gliding—that's for distance. It could have come from a completely different ecosystem. Is that what you came to see me about?"

"No." Jin tossed the bird lightly in the air and watched as it began making short trips around the room, in broad arcs like a paper glider. "You said the ants wouldn't get in our way if we didn't get in theirs, but one of them attacked a convict. How did we get on their bad side?"

Ruchika shrugged nervously. "What have you been doing?"

"Father Theou's been going to their nest. He says they ignored him, but it can't be coincidence this happened at the same time."

"I don't know," Ruchika said, turning away. "Has he taken anything? Touched anyone, annoyed them?"

"I don't know what Father Theou touched, but so far as I know he didn't bring anything back from the nest. The ant that attacked, its body was missing the next morning. Do you think—?"

"They'll be mad? No. It was just a bark-chewer, they probably won't even notice it's gone. As for why it attacked, I don't know. They never hurt anyone on Formicary." Ruchika flicked a key on the console and the monitor views changed to shots of the ant nest. The two screens showing the compound and the sky remained.

"That's strange. There must be something…" Jin stopped, looked at the other woman's face. She looked as though she hadn't slept in a few days. "How did you know what kind of ant it was?"

"I saw it. On the monitor. You didn't need to tell me about it, really, I saw the whole thing. I've been trying to figure it out, but—"

While she was talking, Jin walked over to the bathroom cabinet, put her hand to the door. The smell was stronger here. Ruchika stood up unsteadily, reached toward her. "Don't, I—"

Opening the door, she saw the carcass of the ant hanging from the ceiling. Its shell had been peeled off in strips and she could see the flesh underneath.

Father Theou was lying on the sunken floor of the hut his followers had built. His eye was shut, the lights on his implant blinking as the recordings he had taken of the ant nest flashed before him. He had to make sense of the attack, which went against everything he had learned about the ants. He had seen no evidence of violent behaviour among them; their whole life was a model of cooperation, each of them working toward the greater good like Brothers at the House.

The one that had attacked must have been a rogue, he thought, exiled from the nest for its violent tendencies. Driven from its food source, it had come down to the valley, maddened by hunger, and the convicts' ignorant reactions had enraged it. It was the only scenario that made sense.

He felt a touch on his shoulder and started. Just one of the others, probably Mariela, reminding him it was time to eat. He closed the files playing on his implant and opened his eye. Standing there was the woman they said had killed the ant—Xiang Kao, the assassin.

"What—how can I help you, my child?" he asked.

"You are the pateros who says the creatures have souls."

"Yes." She was looking at him with an intense, unblinking gaze, making Father Theou feel naked. He reached down to feel the reassuring texture of his robe, touched coverall fabric instead.

"I would like to ask you a question, one only you can answer." She had not changed her expression since he opened his eye. He stood unsteadily, trying to gain the advantage of height, but it did not help.

"Of course," he said, as reassuringly as possible.

She stared at him a moment longer. "Do I have a soul?" she asked.

"Of course you do. We all do."

"But my soul comes from the Enemy, and your Church says there is no Enemy. If that is so, how can I have a soul?"

"You—your soul doesn't come from the Enemy. There is no such being. We are all part of the Allsoul."

"But you say the ants are part of the Allsoul, and Brother Bennett says they are not. One must be right and the other wrong. If one is wrong, could not both of you be wrong about there being no Enemy?"

Father Theou wanted to explain to the woman that heresy was not an open bag you stuffed everything into; he had gone through a long and difficult crisis of faith to arrive at his revelation, and it certainly did not follow that he would also start believing in every bit of errant superstition people had come up with in the last six hundred years. She was not likely to respond to an argument on that level, though. Better to address her misguided belief directly. "Why do you think there is an Enemy? What makes you believe in it?"

"It protects me. My parents tried to kill me when I was very small, but they did not succeed."

"Why did they try to kill you?"

"They knew what I was. They knew there was an Enemy. When they saw I was tainted they cast me out of the camp."

"But don't you see—they were the ones who were wrong. It is possible that you might have been possessed by a gwai as a child, but they did not understand, and so they turned to the old superstition of the Enemy." He smiled sadly. "Belief in Tartaris, you know, has caused much more evil than such a being itself might ever inspire. They exposed you to the elements because they could not believe, on such a hard world, that anything could be soft. But the Church is Soft, and you too can be made Compatible, if you wish it."

He felt the woman's eyes burning into him. "I know you believe what you say," she said. "I am sorry you cannot see that I am of a different nature. You offer me Compatibility to soothe my soul. If I have no soul, you cannot help me."

"You do have a soul," he pleaded. "The fact that you can ask the question gives you the answer."

She shook her head. "I am sorry to have taken your time," she said. For the first time he could hear emotion, a trace of bitterness, creep into her voice. "You have important work to do, tending to those who have souls. If you are right, and there are more than we believed, you will have no time to tend to those of us who do not. Goodbye."

Father Theou watched as Xiang Kao turned and left. He wanted to shout after her, to convince her that she was wrong—but what could he say? From what he had heard, the rest of the convicts agreed with her, even if they did not believe in the Enemy. Perhaps when his mission to the ants was well underway, and one of his acolytes could take over the services, he would assign someone to counsel her. There was a proverb, after all, from the early days of the Church: even a stone can be Compatible, if it has a soul. Few others took it so literally as he did—he was where he was for saying silicon and germanium could have a soul—but even the Inquisitors would surely agree this woman had to be reached. It would have to wait, though. There were thousands, possibly millions of souls on this world, waiting for him.

The ant carcass swung back and forth on the hook. Jin turned back to Ruchika, puzzled. "Why did you take it? You could've asked."

"I needed to hurry. Someone would have wanted it. Father Theou would have wanted it. You would have wanted it."

"You didn't have to lie to me about it. People thought the ants took it—that they were going to want revenge, or something. A lot of people are terrified of those things."

"I know. I'm sorry. But they made me leave Formicary; took my first specimen before I could dissect it," Ruchika said, sounding like a child.

Jin sighed, rubbed her eyes with thumb and forefinger. "Well. What have you found out?"

The xenologist shook her head. "No, not 'til I'm sure. I can't release my research until it's ready."

"Can you at least tell me if there's any way we can keep the ants away from the compound?"

"Yes. They don't like the colour red." Ruchika frowned, shook her head. "We learned that on Formicary, but I never found out why."

Jin nodded. That explained the triangles on the outside of the hut. "If you knew, why didn't you—" Jin stopped. There was no point in get angry with Ruchika; it would just make her withdraw, and Jin still needed answers. She took a deep breath before continuing. "The other thing is, we have a food shortage. The food we brought is rotten, and we're going to need to get more somehow. Could we have some of the stuff you put in the hydroponics box?"

"You mean seeds?" Ruchika asked. "You're going to grow your own food?"

Jin shrugged. "I've already survived one death sentence. And we'll all die anyway, waiting for the food ship."

Ruchika stood and fished a half-dozen foil packets out of a drawer. "I'm not sure they'll grow in the soil here, though. You'll have to prepare the soil first, mix in terrestrial bacteria. I hope you don't expect me to help. They may not grow at all."

"I might as well try." Jin looked the other woman in the face. "The rescue ship isn't coming, we both know that. There's only one important person on this planet—and you have all the food and air you need."

As she neared the compound, Jin swerved, taking a detour to pass by the sole hut outside the fence. She saw Ande working on his hut and called to him.

He turned to greet her. "This is a surprise," he said, giving her the quick bow of equals. "Welcome to my almost-finished abode, zi Shi. What can I do for you?"

Jin studied the old man's pleasant face, tried to imagine him giving the order to drop a sky full of ships on an inhabited planet. "Some of the convicts respect your opinion," she said carefully. "Maybe they're wrong in that, but I need your help to make sure—"

"Not interested."

"I haven't told you what I want."

"You've told me enough," Ande said. "We have a lot of history between us, though we never met before coming here. You ought to hate me for what I've done. You ought to call me a murderer, hold me responsible for the deaths of your comrades, the end of your rebellion, the whole process that made you end up on a planet where the sky is yellow and the air stinks." He chewed his knuckle for a second before continuing. "Instead you come to ask me for help with whatever your scheme is. What does that say?"

"It means this is important," she said.

"No," the old man said, turning away. "It means you want it too much."

She reached out and grabbed his shoulder, spinning him around. "So if I didn't want it, if I didn't care whether we lived or died, you'd help me?"

"You don't care about that. This isn't about right and wrong, it's about pride. It's about you wanting to be right more than anything else in the universe."

She let him go. He brushed himself off, walked toward the river. "That's not true," she said to his back.

"That's exactly what I said."

Jason Barr thought for a moment, dipped his trowel in the darker pulpcrete and applied it in a swirling stroke to the side of the hut. It was like poetry, in its own way: the trowel a coarse brush, laying thick and thin strokes on paper. It felt good, working again, doing something other people would see, even if they would only see it as something to live in and not a work of art.

It had been a long time since he had done any work at all, either poetry or painting—since well before his arrest, back on Gemini: the elegies he had written for his wife, the ones that had violated the Emperor's call for "happy and beautiful" art, had been meant to be his last work. Somehow this world, with its reports of strange creatures, had inspired him, and he had designed the new living quarters to fit his imagination's idea of how the ants' homes looked. The others, most of them, only cared that the pulpcrete kept the rain off and the oxygen in. But some might see how he had chosen the mix of orange-browns to create something that would never have been built in the Empire, might never have been built by a human. The layout of the huts was unplanned, little more than pits lined and covered to keep the oxygen in, but they bore an alien aesthetic that could be found nowhere else.

This planet was ugly, they all said. Well, he could not argue with that—but could they not see it was beautiful as well? A sky yellow like the peel of some sweet fruit, a horizon of grass and trees so perfectly straight and vertical they looked like they had been scratched into the landscape with a razor. If the Soul had been in a baroque mood when he had created Gemini, with its glittering buildings nestled in jungle, it had been minimalist here, and perhaps this was the stronger composition for it. It was not a composition of which the Lonely One would approve, of course. The fields of bladegrass, a parchment written with the blood of those that walked in them, were not happy, and they were not beautiful; or if they were, it was a beauty the Emperor would never be able to see.

Jason paused, turned to see whoever it was that was calling. Over the last few years he had increasingly needed to see whoever was speaking to understand them. It was Shi Jin, trying to organize a meeting in the clearing between the pods. Jason shook his head, turned back to the wall he was plastering. He had work to do.

Daniel Wood was hurrying to the far side of the fence when Peter Huyt caught his arm.

"Something's up," he said. "The rebel's calling a meeting."

Daniel looked sadly at the bundle of sticks under his arm. He had heard they gave off a numbing smoke when burned, and had been waiting for an opportunity to try it. It had been nearly two years since he had been arrested and made to stop taking the anhedon, two years of emotion, of caring about things.

"A-all right," he said, dropping the sticks in a nonchalant manner, committing the spot where they had fallen to memory. "W-what's it about?" he asked.

"Don't know," Huyt said, putting on that all-business City Magistrate voice he liked to use. Daniel knew enough about politics to know that City Magistrate was a joke of a job for Huyt's family on Palimpsest, a job given to untalented younger sons in the knowledge that they could not possibly mess it up. That Huyt had nevertheless managed to do so did not speak well of his abilities, though it did explain why his powerful family had been willing to hang him out to dry.

The two of them walked briskly along the circuit of the wall, heading back to the clearing. Daniel hoped he would not have to talk during the meeting. Talking was what had stalled his career, made him settle for the position of Rites and Music Instructor at the Planetary Academy on Xerxes rather than going on to the Imperial Academy, made him afraid that his stutter would make him a perfect target if he did not have some kind of protection. So long as he stayed near Peter, though, people would probably respect the big man enough to leave him alone. *Oh, sweet Soul*, Daniel thought to himself, realizing that Huyt was the closest thing to a friend he had on this planet.

They passed through the open gate, saw a crowd had formed. Huyt pushed through it and Daniel followed, looking for Bennett. He was standing silently at the front of the group, his arms folded, watching Jin carefully as she spoke.

"...found some things out about the ants," she was saying. She held up a triangle of red plastic. "These will keep them away, if we put them up on the wall."

"How do you know that?" Huyt asked, elbowing a small woman aside to get to the front. "Where did you get those, anyway?"

"There was a survey team here before us. They found something out—had these made to protect themselves."

Daniel had been to a dozen voice teachers over the years, knew what that little pause meant. *She's hiding something,* he thought, *but what?* He felt a sharp jab in his ribs, turned to see Huyt looking at him expectantly. *Oh, void.* He took a deep breath, tried to calm himself.

"W-w-why didn't you tell us about this before?" he asked, not listening for the answer. He was tired of being Huyt's party trick, the stutterer who was so incensed that he spoke up despite his disability. He wished he could leave now that he had done his duty. Instead he let his mind go blank, remembering the calm and quiet the anhedon had given him.

"This is open rebellion," Bennett said. He stepped into the middle of the circle, with Nick Leung and Peter Huyt following to flank him. He did not much like having to rely on a brute like Huyt for support, but between Ande's refusal to serve, Father Theou's heretics and Jin's constant needling he could not refuse it.

"It's survival," Jin said, her face betraying no emotion.

"Could we really grow crops here?" Kenneth Fujitu asked.

"Shut up, you," Huyt spat at him.

"I think they could," Malcolm Smith said, ignoring Huyt. "Back on Hesiod we had to mix a special powder into the soil each season to make it produce. I know some of it winds up in the food—we could take the spoiled stuff and use it for that."

"Good," Jin said. "We're going to need to clear a lot of land, though, and take good care of the plants if we want any to come up. We'll all be needed for this. We have to work together—"

"Under your command, I suppose?" Bennett said, not quite managing to conceal the anger in his voice.

"No, vack it, out of your own self-interest."

"Shi Jin is correct," said a voice from someone Bennett could not see. The crowd parted and Xiang Kao stepped forward.

"This is simply not going to happen," Bennett said. He held his hands out in front of him in what he hoped was an authoritative way. "We are still part of the Borderless Empire. There are basic rules we still have to obey."

"You're the only one here with anything to lose—"

Before Bennett could reply, he felt himself being pushed aside by Nick Leung; he fell to the ground and saw Xiang Kao's spear miss him by less than a finger.

Jin took a step forward, put a careful hand on Xiang Kao's shoulder. "Don't."

"She was going to kill him," Huyt said. He and Nick Leung had shaken themselves out of their shock and were helping Bennett back on to his feet.

"No, she wasn't…" Jin could not think of anything to say. Kao was standing absolutely still, holding her spear point down, staring at her.

"Do you see what they will do?" Bennett said as he got to his feet. "Some of you have embraced the second chance you have been offered. Some," he looked at Jin significantly, "have not. They will lead you into error if you let them."

"We can't let someone like her stay here," Liz Szalwinski said. "It isn't safe."

Jin wondered if Kao expected her to speak up. By any standard of right and wrong she should, but if she could not convince at least some of the convicts to help her grow crops they would all die. She hoped Father Theou would speak up—his followers would not abandon him under any circumstances—but he said nothing, an expression of resignation on his face.

Kao finally began walking toward the gate. The crowd gave her a wide berth and then, when it became clear she was going to leave, people began shouting, yelling at her to go and not come back. Jin wondered how many people realized they were sending her to a death sentence—wondered how many of them would have cared. She watched in silence as Kao passed out the gate, which some people in the crowd closed behind her. She could go to Ruchika's hut, she thought, and tried to avoid wondering how she might be able to find it.

She had underestimated Bennett: that much was clear. He was clearly no longer the earnest missionary who had asked for her help. Something had hardened him.

The crowd was beginning to break up, feeling a need to release some of the energy they had built up in their condemnation of Xiang Kao. Jin stayed where she was, looking at the gate. She had never shied away from making sacrifices when they were necessary—she knew a few pawns had to be lost to win the game. That did not mean she did not regret it, that she did not play each move over and over again in her mind, trying to see if the losses could have been avoided. It did not mean she forgot that each and every piece she had sacrificed was a person—usually a friend.

Ande put down his pail of pulpcrete when he heard someone

around the other side of his hut. He had been receiving altogether too many visitors lately, fraying his nerves. He should not have said anything to the young adelfos. He was so tired, though, he would have done almost anything to get him to go away. Something about this planet's air gave him a permanent sinus condition; making it a labour just to breathe and filling him with mucus that matched the sky perfectly in colour.

Had he ever imagined that he would end up somewhere like this? He had studied history, must have known that those who fly highest, fall furthest. Back in his days as a senior scholar, though, that could not have been anything more than a cliché, something one of the instructors would say to a precocious student. For him and his friends it had seemed that life could only be a continuation of their present existence, a long drunken debate held under the warm Hanzi sun. They would all stay together, study to be Fleet Magistrates, the highest office in the Magistracy, and together they would defend the Lonely One against all his enemies.

Where were they all now? Only he and Charlie Soren had continued their studies, the extra years required too much of a deterrent to the others. David Black had gone back to his home planet of Gemini, where he had wound up as Planetary Magistrate. Sei Shimbun had worked with the Colonization Office for a few years and then taken a position at the Xenological Institute. Charlie had had his ups and downs as a Fleet Magistrate, and as for him, he—he was here.

He walked slowly around his hut, wondering who it would be this time. Perhaps that xenologist had the right idea, and he should just go somewhere that no one could find him. He did not recognize the woman waiting for him at the door to his hut. She sat cross-legged on the ground, looking up at him.

"Hello," he said. "Can I help you?"

"I am sorry," she said. "I am Xiang Kao. I…"

He understood now. He had heard that the famous assassin was in the camp: once word was out, it was only a matter of time until they became afraid enough to make her leave the compound. And once they did, there was only one place for her to go. "I don't have a lot of room," he said.

She rose. "I am sorry. I will not impose—"

"No, no. You're welcome to come in. I just meant, it'll be a bit crowded, but that's all right. You're welcome to share the floor, if you like."

She stood still for a minute, considering his offer. "Thank you, zi Linden," she said. She gave him the half bow owed a superior. "Are you sure I am not imposing?"

He smiled, shook his head, giving her the quick bow of an equal. "Being a hermit wasn't working out so well for me anyway. Maybe this'll spur me to make some furniture."

Slowly, tentatively, she smiled. "I learned to make furniture, when I was a child," she said. "I...had to live by myself, for awhile. I learned from a book. I could make you a chair, if you like."

Ande felt her watching his reaction carefully. "I'd like to have a chair," he said. "Maybe you could teach me, too."

Her smile broadened, then faded. "You are not frightened by my...my crimes?"

"We're all criminals here. There's no sense in being snobbish." He gestured toward the other side of the hut. "Now come on, help me get the oxygen pipe connected. Then we can see about making some furniture."

多

Everyone likes being in a mob, Jin thought, watching as others piled branches for bonfires. Expelling Xiang Kao had made the convicts feel in control of their fate for the first time in a long while, and their unity under Bennett, a welcome change from the uncertainty of living on this planet, had charged them up.

She would have thought that his first experience with the stinkfruit would have taught Kenneth Fujitu to avoid it, but the young man had persisted in experimenting and was now revealing his findings to the group, acting with the authority of an Engineer. For days after the incident he had been telling people he had seen visions and colours after eating the fruit: now he was showing other convicts how to burn the wood so that the smoke gave a similar, less intense effect. She remembered he had been arrested on Avalon for selling narcotics and laughed to herself. As Bennett had said, this was the planet of second chances.

With Kenneth's encouragement, the party was soon going strong. The stinkwood burned well, if slowly in the low-oxygen air, and the smoke was having the desired effect on most of those who sampled it. They had been as dry as a Watch Station ever since their ship left Xerxes, not even able to trade for any Traveller voidfire, and tonight was a chance to let go.

Loud whoops could be heard from around the bonfires and Jason Barr, the poet, was singing, a high, hushed song in a language Jin didn't know. He switched to Earthlang for the chorus and the crowd around him joined in with raucous voices.

> I'll go up the highest mountain,
> I'll go down the deepest sea,
> I'll go through the frost and fire,
> But darling, I'll return to thee!

Many convicts danced to the song, fresh voices joining in to replace those that were running short of oxygen. The air was becoming thick with smoke from the fires, and she could feel herself becoming light-headed. Fujitu's instinct was a good one. As improvised intoxicants went, this was near the top.

One of the convicts, leaning over a fire to inhale the smoke more deeply, accidentally dropped his oxygen puffer and was rewarded with a whoosh of flame that singed his eyebrows. Some of the dancers began to return in pairs to their huts, or just to find spots where the light of the fires did not reach.

Jin listened for a while to the singing and then rose and joined in, knowing it was not a celebration but a promise. *I won't let you down*, she said to all of the voices that sang in her dreams. *I won't forget you.*

Sitting at the edge of the firelight, Bennett turned away from the music and dancing and looked up at the stars, embarrassed at all of the excitement around him. He was used to the ecstatic mood that would sometimes occur during a service, but this was entirely outside his experience. He had to remain aloof from the crowd and set a good example—there was no easier way to lose respect than to get caught up in emotion and do something foolish.

He looked back at the fire, enjoying the sight of so many normally solemn faces smiling and laughing. Perhaps he should join in, Bennett thought. He had made sure, tonight, that they were not going to embrace rebellion or treason—that was within his mission. So far as a few minor deviations were concerned, though, he saw no reason to be rigid. From now on he could concentrate on their souls, and turn his attention to correcting the Apomekanids.

After a moment's thought, he turned away from the fire once more. He had not suffered as they had. He did not have a right to celebrate with them. Better to use this time to plan ahead, to think about how he was going to bring the Apomekanids back to Compatibility. Drawing a breath from his puffer, he tilted his head back and looked up, past the thick yellow smoke to the stars above.

"What in the vee is that?" no one heard him say.

CHAPTER FIVE

"You have to see this," Griffin said. "The mass alarm's going off."

Jin rubbed her head, trying to bring the world into focus. Griffin's transmission had awakened her from a deep sleep, and she was still feeling the effects of the smoke. "The rescue ship?" she asked.

"There's a mass out there, but it's only a few thousand li away. The alarm should have gone off hours ago—" He stopped. He was turned partly away from the screen, but she could see his eyes widening. "What in the void is that?" he asked.

"What?"

"There must be something wrong with this mass reading—hang on, I'll switch to the external cam."

He hit a key and the image changed to the view outside the ship. The arc of the planet's atmosphere appeared at the bottom of the frame, the background dotted with stars. In the middle of the screen a large object was hanging in space: it did not look like a ship, but it was not natural either. Its shape was hard for her eyes to follow, a mass of thick and thin curves, pipes, surrounding a roughly oval core. It had a silvery sheen, with flashes of green and blue chasing one another along the outermost pipes. So could see no propulsion, no weapons, and no communications equipment, and it had appeared from nowhere.

"What's the scale on this?" Jin asked.

"It's big," Griffin said, sounding genuinely awed. "If that thing's mass is even half what it looks like, it would take a year of acceleration and a planet's worth of fuel to move it into Nospace."

"What's it made of?" she asked.

"Hang on. I'm getting carbon, silicon, hydrogen, germanium…I'm reading a hundred different elements here. Some of them the computer doesn't even recognize."

She studied the object carefully. When she let her eyes go out of focus she could see the entire thing was changing colour, shifting slowly from red to violet and starting over. The light and dark periods in between suggested it was covering a broader spectrum than she could see. "Any chance it could be one of ours? The Fleet's, I mean?"

Griffin exhaled loudly. "Not unless they hired a new design team, and got themselves some new laws of physics to go with it."

Jin shook her head. She felt confused from staring at the thing, following the flashes running along the pipes. "Is it doing anything?" she asked.

"The whole thing's charged, but I can't read anything specific." He paused. "What should we do?"

"Signal it."

"Are you sure?"

"We have to know."

She waited as he sent the recognition signal that would identify them to any other ship. "Nothing yet...wait, I'm getting a response. I'll put it on."

The screen dissolved into hundreds of small squares of colour, flashing on and off. It made Jin's head hurt. "Turn it off," she said. "Are you sure there's no audio, no files attached?"

"Nothing. Wait—look at this."

He switched the screen back to the exterior view and she could see the pipes surrounding the craft's central core starting to move. They rearranged themselves into a different pattern, with two of the largest ones fusing together where they met. A seam appeared at their junction point, a tiny white sphere emerging through it. As it fell toward the planet, the larger object began to waver in space. The pipes began to spread, covering the oval core completely, and it collapsed in on itself until it had dwindled to nothing.

"Are you tracking it?" Jin asked.

"Yes. It's controlling its descent somehow—I don't see any thrusters—but it looks like it's going to make a soft landing." She could imagine him scratching his head as he paused. "Do you have any idea what's going on here?" he said finally.

"A bit, maybe," she said. "I'd better go—I've got a feeling that thing is going to land nearby. Let me know if anything else pops up."

"Sure. Keep in touch."

She turned off the screen but did not move, still staring at where the image had been. By the time she was out in the corridor, a plan was half-formed in her mind. This time, she would finally have the edge she needed. This time she could make it work. This time she would win.

The crowd had only just begun to notice the object falling toward them when Ruchika arrived. It was descending at a stately pace, like a balloon. They watched it dumbly, standing stunned as they watched the white sphere fall toward them. Ignoring them, she watched it intently, trying to guess where it would touch down.

When it became clear where it was headed, she ran to meet the sphere about a li outside the compound and saw Jin and Bennett walking carefully toward it from the other side. It was larger than it had looked in the air, perhaps forty paces around—a pearl, smooth, pale and translucent. She strode toward it without pausing, up the small rise it had landed on, and reached out to touch it. The sphere felt soft and smooth, like silk, and gave as she pressed her hand to it.

A section of the sphere began to ripple, moving like a fluid. A line of light cut down the middle of the section, dividing it in two halves which drew apart from one another, letting a beam of light shine out from the inside of the sphere. Ruchika stood staring into the light without blinking. Jin, she saw, was shading her eyes, trying to make out what was inside, while Bennett stood staring mutely at the sphere.

Something was moving toward them. It was taller than any human, with long, heavily muscled legs that ended in broad flipper-feet, a barrel-shaped torso covered in loose skin, and small arms that hung limp from its rounded shoulders. Its head was as wide as its body, with flanges of skin running from the top of the head down along the back; no neck, two huge eyes spaced much further apart than a human's, and small, stiff whiskers on either side of them. She could see a sac or pouch of skin hanging from its shoulders on its back. It had grey-green, shiny skin, and two large oval patches on its face, each one slowly changing colour. Each patch had another, smaller patch inside which was also changing. As the creature moved awkwardly past the threshold of the opening, its legs folded in to a crouch. Ruchika realized that the colours on its patches were changing not randomly but in a repeating cycle.

Holding her breath, she extended her right hand, palm upward.

After a pause the alien put out one of its small hands, held it out to her at head-level. The creature stepped forward and opened its wide mouth, showing two rows of small, sharp teeth and pink and yellow membranes within. It offered its hand to her, holding it to her lips.

Ruchika opened her mouth and let the creature put just the tips of its three delicate fingers on her tongue. She noted a bitter taste, an oily liquid on the alien's fingertips, and then went blank. A seal broke in her mind, drawing it and the creature's own into a shared space.

Flashing red!/yellow: Grey/green: Blue/dark blue:

She could no longer see the sphere, or anything else, her mind filled with colours. She struggled against the flow, trying to send thoughts and sounds of thoughts to the other mind.

We communicate like this.

Yellow/blue: grey/grey:

A picture appeared in her mind, of two of these creatures flashing their colour spots at one another. Trying to imagine as vivid a scene as possible, she sent an image of two humans talking to one another.

Communication:

The idea, not the word, had appeared in her head. She tried to think of the idea of "greeting", tried to separate its meaning from its sound.

Greeting.

Greeting: was the response. Otherness: communication: group: question?

She paused for a moment, trying to decode what the creature was sending her and turn it into language. Otherness could mean humans, or it might be her—the idea of any person other than the speaker. If that was right, group might mean humans, or the convicts. Question could mean it was asking her a question—asking if she spoke for humanity?

Affirmation, she sent.

Yellow/red!: Communication: Cooperation: Learning: Question?

The creature began to move backward into the sphere. As it passed the portal they broke contact and the connection ended. The hand that had been on her tongue was drawing an inward circle in the air, as if to pull her into the sphere.

She could hardly breathe. This was the moment she had been preparing for since she was a child, when her parents had read to her from a picture book about the discovery of the Core Worlds. According to the book, when no intelligent life had been found on any of the first colonies, the settlers realized that they were the only beings with souls in the universe.

She had not been convinced. It was only because humans expected other intelligences to be like them, she decided, that none had ever been found. She had spent hours in her room—her nervous parents waiting outside, wondering whether she would ever be presentable to the Gemini social scene—trying to change how she thought, to purge her mind of cultural constructs. It had been almost a mercy to them when she left for the Institute on Mars. They had shown her to all their friends when she was a child, geneworkers proud of their art, and it was better that she be off-planet than embarrassing them by refusing to be put on display.

She wondered why she was remembering, now, the few seconds on the landing pad when she could look out the wayship's portholes and see her parents grieving over their twice-lost child. It had been pulled up out of her mind during contact with the alien, she realized. It had wanted to know why she had been ready.

Glancing back quickly, she saw Jin and Bennett standing frozen, watching her. She smiled at them, turned back toward the sphere, stepped inside as it resealed behind her.

"What in the Soul's name is going on here?" Father Theou had come as quickly as he could, draining two puffers on the way as he ran to where the sphere had landed. When he arrived he saw Jin and Bennett staring at the craft blankly, as if in shock.

"It's impossible," was all Bennett could say.

"It's what we're here for, I think," Jin said, turning to face him. "It's—it's a real alien. I think it was talking to Ruchika."

Father Theou turned on his implant, peered at the sphere though its various sensors. "Where is she?" he asked.

"In there."

He moved closer to the sphere and felt his hair stand up. "Did you hear what they said?"

"They weren't making sounds," Jin said. "They looked like they were…thinking to one another."

Father Theou nodded, scratched his beard. "Soul to soul," he said quietly. He turned to see the convicts still watching, waiting to see what was going to happen. He quickly looked for members of his group, people he thought sympathetic. "This is an answer to my call," he said to the crowd. "I asked the Allsoul to give you the guidance you needed and this is the answer."

"They said there weren't any aliens," Jason Barr said. "They said it was impossible."

Watching the ship, Jason felt something awaken in him that had been gone a very long time. He was curious, genuinely curious. He felt a pang of guilt, as though he was doing a disservice to Anna's memory by letting anything else interest him. But this ship—something about the way it defied reality—Anna would have liked it. It was like her music, blithely ignoring rules that should have applied to it.

He had not written a poem in years, not since Anna's elegies. He was not going to write one tonight, or the next night either, but now, looking at that ship, it seemed to him that someday he might; that there might still be beautiful things in the universe after all.

"And yet here it is," Father Theou said. He reached out to the sphere, almost but not quite touching it. He turned to Jin. "How did she open it?"

"She just put her hand on it. It split right down the side."

He faced the crowd, trying to compete with the spectacle the sphere itself provided. "Brothers, sisters, these beings may never have received Enosis, or they may be close to the Allsoul in ways we cannot imagine. This may be the greatest opportunity to learn or to teach that we have ever had."

Many people in the crowd, not just his followers, were nodding. It was much easier to believe that these beings had minds and souls than to believe the ants did.

"I say we must bring them the word, and take from them what they will give us."

"We don't know if they're dangerous or not," Bennett said, more to the crowd than to him. "Why haven't they let Sister Kaur out yet?"

"She wanted to go in. Maybe she doesn't want to come out," Jin said. She was working something out, Father Theou saw, less interested in the debate at hand than in her own plans.

"We have a duty to bring them Enosis!" he said. "I say the Allsoul guides all things, and this is why we have been brought here—to join with our distant brethren. Are you deaf to the call?"

"No!" Mariela, the youngest and most energetic of his followers, was at the front of the crowd, shouting.

"Do you believe that the Allsoul guides us, gives us life and teaches us virtue?"

It was the first question of the Enosis. All believers knew the answer. "Yes!" some shouted, not all of them his followers.

Father Theou was starting to feel faint, but he could not stop for oxygen and risk breaking the rhythm. "Do you believe that we must bring to Enosis to all who do not possess it, that they may become Compatible?"

"Yes!" Most of the crowd was shouting now.

He put his hands up in benediction. "I will bear the Enosis," he said. "As it has been borne from world to world, drawing the Borderless Empire together, I will bear it across the greatest distance of all." He held his hand up, his palm fingers away from the sphere's surface, near where Jin had told him Ruchika had touched. Closing his eye, he put his hand on the smooth material.

He opened his eye and looked around. Everyone around him was frozen, even Bennett, who was a step away from him. They were all watching carefully, waiting to see what would happen. He paused, lifted his hand, put it down in another place.

The crowd was becoming impatient. He put both hands on the surface, felt around for any mechanism. It was entirely smooth. It was his duty, his destiny to bring the Word to these beings. Something had to be wrong.

"We are not ready," he finally concluded. "We must open our souls more fully to them, before they will let us in."

That seemed to satisfy the crowd, but the moment was clearly gone. Most of the convicts began to slowly walk back to the compound, casting glances over their shoulders at the sphere. The sun was rising on the horizon, turning the sky to a dark orange colour, and the sphere shimmered red with its reflected light. Kenneth came up and put both hands to it, letting the charge make his long black hair stand on end.

"That's enough, now," Father Theou said quickly. "We mustn't bother them. They will show themselves when they are ready."

Kenneth shrugged and turned away, looking like a child denied a toy. Father Theou had to admit he felt the same way. He had been so sure...

"Frustrating, isn't it?" Jin said from behind him. "Not knowing."

"I have faith," he said. "They will reveal themselves, in time."

She nodded. "And how would you react if you found out the aliens don't share your faith? Not a heresy, a heterodoxy, but a completely different belief?"

"I don't know," Father Theou said, rubbing his beard. "I suppose I would think they are as we were, before the Church was founded. Ignorant, and Incompatible, but certainly not beyond salvation."

"But the things they can do, their technology, to call them ignorant—wouldn't it make you question your faith if they weren't even interested in being converted? If they were happy with their beliefs?"

"Is this leading somewhere, Shi Jin, or do you simply enjoy baiting old pateroi?"

She waved the question away. "Forget about faith, then. Suppose they don't want to join the Borderless Empire. Why should they, with what they can do? Suddenly there's another possibility, another way of living people didn't know about before." She paused, short of breath, and took a puff of oxygen. "Do you see? Just the fact that the aliens exist will make us question everything. The Magistracy won't like that one bit."

"Yes," he said slowly. "But we know about the aliens now, and they know about us. What can the Magistracy do about it?"

"They can make sure they aren't friendly. Make them an enemy, and everyone will rally behind the Emperor as she protects us from the alien hordes." She gave a small smile that he knew meant bad news coming. "As soon as the Magistracy finds out about them, we're going to have a war on our hands—and you and I are standing at ground zero."

CHAPTER SIX

A week later, Ruchika had still not reappeared. Jin had gone to work clearing land in an area outside the fence she had marked off with fence posts and comm cable. Some of the convicts—Mariela, Kenneth, and Malcolm Smith—had joined her today, but it was still dawn-to-dusk work. She was on her hands and knees, sawing at a bladegrass root with a sharp piece of scrap metal. The thing was fibrous and incredibly tough.

"Don't just cut it," Malcolm said. "You have to dig the whole thing out, or it'll just grow back."

"How do you know?" she asked.

"It's a weed," he said. "Trust me, I know weeds. Get the whole thing."

She hated to look so ignorant, but knew she was lucky to have his help. He had been a farm supervisor on Hesiod and allowed to keep a garden, so he actually knew something about farming in soil, without machines. She took a breath, wiped sweat off on her forearm and got back to digging her tool under the bladegrass roots. She and the others had stripped to their singlets, and the ribs showing on each of them, even Malcolm, were a graphic reminder of just how important it was they succeed.

It was better to be kneeling, though. Every time she looked up she saw the sphere sitting there, as mysterious as the day it had appeared, mocking her attempts at learning anything about it or its makers. In a way, that was the most disturbing thing about it: it was perfectly featureless, with nothing to connect it to a person or even a pair of hands. Looking at it taught you nothing more than comparing a pawn to a queen without knowing the rules of the game. It was only because she had seen it arrive that she knew it was a machine, a tool built by its makers. The question was what rules they followed, how they moved.

How they moved. The sphere had fallen from space, somehow ignoring gravity, but the ship it had come from had simply appeared and disappeared. So they could move not just in lines, but like a knight—somehow skipping over the space between where they started and where they were going. She had no idea how that could be done, but then she didn't understand the TSARINA either. For all she knew, even the Engineers didn't know how it worked, and crossed their fingers every time they set foot on board a ship. The ball had not moved, but maybe—maybe the space inside it had.

Declaring her work done for the day, she straightened up and began the slow climb up out of the valley. The sky above was a vast yellow bruise and clouds were coming in quickly from the direction of the river. She reached the tree line and started stumbling through the trees in the direction of the old station. Her guess had been right: outside Ruchika's hut, at the end of the path, was an identical twin of the sphere outside the compound. Jin banged her fist on the field hut's airlock and a moment later the 'lock opened without cycling the air out. Ruchika appeared inside, holding an oxygen mask to her face. She opened her mouth but no sound came out. She furrowed her brow, as if trying to remember something.

"What do you want?" she asked at last, taking the mask off to speak.

Jin tried to peer inside the hut. "People are worried," she said.

"That's what you said last time."

"They're still worried. Can I come in?"

Ruchika stood to block her as she tried to step into the 'lock. "No," she said. "But I'll get you your bird. She doesn't like it."

Jin watched as Ruchika turned and went back inside, closing the 'lock beside her. She considered her next move as she waited for the 'lock to open. It looked like Ruchika was the gatekeeper to the alien—she was either going to have to go through her or around her.

The lock slid open and Ruchika held out her hand, holding the black and red bird for Jin to take. "Here." She paused, frowning. "She says it's time to talk to you. Answer your questions."

She took the bird gently. It was not looking well. "She?" she asked, giving it a puff of oxygen.

"The...the alien, you'd call her. Her name is—" She paused, closed her eyes for a moment; her expression changed as she did, becoming blank and then blissful. "Speaks with the light of stars. Sort of clumsy in our language. It doesn't really matter what you call her.

Make it 'Stella'."

Jin nodded, confused. "Is that in her language?"

Ruchika laughed, not pleasantly. "Not even close. It's xenology talk: the language we use to classify animals. It's just easier on the tongue."

"So." She paused to stroke the bird's leathery head, pulling her finger away before it could bite her. "What do they call themselves?"

"They don't really have a word, just a colour. It's—" she shut her eyes again briefly. "Grey-green, but together. Grey-een."

"And you can talk to them? To her?"

"Yes," Ruchika said, smiling. "Not talk, really. We send each other sensory data—so if I wanted to tell you I was hungry, I would just send the feeling of hunger. I'm getting better at it. She's teaching me."

"Okay," Jin said slowly. "Is that how they talk to one another?"

"No. Not all of them can do it; she's sort of an expert on talking to people who don't know how to talk. We've been sharing everything we know about our own species. They are amazing, do you know that? The world they're from—"

"What have you been telling them?"

Ruchika shook her head, sounding giddy. "Don't worry," she said. "We're just another alien species to them. They're in contact with a dozen others; they're all part of this sort of alliance. That's what they want to find out: what we need from them, what we have to offer."

"Tell them we need food. But what do we have to offer?" Jin asked, remembering the huge ship that had appeared and disappeared at will.

"I don't know. That's why she wanted me to talk to you. I mean, my experience with people, besides other xenologists, is sort of limited." She laughed and put the oxygen mask to her mouth.

"Why do you need that? Did your oxygenator break?"

She shook her head vigorously. "No, it's fine, I use it to fill this— she doesn't like too much oxygen in the air. That's why the bird wasn't doing too well, I kept forgetting about it." She shrugged. "Don't worry about me, all right? I'm going to go back in now, but she'll let you know when she wants to see people."

"Can I see her?"

Ruchika paused. "No. I mean, later. She's, tired right now, and that's why she sent me to talk to you. But—later. Definitely later."

"Okay," she said, sighing. "I guess I'd better start heading back to the compound."

"Just a second." Ruchika stepped out of the hut, the 'lock closing behind her. The sphere shimmered and opened as she put her hand on it. "You can go this way."

She looked inside. "Through there? Do I...just step inside?"

"Sure. Try it out."

Carefully, Jin stepped inside the sphere. It was perfectly hollow, with a flat floor to stand on. The inner wall was as featureless as the outer. She closed her eyes, wondering what she could expect to feel. "Ruchika?" she asked. "Is it working?"

Jin turned around. Outside of the sphere, she could see the field where the first sphere had landed and the compound beyond. She stepped out of the sphere, looked around. She had somehow crossed the distance from the station without even being aware it was happening. Father Theou was there with a few of his followers, their mouths open as she emerged from the opening.

"Did they let you in?" Father Theou asked. "Did you—did you see them?"

Jin shook her head to clear it. "No. There's another sphere, up by the old xenology station." She turned back to look at the sphere and saw that it had sealed again. "When I stepped in that one, I came out here."

"How did you get in that one?"

"Ruchika—she's trading notes with the alien. She says they really can talk with their minds, or at least this one can. She calls them the Greyen, says this one's called Stella. It's a private joke, I think."

The priest nodded. "I see. Is it...?"

"She. Ruchika says."

"Ah. Is she willing to communicate with the rest of us?"

"Not yet. Ruchika's keeping her busy for now," Jin said.

"I am sure they will open themselves to receive Enosis soon enough."

Jin raised her eyebrows. "I hope you're not expecting too much, with Ruchika as our ambassador. She's not exactly a believer."

"It doesn't matter. She has a soul, and they will judge her on that," Father Theou said, shrugging.

"You're pretty confident. It might be a long time before we hear anything more from them."

"Faith is my business. I can wait."

She nodded slowly, took a breath from her puffer. "Of course, you might not have to," she said in a carefully offhand way.

Father Theou cocked an eyebrow. "I take it you have a plan to propose?"

"Just an idea. Ruchika said they don't all talk with their minds, the way Stella does. We got a transmission from them, up on the ship. That means that they have a comm system as well."

He tapped his implant thoughtfully. "And this transmission, were you able to make any sense of it?"

"Not yet," Jin said. He had taken the bait. "But you've said you were able to make contact with the network computers, and you've been working on finding a way to talk to the ants. If you can apply that to the Greyen, maybe Griffin can figure out how to transmit to them."

"And your interest in this?"

"Normally Ruchika would be the perfect person to contact the aliens," she said. "The problem is, she doesn't see the bigger picture. What we were talking about, the other night…"

"Yes."

"She can't see that anyone would be less than overjoyed to hear about these incredibly powerful aliens. If we can talk to them ourselves, we can warn them. Maybe keep a war from happening."

"And if that fails, convince them to take your side against the Magistracy?"

As he smiled indulgently, she fought to keep a straight face. He had taken the sacrifice pawn she had set out for him, guessing her 'hidden agenda,' but she knew the idea of communicating with the Greyen was now well-planted in his mind. All she had to do was give him a moment's victory and he would go along.

She put up her hands. "I'm a changed woman, Father," she said. "But you can't deny we're going to need protection when the Fleet comes screaming out of Nospace, guns blazing. That can't be far away, and it's a scene you're familiar with, I think."

"Quite right," he said, nodding sadly. "And not one I'd care to see again. But why are you so sure these 'Greyen' will be willing to defend us?"

She smiled. "I'm not. That's why we have to be able to talk to them. It's hammer and anvil time, Father. If we're not on one side or the other, we're in the middle."

"Not an appealing image, I admit." He paused, squinted up at the darkening yellow sky. "Very well," he said at last. "I can't promise anything, but I'll do what I can."

"Don't worry," she said, following his gaze up to the storm clouds that were gathering. "If it isn't enough, none of us will be alive to blame you."

The clouds filled most of the sky by the time Bennett reached Ande's hut. He had been putting it off for days, but he needed the former Fleet Magistrate's advice. He was not too concerned about Father Theou's rally in front of the sphere—his heresy was too extreme to attract popular support for very long—but the arrival of the alien ship had people worried. The news that Jin had had word from the aliens—she'd said they were called the Greyen—had only increased the rumour-spinning to a fever pitch.

Bennett knocked on the door of the hut, feeling the first drops of rain hit his head. The door unsealed and opened slowly, revealing Ande within. He could see Xiang Kao standing awkwardly in the background.

The old man gave the half-bow due a superior. "Brother Sims, what a surprise. Have you come for more small talk?"

Bennett returned the same bow. "I'm on a more urgent errand, I'm afraid. Some things have happened..."

"Yes, I've heard that. Strange visitors." He paused, moved aside. "Come in, come in. No sense letting all of the oxygen out."

Bennett stepped inside, shaking his head briefly to get the rain out of his hair. The room was cluttered with furniture, a half-dozen chairs and benches. Xiang Kao stood at the extreme other end of the room, looking away.

"Zi Linden, I could step outside," she said quietly.

"No," he said firmly. "I'm not about to accommodate someone else's lack of charity." He turned to Bennett. "Sit."

Bennett stood uneasily over one of the chairs, a fragile-looking arrangement of stinktree branches, and sat down awkwardly. Its legs were too low for him but it was otherwise surprisingly comfortable. *That makes one of us,* he thought.

"Zi Linden—" Bennett began. He stopped, tried to collect his thoughts. "I can see you think I made a mistake, letting her be exiled."

"Not at all," the older man said. "The mistake, the wrong was mine. If I give you a pistol and you go shoot someone with it, which of us is guilty?"

Bennett shrugged. "I am, I suppose. You gave me the means, but I committed the crime."

"Yes, but if I give you the pistol, I am giving you tacit permission to use it, correct? And if I am in authority over you—or if you believe I am in authority over you—then by giving you a pistol I am essentially ordering you to use it. Remember the Book of Shang: it is never wrong to follow the orders of a superior."

"That's right," Bennett said, not understanding.

"So -" Ande paused, sighed. "So, if I order you to use a pistol, and you use it, you are no more than a tool, as the pistol is. And as everyone but the Apomekanids know, a tool is simply the vessel of the action—they have no souls, and so cannot bear guilt." He settled into the chair opposite Bennett. "The victim, of course, is not truly a participant either, in that no choice is made on her part. So we have four parties to our crime: the victim, the pistol, yourself, and myself; but I am the only actual participant, so the guilt is entirely mine."

"But you didn't give me a gun," Bennett said, frowning.

"Yes, I did. And I could prove that to you, if you had another hour, but I expect you would like to leave before the storm begins in earnest. So if we may consider the question of your guilt or innocence settled for the moment, perhaps you could face the prospect of telling me what you want."

"I need you to take command as Magistrate," Bennett said. "I tried to think the way you said, but I just can't get it right, and things are really starting to get out of control."

"Now you know how the others feel," the other man said mildly. "You chose to be here, always knew it was temporary, if you wanted it to be. Now you're in a situation you didn't choose, just like them. Look at it as a learning experience."

"You're a scholar," Bennett said, trying to stay calm in the face of Ande's condescension. "Aren't you the least bit curious about what's going on up in Sister Kaur's hut?"

He raised an eyebrow. "Is that where the alien is staying?"

"That's what Shi Jin says."

"Well, she's the right person for the job. The perfect person, actually." He appeared to consider that for a second before continuing. "It seems to me that things are perfectly in control. The fact that they're not in *your* control is only a problem from your perspective."

Bennett stood, exhaled heavily in frustration. "You have a duty to the Borderless Empire, zi Linden," he said stiffly.

"Yes? Tell me, which is more important, duty to the Empire or duty to the Emperor?"

The last thing Bennett wanted now was to get caught in another of the old man's logic games. "They are the same."

"Of course, of course, so they are. The Lonely One found fault in me, Brother Sims. She, or at least someone acting with her authority, removed me from a post of great trust and sent me here, to a place where I could do no harm and influence no one. That seems to me like a direct order to not give orders or advice ever again, wouldn't you say?"

Bennett couldn't say anything. Talking to Ande was like running in a maze where the walls kept moving around. The right answer was always wrong. "I'm sorry to have bothered you," he said. He waved the old man away as he rose and unsealed the door.

Outside, he leaned back against the wall of the hut and let out a long breath. The rain had picked up and his face was soon wet and burning. It was true, what Ande had said—he was now a prisoner on this planet, the same as the others. All he could do now was pray for salvation.

Wiping the water off his face, he straightened up. He would not forget his duty, even if others did. It had been too long since he had last given a service. That, at least, had not changed; the miracle of Enosis could not be touched. He could do it that night, while the rain made everyone stay inside. It would be a comfort to them, help them forget about the strange and frightening things that had been happening. He began composing his sermon as he walked back to the compound. Faith would be the theme: it was all they had left.

Xiang Kao winced as fat drops of rain stung her eyes. Her body was well covered with the cape that Ande had made out of leaves, but there was no way to keep the water off her face. She regretted having to borrow his cape, and hoped he would not have to go anywhere during the storm. He had been very kind in letting her use it, though he did not understand why she had to go now, during the storm—did not understand why she had to go to Ruchika's hut at all.

She had not known how to explain it. He had been kind to her, giving of his space and oxygen and asking nothing in return. That was not quite true, she realized. It was her company he wanted, for he was as lonely in his way as she was. She felt bad at abandoning him like this, leaving a debt unpaid. She had no choice. She had to know.

Now she had been climbing for half an hour, using her spear as a walking stick. The ground below had turned muddy with the rain and visibility was poor. She had hunted in worse conditions than these, but this was different. When she hunted, she could tune it all out, focus just on the soul she was about to set free from its body. That was not possible tonight, though. She would just have to keep looking.

A flash of movement caught her eye. One of the ants, a large one, was making its way through the forest. Now she began to hunt, tracking it silently and avoiding the gaze of the cameras that had been placed here and there on the path. Blisters along the top of the ant's shell showed that it was not immune to the acid. It was one of the black and gold ones Father Theou had seen in the nest.

The ant moved onward, ignoring both her and the rain, until they arrived at the xenology station. She ignored the abandoned dome huts and focused instead on the shimmering white sphere that stood at the end of the path. The ant, too, went to the sphere first, waving its antennae over its surface, and then turned to the hut. The airlock opened and a woman with dark hair and olive skin—Ruchika, she supposed—put her head out, then went back inside. A moment later the alien appeared. It was not afraid of the rain, stepping out of the hut fully on its long, folded legs.

Kao had not been sure what to expect. She noted its awkwardness, wondered if it was used to a different level of gravity, like the Spacers. It was powerfully built, though its arms were small and weak; it killed with its legs and jaws, most likely.

The ant waved its antennae over the Greyen's outstretched hand, then raised its head and held still. The alien's colour spots flashed, both if them yellow with the small spots turning nearly black. The ant turned slowly, walked back into the forest.

Holding her breath, Kao stepped into view before the alien could return to the airlock. Its spots flashed bright red and blue at her. She heard a jingle as it raised its hand and shook it, noticed it was wearing a metallic chain around its right wrist, the only adornment on its body.

"Stella? What's the matter?" asked a voice from within. The Greyen, Stella, turned back to the airlock, keeping Kao in view. The woman she had seen before stepped out of the airlock, wearing an oxygen mask and shielding her eyes from the rain with her hand. "What is—" She spotted Kao, froze. "How did you get here?"

"I am not here to hurt either of you," Kao said. "I need to speak to the alien." Her heart was beating harder than it ever had on a hunt.

"What do you want?" Ruchika said harshly.

"I need to know—" She stopped, not sure how to explain herself, nor who she should speak to. "The Greyen have souls; they must have an Allsoul. Is Tartaris their Allsoul? Am I...was I meant to be one of them?"

"What are you talking about? Why do you think—" Ruchika froze as Stella put her hand on her lips. She closed her eyes, her angry expression fading. "I'm sorry," she said when she opened them again. "She wants to talk to you. But it's not like talking; it'll just be ideas. Don't try to send back at first. It confuses her, I think."

Kao nodded, stepped forward and opened her mouth. The Greyen gently brushed her fingers across her tongue and she stepped back, breaking contact, overwhelmed by the bitterness and sudden rush of colours.

When her vision cleared, she saw Stella standing still, Ruchika shifting from foot to foot behind her. She took a breath of oxygen and closed her eyes, then opened her mouth again. This time the images were clearer, like pictures; the colours were deep and vibrant, extending into shades she was unable to perceive fully.

After a moment, the shapes grew more solid, forming a group of other Greyen standing around her. She flicked her eyes down and saw that she was a Greyen herself, a tiny version of the others, coated in black mucus. She was lying on a table made of a porous substance she did not recognize, aware of the eyes of the others around her, watching her. Aware of their minds, sending her feelings of security and belonging. Her mother turned to the others and flashed her colour spots at them, and she could sense joy in their minds. They knew what she was and they approved. There was a place for her, here.

She opened her eyes as the images faded. Stella was still standing there, her spots glowing soft shades of blue and green. It was a smile, Kao realized, remembering her mother—Stella's mother—showing the same colours.

"What did you see?" Ruchika asked, lowering her mask.

She tried to prod her brain to think in words. "It's all been a lie, all of it," she said. "I was not born of Tartaris. There was simply no place for someone like me in the Church, in All-the-Stars. But the Greyen have a place for everyone. No one's gifts are wasted."

"Did you see their planet?" Ruchika said, stepping aside to let Stella enter the hut. "Did she show you what it's like?"

"I am sorry," Kao said. She paused, took a breath of oxygen. "I must return now. I have to think." She pulled her cape over her shoulders and turned away. The airlock closed behind her as she began the long trip back to the compound. The rain no longer bothered her. At last, she knew where her home was.

Chapter Seven

Jin sat in the comm room, drumming her fingers over the control panel. She had wanted to talk to Griffin, but the ship's transmitter was too weak to get through the storm. Doing farm work was out, too, since Malcolm had said they had to leave it for a day or two to let the rain soak into the soil. Most of all she wanted to contact the aliens, start her plan in motion, but Theou had still made no progress on his communicator. All she could was wait.

She closed her eyes and began to play a game Fleet pilots played on the long trips into and out of Nospace. Imagine a character—*niao*, bird. Remove an element. Add another to make a new character, flight. Remove an element, add another. Wind. Remove, add. Storm. Again. Chance. Again. Chaos. Again, nothing came to her. That was a bad one to end on. She went over all of her calligraphy lessons, tried adding as many different elements as she could think of and was not able to make a new character. She thought of going back a step, but knew it would not change anything.

Better to start again. Uncarved. Strong. Bending. Change. Loss—
She opened her eyes as the INCOMING SIGNAL chime sounded. She hit OPEN CHANNEL, expecting to receive nothing but static, and a distorted but intelligible voice signal came through the speaker.

"Fleet Shuttle Chuko Liang to Colonial Magistrate, please acknowledge. Repeat, Fleet Shuttle—"

The distortion in the transmission was from velocity, she realized. It had to be a ship coming into the system, but a Fleet Shuttle would not be a food ship.

"The Magistrate isn't here right now," she said into the microphone. "Can I help you with—?"

The transmission cut out. She hit OPEN CHANNEL a few times and then shook her head. She had not been meant to hear this.

She ran through different scenarios in her mind as she went

hunting for Father Theou. She dashed out in the rain, covering her eyes with her arm, and banged on the door to the hut his followers had built.

"Father Theou, it's Jin! We have company!"

The door unsealed and she saw the priest standing behind it unsteadily. "Some of us enjoy sleeping," he said.

"You'll have time for that when you're dead. Let me in." She pushed him aside and stepped in the door, shivering.

"Word from the Greyen?" he asked.

"Other side. We just got a transmission from a Fleet ship—not the rescue ship, I don't think." She shook her coverall where it was loose, trying to dry it.

"What is it here for, then?"

"I don't know, but it wanted to talk to the Magistrate. And that means we can't expect to keep our new friends secret much longer."

Father Theou frowned. "I see. Perhaps we can move the sphere out of sight. How much time until it arrives?"

"Half a blue hour, probably. It'll take a while to decelerate—" A loud boom from above interrupted her.

"You were saying?"

"Lightning. Must be…" She unsealed the door, stuck her head out. "Oh void," she said softly. "Look at this."

He joined her outside and looked up. A ball of flame was visible through the clouds, moving across the dark sky. The compound was shaken by a low rumble as it passed.

"You said it would take half an hour to get here."

"So I did."

"What ships go that fast?"

"Nothing I've ever flown."

The ball of fire slowed. They could hear the whine of thrusters fighting against momentum as it stopped, paused and turned around just before passing over the horizon. People were coming out the pods to see what was going on. The ship came toward them, turned dark as its heat faded, becoming invisible against the night sky. They could still hear its engines, getting louder, and a few seconds later it became visible again, looming over the compound.

It was the smallest Fleet ship Jin had ever seen. It was hardly the size of an orbital wayship, much smaller than even a Traveller sublight. It did not look much like a Fleet ship either. It was long and angular, designed as much for atmosphere as for space. As it passed over she could see it was almost all wings and thrusters, with only a tiny space for a pilot. Seconds after it had cleared the compound its landing thrusters fired, briefly blinding the crowd with their light, and then touched down on the other side of the fence, near the rapids.

The convicts waited for the thrusters to die down and then slowly moved toward the ship, flinching as the rain hit them. Liz Szalwinski was in the lead, urging the others to follow. Jin strained to hear her.

"It's one of ours, that's for sure," Szalwinski was saying. "Those are Fleet markings."

Bennett nodded and said something Jin couldn't hear. A ship like this would not have been sent on a rescue mission. There must have been something in the second message missile—the one nobody admitted to launching—that had made the Fleet very interested in this planet.

As they neared the ship lights under its wings snapped on, illuminating the whole area. Most of the crowd froze. Only Bennett and Szalwinski continued forward as the cockpit unsealed with a hiss and popped open. A person in vac gear climbed out of the cockpit and down a small ladder that had emerged from the side of the ship. He stepped under the ship for shelter from the rain and waited for Bennett and Szalwinski to reach him. Jin stepped forward as the man took off his hood.

"Magistrate Charles Soren, I'm with the Colonization Office. Where's the colonial Magistrate?"

Bennett coughed, gave a hesitant half-bow. "We don't exactly have one. I'm here as a missionary..."

"What's your name, son?" Soren interrupted.

"Brother Bennett. I mean, Brother Sims, zi Soren."

Soren gave him a quick head-bow, the correct address for subordinates, and began shrugging out of his vac suit. He was tall, with tanned white skin and white hair. In his mid-sixties at least, his posture and bearing reminded Bennett of Ande Linden—and, he realized, of Shi Jin. It was clearly something they had all learned at the Imperial Academy, a way of presenting oneself that made people listen to you.

Maybe that was what Ande had been talking about, when he had explained why he didn't want to be involved in the colony—that the same technique, the same voice could serve Jin just as easily as it could someone with real authority.

Soren finished taking off his vac suit and rolled it up in a ball. Underneath he was wearing a two-piece woven paper suit in Fleet black with a stripe of Colonization Office green running down the jacket. He handed his crumpled suit to Szalwinski, not bothering to speak to her, and leaned in close to Bennett.

"Brother Bennett, walk with me," he said, stepping toward the other side of the ship for privacy.

Bennett followed, casting a glance back at the anxious crowd. He would rather this were all done in the open, but could hardly disobey.

"I think you'd better tell me what's happened, Brother Bennett," Soren said. His tone, friendly and reassuring a moment ago, now held a note of disapproval that made Bennett want to beg forgiveness.

"We…well, we think, with all respect to the Colonization Office, there must have been some problem with the survey data."

Soren shook his head, and Bennett felt an urge to straighten his posture and make sure his hair was combed. "What's happened to your Magistrate?" he asked.

Bennett swallowed. "He—well, he—resigned, I suppose you'd say. He, he doesn't even live with the rest of us anymore."

Soren continued to stare at the compound, which was hardly visible even with the ship's lights cutting through the darkness. He held his palm out into the rain and regarded it with an even expression as the corrosive water bounced off his hand. "Dereliction of duty by a Magistrate is punishable by, at a minimum, the loss of citizenship," he said. "You are now the only Citizen on this planet, which means it is your duty to undertake the administration of this colony."

Bennett opened his mouth. His words had fled back into his stomach in the face of Soren's disapproval. He brought his puffer to his lips instead, took a breath of oxygen to help him regain his balance.

"Do you have a respiratory illness, Brother Bennett?" Soren asked. "That's normally a disqualification for deep-space duty."

"No, no," he said, shaking his head. "It's the air here, there isn't enough oxygen. We all have them; it's in my report. Would you like some?"

Soren waved the puffer away. "No need. I have reserve O2 capsules in my sinus cavity. They'll kick in if I get short." He drew his hand in from the rain, a half-dozen small blisters showing on the palm. "It seems to me a lot of things have been allowed to slide since your Magistrate resigned." Soren paused, looked pained. He shook his head and went on. "An unauthorized oxygen generator, housing made of native building materials, no organized plan for meeting terraforming goals—I have to hold you responsible, Brother Bennett. How can you tell me they don't respect your authority when you aren't even wearing your robes of office? I didn't even recognize you when I touched down."

He had completely forgotten that he was wearing coveralls instead of his Soft Church robes. The rain and grass were corrosive, he thought it was best to only wear his robes for Service and for meetings.

"You're—you're right, of course," he said "I'm prepared to accept any punishment you—"

"'Utilize first and foremost your subordinate officers, overlook their minor errors, and promote those who are worthy and capable,'" Soren quoted. "One more criminal is the last thing this colony needs. You have a good sense of responsibility, Brother Bennett—what you just said shows that. For that reason, I am officially naming you Colonial Magistrate of this colony, under the authority vested in me by the Colonization Office."

Bennett blinked. "Are you sure that's wise?" he asked.

"Absolutely. These criminals have gotten a free ride off of you. They need to know that that's over, and this is the best way to do it." He put his hand out to Bennett. Noticing that it was the same hand that had been held out in the rain, Bennett shook it gently.

"I'm just not sure if that's the best way to deal with these people. The times they've listened to me, it was because they thought I was right, not because I had any authority over them. A lot of them feel that we're not even part of All-the-Stars out here—giving me a title isn't going to change that."

"The Borderless Empire is the natural state of humanity. It goes where we go, whether we recognize it or not." Soren sighed deeply, making Bennett feel like a novice who had crashed the system during Enosis. "You're starting from a false premise, that having authority and being right are two different things. You've been letting the criminals decide the terms on which they'll accept your authority, and that has to stop."

"Of course," Bennett said, and gave Soren the half-bow owed a superior.

"Good." Soren turned away, looked out at the compound. "Incidentally, your former Magistrate, you say he's not living in here?"

"No, not quite—he has a hut of his own, just outside the fence. There's a woman living with him there, but there's no impropriety, I'm sure." He paused, trying to read Soren's expression.

Soren nodded quickly and then turned back to face Bennett, all business. "All right, we have a lot of work to do. I have a Colonial Magistrate's uniform in the ship's cargo hold, I'll get that for you in a minute. Right now, I want you to fill me in on everything that's happened since you landed on this planet."

Bennett took a deep breath from his puffer. It was going to be a long night.

Shi Jin wiped her hands on her coverall, fighting the need to exhale. Breathing out meant having to breathe in, and breathing in meant smelling the rotten convict meals she was spreading on the soil. The way Malcolm had explained it to her, besides the drugs in the food that kept the women from getting pregnant, there were also drugs that killed the tiny sickness-animals in the air, which their bodies would have had no defence against otherwise. Mixing the food up into the soil would kill the sickness-animals that lived in the ground, and would let their seeds survive. That was the idea, anyway; there was no way to know if it would work until they tried it. So somebody had to take the job of spreading the stuff over the field. The smell, bad enough in the storage room, had only gotten worse under the hot sun. She was glad Malcolm had warned her not to eat anything this morning.

Finally the pressure in her throat became too strong and she had to let the air out, gagging as more rushed in to replace it. Trying to ignore the urge to retch, she concentrated on working the rotten mass into the soil with her stinkwood rake. The bird she had found darted around her, diving and plucking out bits of still-edible food before she could mix it in. It was slow going, with every muscle in her upper body needed to break up the hard soil, so the bird was not having any trouble getting its snacks.

A shadow passed over her and she looked up. Father Theou was standing behind, covering his mouth and nose with his hand.

"What is that smell?" he asked, his voice muffled.

"It was supposed to be our dinners," Jin said. "With any luck it still will be." The bird, attracted by the glint of Father Theou's implant, landed on Jin's head and watched the priest carefully. "What brings you by?"

Father Theou uncovered his mouth, waved his hand in front of his face. "I wondered if—that thing on your head, where did you get it?"

Jin shooed the bird away as it tried to pull her hair out with its beak. "I found it in the forest a while ago. Ruchika was keeping it for me, says Stella doesn't like it."

The priest looked closely at the bird, which snapped at his nose. "Strange. I haven't seen any animals here other than the ants. Does it have a name?"

"Yertle," she said. Griffin had suggested the name, a character in some old heterodox book he had read.

"Have you been in the compound lately?" Father Theou asked.

Jin leaned against her rake, letting it carry some of her weight. "No, why?"

"Your friend Xiang Kao is back," the priest said. "As you can imagine, her reappearance has caused quite a stir—especially since she appeared, as you did, out of the sphere."

"Really," Jin said.

He nodded quickly. "I heard about it right after it happened— hardly long enough for it to grow in the telling. She would appear to have made direct contact with the Greyen, and is keen to share everything she has learned."

"So what has she learned?" she asked.

Father Theou took a deep breath. "I think you had better hear for yourself," he said.

"They have been lying to us."

The small crowd that had seen Xiang Kao emerge from the sphere—it had been a shell, in Stella's mind—had quickly grown as news of her appearance had spread.

"They have told us that we must fit in," Kao said. She was standing in front of the shell, the small hill that supported it letting her stand a half-bar higher than the crowd. "The Church, the Magistracy have told us that we must make ourselves compatible—but it is they that have failed, they that chose to force us into a mould until we were bent or broken."

She stepped back, turning so that the shell was behind her. "We are not here because we are failures. We are here because we are gifted. They could not accept our gifts, could not use them, and so they sent us here. To die."

Father Theou stood at the back of the crowd, letting others pass in front of him to better see Xiang Kao. He was disturbed to see that the better part of those listening were his fellow believers. He felt bad that he had been unable to soothe her soul, that she had finally been forced to look to the alien for acceptance—but his people did not need to go so far, and he had to remind them of that.

"Sister, there is a place for you and your gifts," he said. "The Church welcomes all."

"You speak of the soul, Father Theou," Kao said, not angrily. "I speak of the world. I have seen a place where we would all be accepted, all valued for the gifts we can contribute—in life, not just after we die. This place was shown to me by the Greyen, Stella. The Greyen have offered to let us join them, as other species have joined. We can live here while they teach us, then join them in the stars."

"This planet and all of you are property of the Imperial Colonization Office," Magistrate Soren said, stepping forward as the crowd moved aside to let him pass. Bennett followed a half-pace behind, wearing a uniform that looked like Soren's but was made of cheaper paper, with a much broader weave. "You ought to think twice before making such irresponsible remarks, young lady."

Daniel stepped behind Bennett and the Magistrate, standing as close to them as he dared. He felt more comfortable now that there was some real authority on this planet, but he knew that it wouldn't count for anything out of that authority's sight. He wished he didn't care, didn't have to care, but the stinkwood smoke had been a disappointment. It had made him feel more, instead of less; he had started out feeling happy, celebrating with the others, but before long they were all making fun of him, threatening him. As he staggered around he saw couple after couple and they had all been him and Marise, not that final image but the way he remembered them in the days right after their contract marriage. He had felt something, then. In the time since then the memory had scabbed over but he could not resist picking at it, bringing that mocking image back over and over again.

"You see how they want to bend you. If they cannot bend you, they will break you," Xiang Kao was saying, ignoring the Magistrate and speaking to the crowd instead. "We have been given a choice. The Greyen have come to us to let us choose our destiny."

He was amazed by the way her voice had changed. The few times he had heard it before it had been weak, hesitant, almost a whisper. Now, though harsh, it had a certainty to it that had not been there before.

Soren deepened his voice slightly in response, giving it an undertone of command. "This is an illegal assembly," he said calmly. "In addition, any convict who remains here for one more minute will be guilty of listening to seditious material. Brother—Magistrate Bennett, please take down the names of every convict attending this meeting. Starting with…"

Soren looked the crowd over. Finally Soren pointed to Kenneth Fujitu. "…him," he concluded.

Xiang Kao took a step forward, put her hand on Kenneth's shoulder to reassure him. He had paled when the Magistrate had looked at him, and was now shaking involuntarily. Daniel imagined himself in the young man's place, took a hesitant half-step closer to Brother Bennett.

"You have no power here," Xiang Kao said. "Your ships and soldiers are all very far away. If we were to kill you, no one could stop us."

"I have the authority granted me by the Emperor. There is no other power," Soren said simply.

Xiang Kao turned and put her hand on the sphere. It opened under her touch. "There is now," Kao said, in a voice as sure as a bell, and stepped inside.

Liz watched as a few of the convicts, Kenneth and two others, followed Xiang Kao into the sphere before it closed. Soren turned to the crowd, not showing any reaction to the convicts that had disappeared through the sphere.

"You may all remain until I finish speaking," Soren said. "First, all unauthorized agriculture will cease. Secondly, by order of the Colonization Office Brother Bennett is hereby granted Imperial Citizenship and appointed Colonial Magistrate. He is now officially in charge of this colony."

Liz stepped quickly to flank Bennett when Soren introduced him. It was important that she show the Magistrate where she stood, right off the bat.

"Well. I—you all know me, of course, and I hope you know I've always wanted what is best for you all," Bennett said. He cleared his throat. "We've had some problems, of course, but I think—"

"Thank you, zi Bennett," Soren cut in. "In addition to his duties running this colony, Magistrate Bennett will be acting as my liaison for as long as this planet is a basis of Fleet operations."

Liz's heart jumped at that. Before her arrest she had worked servicing ships; if the Fleet came they would surely need mechanics. "What kind of operation?" she asked, craning around to see the two Magistrates.

Sims opened his mouth. "That's classified," Soren said before the younger man could speak.

Liz turned away, not wanting to look impertinent. She didn't want to risk ruining her chances. Soren had been disgraced at the Battle of Tallinn, tricked by a rebel just like she had, and he had been forgiven; now she would be forgiven too. It was only fair.

"Classified or not," Jin said, "it's not hard to guess what you have planned. You want to use us as a base for fighting the Greyen, and I don't recall being asked."

"This planet is under direct Fleet administration," Soren said. "Whatever right to consultation you might have had as colony preparation workers—which would have been slight, I assure you—is no longer an issue."

She knew the tone Soren was using, having been taught to use it herself. It was a miscalculation on his part, she thought, a tactic suitable for docile colonists but not for convicts that were already half wild. "Oh, I get it," she said to the crowd, adopting a more casual tone. "We're supposed to just let them turn this planet into a smoking crater. I'm not sure I want to let that happen."

A few people in the crowd voiced their agreement, but quieted down when Soren looked at them.

"You don't have that choice," Soren said.

"Yes we do. We can refuse to help you—sabotage your effort." She turned to the crowd again. "We don't have to get into a war we don't want."

"What do you want to do, give the planet to the aliens?" Liz Szalwinski shouted. "Sell out our own people so we can be friends with—with—whatever they are?"

"They don't have a war fleet on the way," Mariela cut in. "We don't have any reason to be afraid of them."

"No, they're just taking people into that sphere and brainwashing them," Peter Huyt said.

Soren was hanging back, watching the discussion go back and forth. *He's probably never seen anything like this before,* Jin thought. *I hope it scares him.* Soren touched Bennett on the shoulder and nodded toward the crowd.

"People," Bennett said, trying to be heard. He coughed, drew a breath from his puffer. "Excuse me," he said, more loudly. Some of the convicts turned to listen, though a few still arguing with one another. "I think—I am ordering you all to cooperate with any and all Fleet plans, in my power as Colonial Magistrate."

"Is that why you sent off the second missile, Bennett?" Jin asked. "So you could trade in your robes for a new suit?"

He reddened. "I have not abandoned my calling. And I did not send that missile."

That was strange—it did not make any sense for him to deny it now. But if he had not done it, then who—

"Bet that alien-loving xenologist sent it," Huyt said, crossing his broad arms.

"Yeah—or the Traveller."

Of course. That was why he was denying he sent the missile—so long as people were curious about it, the question would divide them. It was, for Bennett, a surprisingly canny tactic. She had one more piece to play, though; something to let them know the game was not over.

"Okay," she said. "We'll consider your suggestion. What do you think, everyone?"

Soren cleared his throat, but before he or Bennett could speak Daniel Wood called out "I-I say M-magistrate Sims is right!"

A half-dozen other people noisily expressed their agreement. Soren cast an angry glance at Wood who shut his mouth, chastened and confused.

Jin smiled, covered it with her hand. She had known one of Bennett's followers would take the bait. The fact that the support of the crowd had gone to Bennett wasn't important; the important thing was that it looked like the group's decision, not Bennett's order. They were less tied to Soren's authority now than they had been before the meeting.

Jin put her hands up in mock surrender. "I guess the group has spoken, Bennett. We're still on your side, after all."

No longer able to hide her smile, she turned and began to walk back to her pod. She forced herself to remember that no matter how good it felt she had only won a tiny victory, with most of the war still ahead of her.

"I'm beginning to understand how you won all of those battles," Father Theou said, turning her attention back to the present. He was half a step behind her, walking away from the rapidly dwindling crowd.

"Let's just hope I don't show you why I lost the last one."

Chapter Eight

They came out of the shell not at the field hut, but just inside the forest on the other side of the compound, near Ande's home. Kao had not known there was another shell near there, but concealed her surprise from the others. They had to be able to feel confidence in her, after what they had just done. She led the others to the door of Ande's hut and knocked on it.

"Kao, is that you?" Ande said as he unsealed the door. "I was wondering—oh, you brought friends."

"May we come in?"

"Of course, of course." He stepped aside, gave them each a quick bow. "We can finally use all of this furniture. I'm afraid I don't know any—"

"Elaine Koch," the other woman interjected. "I used to work two floors below you, actually, in the library."

He smiled slightly and nodded. "I'm sorry. That's a poor reward, I'm sure, for all the books you must have helped me find." He stepped over to Kao, who was resealing the door. "Are your friends staying?" he asked.

"I believe so. There will be more coming, I hope." She slid the round door into place and felt it seal as the higher pressure in the hut pushed it into the frame.

"You've been telling people, then," he said. "About what the Greyen showed you."

"About what I saw. Yes."

He paused, scratched the bridge of his nose. "Is this a good idea?" he asked in a low tone. "Making people listen to you—believe in you—is a responsibility. If you're not sure—"

"I have a responsibility to show what I saw," she said, not looking at him. She owed him too much to show anger. "You are exactly the sort of person I am talking about. A hero of the Empire thrown away like garbage—your talents would not be wasted if we were like them."

"That's what I'm afraid of," he said.

Bennett watched as most of the convicts went back to their huts. Some of Soren's more devoted supporters—Huyt, Wood, and Szalwinski—were standing by expectantly, waiting for instructions. Wood, in particular, was like a dog that had been whipped and did not know why.

He gave them a weak smile and waved them off. It was strange how having authority did not make telling people what to do any easier. The trio reluctantly wandered away, Wood occasionally looking over his shoulder in case Bennett should call them back. He gave the man another little wave—hoping this would reinforce his obviously fragile ego—and was rewarded with a smile and a nod.

"He likes you much better now that you've kicked him in the teeth, doesn't he?" Soren said quietly, not turning to face him. The old man was looking toward the forest, straight into the sun. "Go easy on the treats, though. You don't want to devalue them."

"I hadn't thought about it that way."

"Food tastes better when you're hungry, right? Keep them hungry." Soren looked at him. His eyes were black, like polarized lenses; they lightened as he turned away from the sun. "Not a problem around here, I guess."

Before Bennett could say anything, Soren began marching away in the direction of the forest. Bennett had to run to keep from being left behind, his careless steps letting the bladegrass cut into his legs. Once he was in stride with the older man, he drew a breath from his puffer.

"Where are we going?" he asked.

"To get some first-hand intelligence," Soren answered, not slowing. "This is a Fleet mission, not Colonization Office. You don't have to come if you don't want to."

"No, I'd like to help," Bennett said, watching the ground carefully to avoid cutting himself any further. "I've been up here before."

The other man nodded offhandedly, continued his march. The two continued up out of the valley, Bennett's laboured breathing the only sound. What made this planet feel so unnatural, he realized, was the quiet. Until he heard about Jin's bird, he had believed this world held no animals, no small insects, only the silent ants.

"I thought implants were illegal," Bennett said after a few minutes of silence. They were partway up the rise at the edge of the valley, where the grass began to give way to thick clumps of stinktrees.

"Unauthorized implants are illegal," Soren said. He stopped, turned and looked over the compound below. "Just like genework. When you come down to it, all of us are Imperial property, so you need permission from the Emperor to tamper with it." He paused. "That's why suicide is illegal, of course."

"Suicide is a denial of Compatibility," Bennett said.

Soren raised his eyebrows. "Joke."

Bennett nodded slowly. He could not help feeling the joke was on him. Working for—with—Soren was like talking to Ande all the time, constantly feeling as though he was out of his depth. He paused to scratch under his arm—his new uniform itched terribly—and stopped, realizing how he must look. "Sorry," he said. "I don't hear too many jokes these days."

"Don't worry about it. Here's another one: how many Apomekanids does it take to change a lighting panel?"

"How many?" Bennett asked carefully.

"Just one, but first they have to decide if changing it would be murder." Soren's deeply tanned face creased into a smile at his joke. "No? Thought you'd like that one." He leaned forward, pressed his hands against his thighs and stretched.

"It's very funny," Bennett said quickly, unable to make himself laugh. "I'm just not—"

"Don't worry, I understand. You're still young. When you get older, if you see a little bit of the universe, you either learn to laugh at it or you just give up."

He nodded, thinking of Ande's quiet refusal of his duty. He had clearly made the latter choice, if it was a choice.

"Come on, we've got a lot of ground to cover," Soren said, straightening up and turning toward the forest. He wrinkled his nose as they passed under the stinktrees but made no comment. Bennett followed him, thankful that the older man had decided to slow his pace.

"Can I ask you a question?" he said after a few minutes.

"Of course."

"Why did you talk the way you did at the meeting? To the convicts,

I mean?" He watched Soren's face for signs of offence, went on. "When we talk you explain things to me, you convince me, you tell jokes. With them you just gave orders, like you didn't care whether they agreed or not."

"If I try to persuade them it gives them the idea that they need to be persuaded. We can't afford that. Besides which, if I'm the harsh master, you get to be the kind master. Makes your life easier. Any other questions?"

He thought for a minute. "Are we at war? With the Greyen?" he asked at last.

Soren's pace slowed. "Why do you ask that?"

"Zi Linden told me about the book he wrote. He said the most important thing—"

"Yes, I know. I've read it," Soren said. Bennett could not quite identify the emotion in his voice. "What do you think the answer is?"

His heart sank. Another trap. At least Soren was only toying with him for amusement, rather than refusing to help like Ande. "I don't know," he said. "Maybe that's what you're here to find out."

"Good answer for the Academy," the old man said, smiling. "Bad for the real world. How much of the book did you read?"

"I didn't read it at all, actually. He just told me that first part."

"He didn't tell you all of it." He stopped, took a small instrument out of his jacket pocket. It looked like a miniature datapad, about a hand and a half long, with a loop of gold wire coming out the top. He waved it slowly in a circle around him, watching the screen. "If you don't know if you're at peace, you're at war. It's a lot safer to be at war, so peace is the one that has to prove itself."

"What do you mean, war is safer?" He instantly regretted the impudence of his question, but he was learning that Soren was not sensitive about such things.

"Nobody ever got killed by a surprise peace treaty," Soren said, running his thumb over the instrument's controls. "If you think you're at war and you're wrong, so much the better. Think you're at peace and you're wrong—ah. This way."

Keeping his eye on the instrument, Soren moved rapidly through the forest, turning every few paces. Bennett followed, trying to coax his mind along the path the older man had laid out for him. He wondered why Ande had not told him the rest of the principle, then remembered that getting that much advice out of him had been a struggle.

Ahead of them lay the xenology station. At the far end of the path was another alien sphere, identical to the one outside the compound. They moved carefully down the path until they stood in front of it.

Soren waved the small instrument at the sphere. "Hm," he said, without elaborating further. He turned to the hut's airlock, then reached into another jacket pocket and drew out a small metal disc, only a few fingers around. Running it along the surface of the airlock, he found whatever spot he had been looking for and gave the disc a sharp jab with his palm. The airlock opened with a whine, revealing the small space within.

There was next to no furniture in the room, just a strange sort of swing-and-harness that stood on six poles, made out of a dark purple material. Ruchika and the alien—Stella, he'd heard her called, though he did not know where the name came from—were at the instrument panel. Breathing in, he realized that the air in here was no different from the air outside, low in oxygen and reeking of sulphur. Ruchika was wearing a small air mask with a hose that ran to the portable oxygenator in the corner. The two turned to face them, the alien's large colour spots flashing an angry red, the smaller ones colouring two different shades of blue.

"Get out of here," Ruchika barked.

"Not very hospitable of you, zi Kaur," Soren said as he strolled over to get a better look at Stella. The Greyen rose from its seat, standing nearly a bar taller than the Fleet Magistrate. "This is your new specimen, is it?"

Stella's colour spots changed to a dark, bruiselike purple, the inner spots turning to red and yellow. Her mouth opened, giving a glimpse of the teeth inside, and her broad nostrils flared.

"She won't talk to you," Ruchika said, stepping between Soren and the alien.

"Can't she speak for herself?" Soren asked over her head.

"She talks through me. And we don't want you here."

The Magistrate lowered his gaze, looking directly at her. "We?" he asked. "You were sent to make contact, not make friends. Your cooperation is a condition of our offer of amnesty."

Surprised, Bennett stepped closer. There had been rumours flying around that Kaur's deal was not the same as the others', but he had not given them much credence. Now even they were not the whole story, if she really had been sent to make contact with aliens. But if this was their first contact, how had they known—?

"I already have what I came for," Ruchika was saying, interrupting his train of thought.

Soren cocked an eyebrow, keeping a watchful eye on Stella. She was standing lower now, her legs more bent, and Bennett noticed that the flap of loose skin hanging from between the alien's shoulders had grown since he first saw her.

"We need this specimen," the Magistrate said. "If you don't hand her over, we'll take her."

"Try," Ruchika said, looking past him.

Bennett turned and saw Xiang Kao standing in the 'lock. She was holding her spear low, ready to strike. He cleared his throat and Soren turned as well. He nodded fractionally and began to slide his hand under his jacket.

Before his hand could get inside she was between Soren and Stella, the point of her spear under his chin.

Soren stepped back, nodded at her respectfully and lowered his hand. Turning to Ruchika, he looked at her for a moment longer and shrugged. "Fine. You don't have to make this easy if you don't want to." He turned back to Bennett. "Please note that convict Kaur is impeding the progress of a Fleet operation. All arrangements made with her are accordingly cancelled and sentence of death hereby reinstated."

Bennett nodded automatically. He drew a breath from his puffer and took a step backwards toward the open airlock.

Soren turned back toward Stella, gave the quick bow of equals. "A pleasure," he said. "Convict Kaur, until we meet again."

He spun on his heel and marched out the 'lock, not bothering to see if they were watching him go. Bennett followed after a moment. He did not the willpower to keep himself from looking over his shoulder: Stella had dropped to a low crouch, one of her hands in Ruchika's mouth as she watched him and Soren go.

They walked on in silence for a few minutes, keeping up a quick pace through the forest.

"I'm sorry about that," Bennett said once he had worked up the courage to speak. "I haven't been able to keep an eye on her—I had no idea she would just betray you like that."

"I did," Soren answered, not without a touch of smugness. "Her profile showed very little loyalty toward people, groups or institutions, and a firm commitment to her science. That's how the Institute trains them, of course, but she was an extreme case." He stopped and looked around, trying to retrace his previous path. "If we'd sent someone who was loyal to the Magistracy, they'd hardly be likely to gain the trust of any aliens they encountered, and they wouldn't get any useful information. Whatever bond there is between those two, I've just strengthened it. Kaur is completely on their side now."

"I understand," Bennett lied. "But—if she won't tell us what she finds out -" He stopped, nodded slowly. "Oh."

Soren smiled. It was not a pleasant smile—in fact, it looked uncannily like the expression Stella had when she showed her teeth. "You really do need to read the rest of that book," he said.

"This is bad. This is really bad."

Jin turned to Father Theou for confirmation. They had been discussing the progress of the communicator with Griffin, and he had not had good news for them. The ship's computer had been unable to make anything of the transmission they had received from the Greyen craft, which meant they were no closer than before. If Soren was here, that probably meant that the more massive Fleet ships were already starting to slow down out of Nospace—and that meant they were running out of time.

"The problem is, we don't have any kind of context to make sense of the transmissions," Griffin said. He was stretched out in front of the vidscreen, turning slowly. A half-full ampoule of Traveller coffee floated nearby. "We know the colours mean something, but it's like looking at a screen full of characters and trying to figure out what they mean based on what they look like."

Jin nodded. A sudden flash of childhood memory came to her, wanting to make the character for "monkey" look more like it had a monkey in it. Yertle soared in from the corridor, landed on her shoulder and began pulling at her hair with its beak.

"Wait a minute," she said. "We have a way to get a context—go see Stella. The colours in the transmission must be based on their spots. If Theou uses his implant to record what she flashes and connect it with what she means—"

"How will we know what she means?" Griffin asked.

Jin thought for a second. "I'll ask Ruchika a question while she's in contact with Stella. The colours she flashes will mean the answer we get." As she batted the bird away it jumped off her shoulder and began hopping around the room, cackling in the back of its throat.

"That is assuming sister Kaur gives us an accurate version of the answer," Father Theou said, steepling his fingers thoughtfully. "And assuming you can remember all of the colours Stella displays. Perhaps I should come with you, to record."

"No," she said. "Ruchika's very protective of her. Two of us might be too many—but you're right, we need to record it."

"Father Theou could go alone," Griffin suggested.

"Maybe," Jin said. "I wonder, though—the two people we know she's been in contact with, Ruchika and Kao—"

"We have only Xiang Kao's word on that," Father Theou pointed out.

"Still—they're both women. Ruchika was very sure that Stella was a she. I'm not sure she's interested in talking to men."

"That's a bit of an assumption," Father Theou said, sounding genuinely hurt.

"It's just a coincidence, Jin," Griffin said. "How many xenologists do we have?"

"I know, I know," she said, putting up a hand. "It's a hunch, a feeling. Think about it, though. If you were going to make direct contact, mind-to-mind, wouldn't you want to be sure there was at least one point you had in common, somewhere to start from? Even if they don't have sexes like we do, every species must have some individuals that give birth or lay eggs or whatever."

"So how do you propose to record your encounter?" Father Theou asked, obviously annoyed.

"I'm not sure," Jin said, cupping her hands to let Yertle jump onto them. "Any ideas?"

Griffin stretched and yawned, his long spider legs reaching outside the viewscreen. "You could link your 'pad to the comm, leave the channel open. Take a lot of power, resolution won't be great, but it should work."

"Not much point in saving power now," she said, nodding. "We may only have another week or two before the Fleet gets here." Jin rose, deposited Yertle on the comm panel where he began hopping around, snapping at the various keys. "We'd better get it hooked up so I can be there before nightfall."

"Well then," Father Theou said, rising and brushing imaginary dust off his robes, "if I'm not needed here, I must tend to other affairs. Do let me know when you have results—and also when you come to thinking about exactly what it is you're planning on saying to the aliens." He gave a small wave to Griffin in the monitor and went out into the hall.

Griffin looked thoughtful. "That's a good question, actually. What *are* you going to tell them?"

"Vacked if I know."

Bennett followed Soren down from the forest in a broad arc, arriving not far from the hut Ande had built. He had not asked where they were going. It was obvious that Soren and Ande knew one another, and that the Magistrate had delayed their reunion as long as he could. As they approached they could see a few convicts building another structure next to the hut. Soren narrowed his eyes.

"It's them," he said.

Bennett was unable to make out any detail.

"The ones that went with Xiang Kao?" he asked.

Soren nodded, picked up his pace. A few moments later Bennett was able to see Kenneth Fujitu and Elaine Koch connecting stinkwood poles. As soon as they saw Soren they froze, watching him carefully. Unconcerned, Soren walked up to Ande's hut, rapping three times on the door.

"Just a second," a voice came from inside.

The round door unsealed with a hiss and then opened partway. Soren cocked his head, waiting. A moment later the door opened fully.

"So, it's you," Ande said.

Soren smiled, gave a quick between-friends bow. "May I come in?"

Ande paused, returned Soren's bow. "Of course," he said, stepping aside. "Brother Sims, you've found your new instructor. Or should I say Magistrate Sims?" He turned to welcome Soren. "So, Charlie, what brings you to this part of All-the-Stars?" he asked.

"Oh, you know. Never miss a chance to mix business with pleasure." Soren reached into his jacket, drew out a thin black flask. "Speaking of which, I brought you something. Probably better than whatever they have here."

Ande leaned out the doorway and waved to the other convicts. He put the door back in place and gave it a shove to complete the seal. "They burn sticks," he said. "The smoke makes you funny. The boy out there, the one with the long hair, figured it out. Pure genius."

"I knew it would be something," Soren said, nodding appreciatively. "Wherever we go, we find some way to get funny. I heard once that on Setebos they actually suck rocks."

"It's a tough world. Some sort of chemical…" Ande said. "Sit down if you're going to drink."

"'The virtuous man shivers with delight when asked to dine with his superior,'" Soren said, sitting in one of the roughly made chairs.

Bennett looked from one man to the other. Ande was shorter, his skin lighter and more wrinkled, but they were clearly cut from the same cloth.

"Nice place you have here," Soren said. "You seem to have chosen carpentry as a second career."

"It chose me," Ande said. He brought three small plastic cups, salvaged from the mess room, handed them to Soren.

Soren's flask opened with a pop of broken vacuum as he twisted the top off and then poured two cups full of dark liquid. "You'll like this," he said. "After I got it from the distiller I had my people put it in orbit and forget about it for ten years. Zero-gee lets it ferment in ways you just don't get in a gravity well." He looked over at Bennett and frowned, hesitating over the third cup. "Do you drink?"

"Uh, yes, please," Bennett said. He had only had alcohol once before, on the Lonely One's birthday, four years ago, when Father Dionides had acquired some Spacer voidfire to liven up the celebrations. It had had a strong effect on the novices that had tried it, and he could still remember the headache that had greeted him upon awakening. He took the glass, being careful not to spill, and sniffed at the liquid. Honey and coolant fluid filled his sinuses, already making him cough.

"We were great drinkers, back at the Academy," Soren explained as he passed Ande his glass.

Ande took it with his right hand in an unnatural position, the last two fingers held inward. "You have to learn to hold your liquor to be an Imperial Scholar," he said when he saw Bennett staring. "We were taught all the drinking rituals by a Senior Scholar who'd been around forever and gotten so fat he couldn't even take a wayship into orbit. He would bring just one bottle of wine for his demonstrations, and by the end of class he'd have drunk it all. Then he'd turn to us and say,"—deepening his voice, adding a rolling burr—"'Class, there's no time for you t'try it out today. You'll have to take care of this—'"

"'—as independent study,'" Soren chimed in, both men laughing. After a moment Soren sighed. "I should come to the point," he said.

Ande put up a hand. "A bit more small talk, please," he said. "You owe me that much."

Soren nodded. "Of course. You…look well," he said.

"'Incorrect, Junior Scholar Soren,'" Ande said, this time adopting a sharp, nasal voice. "'Contradicts the facts—could be taken as criticism.'" He paused, returned to his own voice. "Let me try. I see you're wearing a new uniform—have you decided to leave the Fleet for greener pastures?"

"I'm still Fleet," Soren said. "This is a ColOff mission, at least officially, so I'm flying their colours. 'The virtuous man arrays himself properly in his robe and cap, and throws a nobility into his looks, so that men looking upon him stand in awe of him.'"

"And what is the mission, Charlie? Now that I've resigned my commission, can you tell me what I wasn't allowed to know as a Magistrate?" Ande said.

Neither man spoke for a moment and Bennett shrank down in his chair, feeling more and more the outsider. He took a careful sip of his liquor, trying to hold his hand the way Ande did. The thick liquid burned his throat on the way down, making him cover his mouth with his hand and swallow a cough. He wondered how rude it would be for him to put the cup down.

"'The usual. Protect the Borderless Empire.'" For once Soren was quoting not the Book of Shang but a vid series popular enough that even Bennett had seen it.

"Aha. And have your simulated Fleet Pilots run this mission through the simulator?"

"There is no simulator for this situation," Soren said. "We have no data to even start making one."

"Good," Ande said, taking a long pull from his cup. "That machine's the worst thing that ever happened to the Fleet."

"The simulator's proven its usefulness over and over," Soren replied, annoyed. This was obviously an old argument.

"In war games, yes—but it's no preparation for fighting someone who doesn't use Fleet tactics. Which, I can only assume, is what you're once again preparing to do." For some reason that 'once again' sounded like a jab at Soren. Both men were angry now, hurt over something that had happened between them long ago.

"We need you, Ande," Soren said. "Your being sent here—it wasn't personal. We needed to get you in the right place, needed the fact that you don't trust the simulator, that you think things nobody else does."

"And was there some reason you couldn't tell me this at some point during the investigation? Or the hearings?"

Soren sighed. "It needed to look convincing. We couldn't risk anyone knowing how important this place is. Just the idea of intelligent aliens—"

"Is treasonous," Ande finished for him. "So why did I end up here and not you? You seem to have known all about this from the beginning."

"I have someone in the Records Office at the Institute—sends me the first data from all the missions. When I got the results from the Formicary team—what Sister Kaur learned about the ants—I knew at once what it meant. And I remembered what you said that time, about food and ships."

"You think the Greyen are going to go into the business of shipping food to the Outer Worlds?"

"Probably not, but it might be enough to encourage colonies to revolt, if it looks like there's someone outside the Borderless Empire. It might encourage rebels—or even some people in the Fleet—to try to make a deal with them."

"And so now that they're here," Ande said, slowly sipping his drink, "I'm to be restored to my former status? All crimes forgotten, sins forgiven?"

"Of course," Soren said, a smile beginning to form on his lips.

"This will make the Nine Dragons war nothing more than a footnote."
He paused. "'The virtuous man fears that after his death his name will
not be honoured,'" he quoted.

"Ah, but who will honour it? And for what? Funny how we never
asked that question." Ande looked as if he was going to continue, but
shook his head. "In any case, my answer is no."

Soren stood up. "This isn't a joke, Ande."

"I'm not treating it as one. I just can't do it." He shook his head
sadly. "'The virtuous man knows enough not to exceed his position.'
I was found guilty and demoted by the Lonely One herself. To pardon
me, she would have to admit she made a mistake, and if the Emperor
can be wrong our whole system falls apart. I can't let that happen."

Red-faced, Soren threw his hands up in the air. "That isn't your
reason. You're just doing this to spite me, aren't you?" Bennett had
not seen before just how menacingly Soren could use his height. "I
offer you a chance to forget everything that's happened—"

"I can't forget," Ande said, not looking at him. "I knew, Charlie, I
knew all along. That made it worse, don't you see? If I'd thought you
really believed I'd done those things—that you were acting out of out-
rage, or even jealousy—it wouldn't have been so bad. But I could
have been anyone, just a piece in the game." He took a deep drink
from his cup. "If you want to serve the Magistracy, leave the Greyen
alone, Charlie, and pray they return the favour. Your fight will destroy
All-the-Stars, and I'll have no part of it."

"And is there anything you will be part of?" Soren asked. When
Ande did not answer him he turned to Bennett, his face a mask. "Magistrate Bennett. We are leaving now."

Bennett paused while Soren opened the door. "I'm sorry we
couldn't work something out, zi Linden," he said.

"It's all right," Ande said, rising from his chair to see his old friend
go. "We all have our duty."

Taking a step toward the door, Bennett stopped, turned back. "Do
you think I'm doing the right thing?" he asked, keeping his voice low.
"Not as a Magistrate, I mean—as an adelfos?"

"I don't know," Ande answered. "Are you here to minister to the
weak, or to serve the strong?"

Soren's voice came from outside the hut. "Magistrate Bennett," he
said.

"You're so angry at him," Bennett said. "What—what did he do?"

"I'm not mad at him. I'm mad at me." Ande drained the last of his liquor, choking it back.

"Why?"

"Because after everything we did—everything I did—when he comes in the door I'm ready to go back to the way it used to be, ready to be young and to take on the universe again." He tossed the plastic cup away, watching it bounce off one of the low tables. "That's why I had to say no."

"But what—"

Soren called again, anger in his voice. "Magistrate Bennett!"

Bennett looked at Ande, saw the old man wave him off. He took a breath and then turned and left the hut, pulling the door closed behind him as he went. Soren was waiting for him outside.

"What did he tell you?" Soren asked.

"Nothing." Bennett shook his head. "Nothing at all."

Ande watched them go, remembering the moment it had all started to go wrong; the moment that had set him on the course that brought him here. It had been so many years ago, it hardly seemed that it had even been part of the same lifetime. It was almost impossible to remember being young, but they had been once, he and Charlie Soren and their friends. The Academy's best and brightest, they had lain on the grass—so soft in retrospect, and how odd that he would miss such a thing—in the ornamental garden, enjoying the endless Hanzi afternoon. Senior scholars were permitted many liberties, and a few words had arranged things so that cups full of wine floated periodically down the stream beside them. David Black had brought a custom from his home on Gemini which appealed to them: each time a cup floated by one of them would take it, drain it to the bottom, and compose a poem on the spot.

Charlie had been there, and David, who would go on to be his homeworld's Planetary Magistrate, and Sei Shimbun, whom they had all been openly secretly in love with—and a good thing too, or who would all of those fine love poems have been written to? There were others, too, two or maybe three men whose names and faces were no longer even a blur in Ande's mind.

As the sun finally began to redden and sink poetry was abandoned and a new challenge was offered. An impossible riddle was put in each cup, and whoever drew it out of the stream would have to answer it. They had been such children, he saw now, using what they had been taught as toys. The predictable questions—how men could be evil if the Allsoul were good, how the TSARINA could make ships go faster than light without accelerating them—had already been chosen and answered to their drunken satisfaction when Charlie leaned over and pulled a cup out of the water. He drank, fished the plastic tag out of the bottom and read. After a moment's incomprehension his face darkened and he said, "This cup is not for me."

Eager to show off—he and Charlie had been friendly rivals since childhood, and though neither of them truly desired Sei they wanted her favour all the same—Ande caught the cup before it hit the ground and read the tag himself. It said:

HOW CAN THE EMPEROR BE OVERTHROWN?

He looked around quickly, wondering who had been brave or foolish enough to write this. Even the question was treason, but senior scholars are permitted many liberties. He passed the tag from hand to hand, so as to avoid repeating the question aloud. When David Black received it he said, "That's not a fair question. There's no way for anyone to challenge the Fleet."

"The question doesn't say anything about the Fleet," Ande said. Black's dismissal had made him determined to work it out. "It isn't really what holds the Borderless Empire together, the Equitable Marketing System is—it's what makes the planets dependent on the Empire. If they had another source of food, they'd be as likely to follow whoever provided it as the Emperor." Viewed this way it seemed obvious, like the decaying orbit of a disabled ship, spinning inevitably out into the chaos between suns.

Soren spoke up. "If the colonists are truly so fickle in their loyalty, why would they risk execution to support a rebel? Where would he find people loyal enough to him that he could trust them to crew his ships?"

Ande thought about that for a minute, wondering if his solution had only looked perfect when viewed through the wine glass. "There are many crimes besides treason which carry the penalty of death. A crew of criminals would have nothing to lose in following him, and no motivation to turn against him—a successful revolt would be their only hope of survival. Actually…" He turned, looked at his cup floating downstream, slowly turning in the water. Suddenly he saw the Borderless Empire like that, a spinning system doomed to fall to pieces. "You wouldn't even need a rebellion. If everyone had their own food source it'd just be a matter of time before people realized they didn't need the Empire anymore."

"I'm sure it's not that simple," David said, draining another cup without bothering to read the riddle. "There are other things—the Fleet—"

"Salt and iron," Ande said. "Food and the Fleet. The Empire turns a blind eye to Travellers smuggling everything, except food—why is that? Because if they could the Distant Worlds wouldn't need the Fleet—they could grow their own food, develop into fully colonized planets—"

"Just like the Core Worlds did," Charlie interrupted. "Different cultures, different laws. Different religions. People on one world weren't even able to talk to the people on another. What you're talking about isn't just the end of the Empire, it's the end of civilization."

"In that case," Sei said, ever the peacemaker, "it is fortunate this is just a game, and not reality. But I think we would all concede Ande has won his challenge, don't you think?"

Even Soren could not argue with that, and the evening went on, the mood only slightly dampened. Ande, though, had felt guilty the rest of the night. That image, the worlds of the Borderless Empire spinning away from the centre, had never left him, and when he wrote his famous book, many years later, it was out of a fear that someone else would have that same vision and act on it. From that afternoon, though, he knew that what he had done was much worse than simple treason. He had imagined the end of All-the-Stars.

CHAPTER NINE

Jin stood in front of the sphere, holding her palm a few fingers above its surface. She wondered if her touch would open it again, and whether she wanted it to. She preferred to come to each partnership as an equal; if the Greyen were going to help her, though, it would not be because of anything she had to offer.

She straightened. Maybe she was coming to beg at the door; nothing was keeping from doing it on her own power. Turning away from the sphere, she began the long trek up to the station.

Two hours later, the afternoon sun was warm and the air thinner than ever, more than half her puffers empty. Reaching the station's path she saw the sphere ahead, a rainbow of late-afternoon sunlight reflecting off its surface. She walked up to the hut and knocked on the 'lock. Inside she could hear the sound of something heavy being moved before the 'lock opened, revealing Ruchika standing behind a pile of debris that blocked the entrance.

"What do you want?" Ruchika asked.

The annoyance on her face told Jin there was no point in trying to be friendly. "Where's Stella?"

"Out."

"I need to talk to her," Jin said.

"I said she's out." She paused. "With Xiang Kao."

"Kao really did talk to her, then?"

Ruchika nodded. "Hang around, she might talk to you too. It seems her standards are dropping rapidly."

"I don't think so," Jin said. "I like to keep my mind private—I was hoping to use you as my interpreter."

"It's not the same," Ruchika said, a dreamy look coming over her. "Most of what we share I couldn't translate into words. It's direct communication—just ideas and images, back and forth."

"And these images, you're sure you can trust them?"

"Come on, Jin" Ruchika laughed. You can't lie with your mind."

"How do you know?"

Ruchika frowned for a moment, then shook her head. "Anyway, they've got no reason to lie to us. You've seen what they can do."

"Yes, I have," Jin said, nodding slowly. "So why would they want anything from us, at all?"

Ruchika smiled triumphantly, given a chance to lecture at last. "They believe that everyone—every person, every species—has a unique potential." Her expression darkened briefly. "You've probably heard zi Xiang talking about that. Anyway, not every species achieves theirs right away. They can help us, like parents—teachers. Let us find our own potential, so we can contribute, pay them back for their help."

Jin raised an eyebrow. "Pay them back how?" she asked.

"She just put it that way in my head, so I'd know what she meant." Ruchika paused, raised her oxygen mask to her face and took a deep breath. "Some of the species they've contacted were just barely sentient at the time. Imagine how different things would have been if we'd met them right after we got the TSARINA. We never would have had the Corp Wars, never would have needed the Magistracy."

"And we wouldn't have the whole Fleet breathing down our necks right now," Jin agreed.

"Is that what you're here about?"

"Kao may have told you, we had a new arrival touch down a few days ago," Jin said. "He was a Senior Scholar during my first year at the Academy. He's wearing Colonization colours now, but he's a Fleet Magistrate for sure."

"I've met him. I wouldn't worry."

"You sure about that?" Jin asked. "He's here to start a war, you know. Isn't Stella interested in the fact there are a dozen warships headed this way?"

Ruchika smiled. "She knows, and she doesn't care. They might as well be sending soap bubbles."

Jin began to speak, but thought better of it. "Maybe Stella knows that, but Soren doesn't. And whether or not they can hurt the Greyen, they can certainly hurt us."

"No. Stella wouldn't let us get hurt."

Won't let you get hurt, Jin thought. The xenologist was like a child, unable to believe that her parents could not protect her from every danger in the universe. If Xiang Kao really was in contact with the alien, though, she would be a better person to talk to: she knew how easily death could claim anyone, even aliens with magic tricks. "Maybe you're right," she said at last. "Do you know when Stella is coming back?"

"No," Ruchika muttered. "They went through the shell. They didn't say where they were going."

"I thought you couldn't lie with your mind."

"She didn't lie. She just didn't tell me."

Jin nodded, waited for Ruchika to offer to refill her puffers. After a minute she turned away, stepped over to the sphere. "Can I use this?"

"It's not up to me," Ruchika shrugged. "Try it."

Jin put her hand out to the sphere, its charge making her tingle from a few fingers away. The surface flexed and folded as she touched it, parting to allow her inside. Somehow the lack of show about it—you went in, turned around, and when you came out you were somewhere else—was disturbing. Something that did the impossible, she thought, ought to have a little flash to it.

Thinking of the ship, though, it became clear that the Greyen were not without their limitations. The sphere had not suddenly appeared here: it had been brought by the larger ship and had moved through space before setting down. That made her feel better—it was technology, that was all. She did not understand how it worked, did not yet know everything it could do, but in the end it was worth only as much as the use you put it to. It was a tool, nothing more.

The sphere opened and she stepped out into the clearing, just outside the fence around the pods. She was stymied for the moment so far as the Greyen were concerned, but more convinced than ever that the Fleet Magistrate was more of a threat than Ruchika thought. She could not move against him openly, of course. For one thing, he was certainly armed, but more importantly he had many of the convicts hoping a Citizenship might fall out of his back pocket. She remembered Lieutenant Wiesen explaining king strategy to her: the king can't be killed, he had said, but if you can keep him on the run you control the board.

She looked back at the pod and suddenly the board was clear to her, all of the pieces in place. She had made the mistake of thinking of the Fleet and the Greyen as being on opposite sides—but they were really on the same side, standing between her and what she wanted. Now that she knew who the pieces were, she could afford to leave the queen alone for a while. It was time to rattle the king a bit.

Soren awoke, stiff and claustrophobic. He struggled briefly, trying to throw off his sheets, and remembered that he had spent the night in the cockpit of his ship. Unlike the other mornings he had awakened there he also had a pounding headache. He reached for the waste hose and realized he was still wearing his duty uniform rather than the flight suit; he was going to have to go outside. He hit the RELEASE key, heard the cockpit locks hiss as the seal broke.

The smell of the air assaulted him and he vomited, barely managing to keep it clear of the ship's hull. He climbed out onto the landing ladder and lowered himself down to the ground, stepping carefully to avoid the puddle that had spread over the ground and made the sharp grass fold inward on itself.

After taking a moment to ensure that he was alone Soren pulled down his pants and relieved himself, watching the grass curl in shock as the spray hit. He had not done that since his year in the wild on Cicero, a very long time ago. He wondered if he could still write his name in the snow. Certainly not with all of the titles and honoraria attached—'King of Military Pacification,' his official rank, would by itself take more than his bladder could hold. He supposed that Ande could now do it without difficulty.

He pulled his pants up and then felt in his jacket for his flask. It was light, too light to have any good news inside. He had not intended to drink it all, just enough to take the edge off the headache seeing Ande had given him, but there had not been enough in the bottle for that. He went over the day's plans, patting his jacket smooth. It would be a relief to be by himself for a few hours. 'The virtuous man is an inspiration to others,' said the Book of Shang, and being an inspiration could be very tiring.

He drew his pistol from inside his jacket, set it to flash and burned the puddle of vomit away. After holstering the pistol he reached up the ladder and pulled himself into the cockpit with only a slight protest from his shoulders. He hit SEAL and paused to enjoy the sweet ship air rushing in before beginning the ignition sequence. As soon as the engine was warmed up he punched it, making the ship shoot straight up at a stomach-lurching rate. Just below the cloud level he switched to the horizontal jets, confident that the sudden thruster-blast had rattled the convicts in their beds and reminded them of the power at his disposal.

He left the controls on manual for a while, reacquainting himself with flying in the atmosphere. After so long a time in the boring sameness of space, having the wind fight back when you tried to bank was an exciting sensation. More importantly, if anything went wrong with the autopilot he would have to take over. He knew it would never happen, though every time he went up he wished it would. Unlike most of his colleagues, who would do anything to get out of the annual flight hours they needed to be certified for Fleet service, it was the one part of his job he never tired of. There had been a story, back when he had been a Senior Scholar back on Hanzi, that on his days off he would bribe wayship pilots to let him take their place on the trip up to the waystation. He had always encouraged the tale, reasoning that the more outlandish it became the fewer people would suspect that it was true.

Reluctantly he engaged the autopilot and called up the mission data, selecting the parameters for the ship's search. There had been no useful spectrography off the alien spheres, and they had only a small electrical charge; if there were other ones on the planet it would take hours to find them. With no other option he resigned himself to a long day in the air; he closed his eyes, but did not feel much like sleeping. He pulled gently on the throttle to make sure the autopilot had disabled it, then plugged his datapad into the ship's computer and called up the tactical simulator. He set the alarm for when the scanner got a hit and put in his tactical display lenses.

When he opened his eyes, he saw not the dirty yellow sky of this planet but the darkness of space. Pushing the dummied throttle away from him he began a simulated dive, watching as a planet's arc crept up from the bottom of the display. He checked the mass readings, found a good orbital slot and powered his ship-to-surface weapons. Suddenly the simulation's mass alarm sounded, showing dozens of Corp War-era battleships appearing seemingly from nowhere, pinning his ships down before they could get out from the planet's gravity. It was his rule that whenever he used this simulator he would play the way it had happened up to this point. Up to that point, he had only done what any other Fleet Magistrate would have done in his place; only after that could he be held responsible for losing the Battle of Tallinn.

He was leading the remnants of his force on a suicidal uphill attack on one of the bigger ships when the tactical display vanished, returning him to the yellow sky. Looking out the side of the cockpit he saw a completely different world from what he had seen at the prisoners' compound. It was a broad plain with a variety of plant life, mostly shrubs and flowers. The spindly trees that covered the area near the compound were nowhere to be seen. Off to the northeast a series of low, rocky hills began, the location of whatever it was the ship had found.

Soren switched over to manual, pulled the ship into a gentle descent spiral and touched down. He quickly ran an atmospheric analysis, found that the oxygen levels were higher, the sulphur levels much lower—the reading in general was closer to what the initial survey team had recorded. He unsealed the cockpit, stuck his head out cautiously. The air did not smell anywhere near as bad as it had back at the compound. Scratching his head, he climbed out of the cockpit and down onto the ground. Tiny, multicoloured flowers surrounded the ship, carpeting the plain everywhere but where the ship's thrusters had burned their signature. He heard a buzz, leaned down and saw a small insect flying from flower to flower. It was black with a pattern of green diamonds on its back, a thin tube of a body supported on six gauzy wings.

He drew his field sensor out of his jacket pocket and charged the wire coil that let it detect nearby power sources: there was a positive reading in the direction of the hills. He bent deeply and stretched his back, waved his arms to shake the stiffness out. It got harder every year, especially now that he spent so much of his time in space without gravity to pull against.

As Soren strode forward he saw a dark shape above in the sky and looked up, his eyes darkening in the sunlight. It was a bird, black and red with wings like a child's kite, soaring in circles above him. Bennett had told him about the bird Shi Jin had found, and here was another, looking thoroughly at home. He frowned, wiped sweat off his forehead. There were definitely more pieces to this puzzle than he was aware of. He felt the heat of the sun beating down on him, remembered how much further south he had gone and debated the propriety of unbuttoning his jacket. He had already violated several rules of conduct that day, he thought, undoing the topmost button. After all—absentmindedly opening the second button with his left hand—there was no one to see him here, and 'the commander in the field is not bound by all the rules of custom.' On the other hand, he thought, his jacket half-open, there was a principle at stake here. He had not come to join this mob, but to bring them rule of law and the protection of the Emperor. Fortified by that thought, he buttoned up his jacket, straightened his back and walked on.

Ten paces later he stopped, took his jacket off, pulled down his pants and pissed on the flowers.

By the time the field sensor showed he was near the source, his jacket was back on, keeping out the strong wind that had come up. The hills that had looked so peaceful from the air were actually jagged crags, some of them five bars or more above the ground, covered in a slippery green moss. There were deep cracks in the rock an unwary traveller might fall into—or that something might crawl out of.

Below him was a miniature valley formed by the rise of two huge rocks on either side of it, each about four to five bars high. The floor of the valley was ten paces across and nearly a li long. One of the alien spheres had been planted in the end to his left, and at the other end was something that looked like a small coffin, balanced on poles and cords like the sling he had seen in Kaur's hut. The coffin was made of a void-black substance that had a shimmer like the sphere's.

He turned, drawing his pistol, as he heard a sound to his left. The sphere had opened noiselessly and one of the ants was coming out. It was large, black and gold, and its antennae were waving wildly. A second later four smaller, bright green ants emerged, following it. They moved to the other end of the valley, near the coffin, and pressed their mouths against a section of the rock.

Soren watched as the creatures' secretions began to burn through the rock. Kaur's initial report had been right: these creatures were either in league with the aliens or served them. He drew his pistol, set it to blast, levelled it at the black ant and fired. The ant's shell smoked as the beam struck it but the creature kept moving, turning in his direction and hissing. Soren thumbed the pistol to flash and watched the ant's shell begin to melt. The smaller ones turned and began spitting gobs of liquid at him; one caught him in the chest, burning through his jacket.

The ants loosed another volley and acid spattered onto his face, blinding him. He tore his jacket off and threw it away before the acid could finish burning through, and then ran at a halting pace, stopping every few seconds to feel ahead for a sudden drop.

He could no longer hear the hissing ants, but could not be sure that he had lost them; he dropped to his hands and knees and crawled along the rocks, finding his way by touch until his vision returned. He regretted having left the ship in such a hurry, without even a flask of water to wash his face. He had been put off guard by the more familiar scenery and plentiful oxygen here, had been tricked into thinking this was a safe place. He ought to know better by now. There were no safe places.

The sun had nearly finished crawling to the far horizon by the time he made it back to the ship. For much of his journey he had been thinking paranoid thoughts, afraid that it would be destroyed or simply gone, but it was untouched. As soon as it was in sight he pulled his datapad out of his pants pocket—it was the one item he never kept in his jacket—and used the remote start to pop the cockpit and begin the ignition sequence.

Groaning with the effort, he pulled himself into the ship and fumbled for the first aid kit. He pulled on the eyewash goggles, flinched as they sprayed him with saline solution. When it was empty, he peeled off the tactical display contact lenses: the hard plastic was nearly burned through.

He waited for the launch indicator to flash green and then punched it. This time he welcomed the g-forces that pulled him toward unconsciousness. He was tired, tired from running and tired from thinking. Just one more job to do and he could rest.

Keeping the ship low, he skimmed over the hills until he found the small valley where the ants had been. He circled around and did a bombing run, releasing a half-dozen incendiary charges. When he looked back, he saw that only the sphere was still there, everything else burned to cinders. With a deep sigh he activated the recall function and lay back in his seat. A minute later he was asleep, dreaming of sharing a cold night in the Cicero wilderness with a friend, writing their names in the snow.

It did not take long for word to spread that Stella was receiving visitors in Ande's hut. Too many people were crammed in the small building, making Kao feel claustrophobic. As they waited for her to speak, she felt a pang of doubt; how could she hope to convey in words even a fraction of what she had learned from Stella? The Greyen turned to her, reached out with her tiny hand and touched it to Kao's tongue. Stella sent a burst of approval and Kao found herself again on the stone table, surrounded by friends. The Stella withdrew her hand and the vision was gone, but it had been enough. Kao took a deep breath, smelling the sweet air of her home, and began to speak.

"Convict Szalwinski. I have need of you."

Liz started at the sound of Magistrate Soren's voice and turned slowly, taking a casual side-step away from the door she had been fitting to her hut. She knew the Magistrate did not approve of using shelter outside of the pods, but she simply could not stand her idiot bunkmates another night. "I am at your disposal, Magistrate," she said.

"Good. I will, of course, require absolute discretion in the matter." This was serious, whatever it was, but the Magistrate's face did not betray a flicker of emotion.

"I understand."

"I am not entirely sure you do, and you should not say you do unless you are sure."

She fought to keep her confusion from showing on her face. "Magistrate, I…I do not understand, you are right."

"Yes. Here is what you must understand: I need you to perform a duty to me that will be a risk to your life. It may also require you to use deadly force against others, some of whom may be friends of yours. Throughout, you will be required to obey my orders without question or hesitation. Now, let me ask you again. Do you understand?"

"I—yes, zi Soren. I do."

"And what do you understand?"

She smiled a little. "As much as I need to."

"Good." He did not smile. "Do you have any questions?"

"I—no."

"Yes, you do. Here are the answers I can give you. Just outside the forest gate, two golden hours after sunset. Meritorious citizenship." Without waiting for a response he moved on, showing as little concern as though they had been talking about the weather.

Liz didn't care. Meritorious citizenship—that was enough to let her be a mechanic, maybe someday work with ships again. She imagined leaving all the others behind, being sent back to Jericho or maybe even to one of the Core Worlds. She had been right: that was all she needed to know.

Jason Barr watched, fascinated, as the alien put its hand on Xiang Kao's tongue. He had seen some strange things in his life, from the ice fields of his childhood on Lysander to the exotic things produced by the artists on his adopted home of Gemini, but nothing like this. It was an entirely new form, a new medium.

The alien took its hand out of Xiang Kao's mouth and the woman turned to speak. She spoke in an oddly affecting way, awkward but powerful.

"You have all heard what I told you," she said. "The Empire is a lie. There is a better way to live, and the Greyen have brought it to us. They do not seek to rule; they seek to explore. Their power does not come from weapons but from the imagination. Everything they do— all of the wonders you have seen—they do because they imagine they can do them."

Jason found himself nodding. He thought of how he had never noticed how beautiful his home planet was—the way the sky was sometimes so blue it hurt your eyes, the way the skies at night stretched into streaks when the dome was covered with frost—until he read a book of poems by Zheng He. Zheng's poems had been about the urban delights of his home on Hanzi, but they had let Jason see his own world with different eyes, opened the door to a Meritorious Citizenship and life as a poet rather than an icecracker. The world had been changed that day, changed by nothing but a book. Who was to say it couldn't be changed again?

"Some of you will be sceptical of my words," Xiang Kao went on, as though she had been reading Malcolm's mind. He had arrived just after she had started to speak, taking a break from weeding the field to hear her. "You are right to be so. We have all been promised things by the Empire and been disappointed. Work the mine and the food ship will come. Work well and you will be rewarded. Do your duty and you will be accepted. We have all been lied to by the Magistracy, and we know they will give us nothing without taking twice as much in return."

She's not really a dreamer, Malcolm thought, straightening up and rubbing dirt off his hands onto his legs. She was talking to their stomachs as well as their hearts, reminding them of the food stores that were nearly empty. Though the crops were starting to grow, it would still be weeks before anything they could eat came up.

"So you who are sceptical will ask me," Xiang Kao went on, "what do the Greyen want? What must we give them to be given our place among them? What could we have that they need?"

That was the question. Back on Hesiod, the equation had been simple: give us your harvest and we'll give you tools to work your farms, clothes to wear, and vids to entertain you and school your children. You can keep enough to feed yourselves—unless, of course, there's a war on. Then you get the honour of going hungry to keep the Fleet fed. But the Greyen didn't seem to have the same transportation problems the Empire did: Jin had said their ship just appeared and disappeared out of vacuum. What could they need from anyone here?

Daniel was cold. It was never this cold on Hellespont, certainly never windy like this. For all the good his clothes did him he might as well have been naked. He had heard some of the convicts talking about other planets, colder even than this; it seemed impossible to him that anyone could live in places like that.

He scratched at the scab on the back of his neck, wiped his thumb on his pants when it came away bloody. He was crazy to be out here. The whole thing had been a trick, a prank Huyt was playing on him.

Why would Soren ask him to help with some kind of Fleet mission? He had been a Rites and Music instructor, for Soul's sake. Now he was nothing.

His hand reached up to his neck again and he forced it down. Nerves, that had always been his problem. They made him stutter, kept him from getting a good job in the civil service, kept him from even being able to ask Marise to make their marriage legal. Of course, she would probably have said no. Why she had even agreed to the contract marriage had always been a—

"Ready, Convict Wood?" Magistrate Soren asked from behind him in confident, perfectly pitched tones, with just enough reproach in them to make Daniel feel like Soren had been waiting for him instead of vice-versa.

"O-of course, Magistrate. Anytime you are."

Soren nodded before he had even finished talking, moved on. Daniel followed a few steps back, trying to look inconspicuous. Soul, but he hated that voice.

"They need our dreams," Kao said. "That is the one thing we have that no one else can give, because no one's dreams are the same. That is what they receive from their other partners, the dreams that are the unique possessions of each species. The dreams that we can give them—the songs, the paintings, the stories that will carry us to the stars."

She crouched down and opened the case that lay at her feet, drew out a half-dozen paper packages.

Mariela was the first to step forward and take one. "It's food," she said as she opened it.

"It is a gift," Kao said.

Almost without realizing, it Malcolm had accepted one of the packages. The smell was almost intolerably strong, so different from the tiny portions of reconstituted food he had been eating for so long. It smelled like…

"Meat," he said in wonder. "From an animal." He had never eaten real meat; nor, he was sure, had any of the other convicts—it was simply too expensive to transport offworld. He peeled the package open slowly and saw a lump of dark, reddish-brown matter inside.

"Tastes kind of familiar," Jason Barr said, nibbling carefully. "Sort of smoky…"

"Tastes like soymeat," Kenneth said, answered by a peal of nervous laughter from the others.

He let the corner of the hard brick touch his tongue. It was strong, not at all like soymeat. It tasted like smoke and fire, like earth.

He had meant to save half for later. Oh, well; he was sure there would be more.

"Thank you for coming," Soren said.

Liz looked from him to Daniel Wood and Peter Huyt, the other two convicts Soren had recruited. The choice was an odd one: so far as she was concerned Daniel was useless and Huyt worse.

"The mission I have for you is this: the Fleet requires more information about the aliens, particularly their language and technology. To that end, we are going to take the alien prisoner and seize any items of alien technology it may have in its possession." He reached into his beltpouch, took out three thick black rods, each with a barely visible metal contact at one end. He handed them to each of the convicts and then went on. "Any and all methods up to and including lethal force are approved for any convicts that get in our way, but the alien is to be taken alive. Convict Kaur is also to be taken alive if possible, so that she may be interrogated."

Daniel put his hand up. "Ex-c-cuse me, zi Soren—what happens if the alien tries to d-defend itself?"

Huyt shook his rod in Wood's direction. "That's why we have these," he said.

"Please be careful, Convict Huyt," Soren said. "To answer your question, Convict Wood, our intelligence suggests the alien does not have any defensive technology we will not be able to counter. Are there any other questions?" He paused, looking around at their faces. "Good. Please maintain silence and follow my lead."

Liz sighed, reminding herself that the Magistrate knew what he was doing. She waited until the others had gone and then trailed after them, taking up the rear. *There's no disloyalty,* she thought, *in being cautious.*

Soren's ship loomed ahead, just barely visible against the dark sky. Jin approached it slowly, staying low; few people would be out with the bitter wind and the harsh scent of rain in the air, but she was not inclined to take chances. She was out without a guidelight, putting each foot down carefully to avoid stepping on the wrong side of the bladegrass. A few paces from the ship she stopped and looked around. This was the closest she could come and still say she had just been out walking if someone saw her.

Seeing no one around, hearing nothing other than her own breath and the wind, she moved closer to the ship. She had watched Soren carefully every time she had seen him near it and had decided it probably did not have a proximity alarm. That made sense, since an alarm really couldn't summon anyone but him. Still, she felt nervous as she came close enough to touch its smooth ceramic hull, to read the characters *chu ko liang* embossed in gold under its left wing. A tiny spark of electricity ran up her finger and along her spine, making her shiver.

She shrugged her shoulders to throw off the feeling and then ran her hand along the ship's hull until she found the landing ladder. The ladder was locked in the up position, so she had to hang by her right arm as she fished her datapad out of her pocket with her left. She thumbed it on and turned the brightness up to maximum so that it cast a soft blue light that would not be visible more than a few paces away. Waving it over the hull just below the cockpit canopy, she found the manual input jack. She held the 'pad up to her mouth, pressed the release button, gripped the gold-and-glass comm cable with her teeth and pulled it out to its full length.

Her right arm was beginning to cramp as she lowered the 'pad and gripped it between her knees. She started to swing back and forth involuntarily, each swing weakening her hold on the ladder. Holding the end of the cable with her bad hand she fumbled for the jack. Finally she had it connected, the 'pad beeping quietly in response. She swung her free left arm against the ladder and let go with her tired right. The 'pad slipped from between her knees and fell for an agonizing instant before she caught it with her feet, hanging a half-bar above the ground.

She squinted at the jack, trying to see if the cable had been pulled free. Feeling her left arm beginning to tire, she checked the 'pad screen to see if the connection was still good, then began clumsily programming the manual override with her thumb.

Quantum Dynamics Engineers, the arm of the Magistracy responsible for building and maintaining ships, was the most conservative organization in existence: this had been proven true when her salvaged Corp War ships had turned out to be almost identical in design to the Fleet ships she had trained on. The back doors Griffin had shown her were still there, too: after an agonizing few seconds' wait the canopy popped open with a hiss of air.

Blinking back tears of fatigue she pulled herself in and settled down in the seat, resealing the canopy and gulping down the air that was pumped into the cockpit. After a brief moment's rest, she looked over the control panel. All of the ship's innovation was on the outside: it was not much different in its controls from other ships she had flown. She flicked on secondary power, leaving the engine idle; all she needed was computer access.

On the other hand, this ship was almost certainly faster and better armed than any other in the Fleet, perfect for hit-and-run. If she started primary ignition now she could be in orbit and out of range of Soren's remote before he even knew what was happening. It was like a present that had been dropped into her lap, a chance to start again— contact her people in the Fleet that had never been found out, start disrupting shipping lines. The main Fleet would be tied up with the Greyen for weeks or even months, and this ship—

—had only enough room for one person, she realized, and the whole future history of her next rebellion dissolved.

She connected her 'pad to the ship's computer and selected as many files as she could. A noise nearby caught her attention: listening carefully she heard the unmistakable sound of someone drawing breath from a puffer. Unable to move without being heard herself, she pressed herself down in the seat, forming a fist with her right hand.

Soren held up his hand, signalling them to stop. He pointed to his left where they could see the outline of the old xenology station huts. He held up a finger—wait—then closed his fist and counted off, one, two, three, four, five. Then he moved away toward the station, taking something Liz could not see out of his pouch as he did.

Her heart was beating quickly now, her palms sweaty. She gripped her shockstick in both hands as she slowly counted to five and then followed Soren's path. Ahead, she could hear Wood's ragged breathing becoming louder.

She came to the foot of the concrete path, peered down the double row of huts. She did not see Soren anywhere and could not tell which, if any, of the huts was inhabited. Huyt held up a hand to signal a stop; she ignored him and continued on, and after a moment Daniel did as well. They moved slowly down the path until she heard the rush of air coming from the next-to-last hut on the right. They stood there for a moment, waiting for instructions.

"Well, are you coming inside?" Soren's voice came from within.

Liz stepped inside, squinting to see in the dim light cast by the vidscreens. In the middle of the room Soren was standing over the fallen bodies of Ruchika and the alien.

"Pick them up," Soren said. His eyes were almost black, all pupil. "Szalwinski, you can carry Kaur by yourself. Huyt, Wood, take the alien and for the Emperor's sake be careful."

The tension Liz had felt had not dissipated; instead it settled into her stomach, a ball of worry that made her wince. Huyt positioned himself by the alien's head while Daniel stood at its feet—flippers, really. The colour spots on its face had faded to a neutral grey.

"Turn it over," Huyt hissed.

"A-all right."

When they rolled it onto its stomach, Liz noticed it had a tiny stem of a tail and some sort of loose sac of skin hanging from its shoulders, about a half a pace across. She could not resist reaching out to touch it: it was firm, like a blister, but felt spongy as well.

"Do you mind?" Huyt said.

"Sorry." She reached under Ruchika's armpits and hoisted her up; Daniel and Huyt balanced the alien across their shoulders like a yoke, Huyt with his arm around its chest and Daniel holding onto the legs. Moving awkwardly, their two-man carrying method forcing them to remain in step or let the alien drop, they shuffled out of the hut.

Half an hour later, Soren called a halt. They were still deep in the forest, but they were all beginning to tire from carrying their captives.

"Rest until you are able to go further," Soren said. Liz could not see more than a pace in front of her, had no idea what the Magistrate was thinking or doing. "We have three more hours until sunrise. Will you be able to make it back to the compound by then?"

"Y-y-yes, M-magistrate," Daniel said. "We'll be fine."

"What do you think it is?" Huyt asked.

"What do you mean?" Liz asked. "It's an alien."

"I mean, what is it? A frog or a fish?"

"It's warm, though," Daniel said. "Maybe this i-isn't even its skin. Maybe it's like a v-vac suit."

Peter nodded. "Yeah, maybe. Or maybe it's always cold, like a lizard, and the suit keeps it warm."

Daniel laughed nervously. "I c-could use one of those."

"Me too," Liz said. The two men looked at her in surprise and she turned away.

A rustle came from the darkness. "Magistrate?" she said, keeping her voice low.

Her eyes shut involuntarily as a light beam crossed her face. A few seconds passed before she was able to make out Soren waving his guidelight around the clearing. There was an ant there, about half her height with a dark green shell, waving its antennae at them.

Suddenly the alien held its head up, its colour spots flashing bright red. The ant began waving its head side to side and moved toward them with surprising speed, drops of goo dropping from its mouth along the way.

After what felt like a long time, Jin let herself breathe again. She waited a few more minutes but heard no more sound.

Deciding not to press her luck, she pulled out the comm cable and turned off secondary power. She sat for another minute, letting her eyes adapt to the darkness now that the displays were off, and then carefully peered over the edge of the cockpit. Holding her breath, she popped the canopy and wormed out onto the nose of the ship. She found the ladder with her feet and started to inch her way down; partway down she heard a noise and let go, landed hard.

Somebody was running away from her, away from the ship and the compound. She took a step after whoever it was, stopped when she felt a stabbing pain in her ankle. Two more steps told her she could walk if she had to but not run, and she resigned herself to letting the fleeing figure go.

She reached down to feel her ankle and decided it was just a sprain. She drained her last puffer, bit her tongue and began limping back to her pod. She was exhausted but far from finished for the night. As much as sleep beckoned, the files now stored in her datapad meant it would have to wait.

"Move!" Soren was shouting, but Liz was frozen.

She watched dumbly as the ant rammed Daniel, knocking him off his feet. She raised her shockstick but Huyt was in the way, rushing at the ant. He rammed the contact into the creature's side, but nothing happened; he poked the ant again and turned to look at Soren as the beast seized his right arm in its jaws. The stick dropped from his hand as the ant bit through flesh and bone. He screamed, breaking the night's silence at last. A second later and Daniel was screaming as well.

"Vack it, try it now," Soren said.

Liz could feel her shockstick humming with electricity as it charged. It had not been on; Soren had not trusted them with active weapons.

"Hit that thing," she heard Soren say. "The pistol takes too long to cut through the shell."

Another ant had appeared, a larger one; a moment later the clearing was full of ants, a nightmare's worth. She turned and sprinted into the forest, ran until her lungs burned with sulphur and shame.

Chapter Ten

The alarm on Jin's datapad chimed, letting her know it was ten minutes before sunrise. She rubbed her eyes and drained her plastic cup of the last of the thick, sweet Traveller coffee Griffin had sent her. She had spent most of the night breaking the encryption code on Soren's files, and it would take hours more to read them all; already, though, he had learned some surprising things about Soren's mission, and about the planet itself.

She rose, stretching, looked over at her undisturbed bed. There was no point in trying to sleep now, with another day already started, but on the other hand more coffee was not going to do her any good either. She walked over to the beds and looked at the top bunk where Yertle was sleeping, his wings folded up like an umbrella. One mystery solved, only a million more to go.

A sudden yearning for sunlight seized her and she decided to take a walk. She tossed a few puffers into her pouch, refilled Yertle's water bowl and walked out to the corridor and through the airlock. The sun was just rising over the hills to the east, dark red against the pale yellow sky. There was no sign of activity from any of the huts yet, no sounds of washing from the river. The smell of the air was less pungent that usual, probably due to the strong winds the night before.

Stepping carefully to avoid putting too much pressure on her injured ankle, she made a slow circuit of the huts and passed by the gate. It was open, though it had been closed when she had returned from Soren's ship the night before. There was a dark stain on the ground, and when she crouched to inspect it she saw it was blood, the end of a trail that reached out to where the bladegrass began.

She followed the trail until it reached the outskirts of the forest. Suddenly nervous, she picked up her pace and began walking toward the sphere. If anything had happened to Stella, she might soon be wishing she had escaped in Soren's ship when she had the chance.

A moment later, she saw Ruchika coming out of the sphere. The xenologist looked even more tired than Jin felt. Her coverall was badly torn, her left eye swollen shut, and there were bloody scratches running along her legs. She was dragging two bodies wrapped in sheet plastic out of the sphere. "Ruchika?" Jin called, keeping her distance.

"You were right," Ruchika said looking up. "It's war, and they just started it." She rolled Peter Huyt out of one of the sheets. "I just brought these two back in case anybody cares enough to bury them."

Jin took a step forward and saw Daniel Wood's waxy face. "What happened?"

"They came after us—after Stella. It was the Magistrate, these two, and another one that got away. They drugged us, then…" She trailed off.

Huyt groaned softly. Jin watched Ruchika's face, wondering if she had noticed he was still alive. "Did Stella…?"

"No. She told the ants—"

"You mean, like she talks to you?" Jin could now see that Wood's body was being held together only by the clear plastic sheet wrapped around it. A thick line of dark red smudged against it showed where he had been cut nearly in half.

"No. She flashed her colour spots at them, like the Greyen do with one another."

"And they did what she told them?"

"Yes. I think so." Ruchika straightened up and put her hand to the side of her head. "The Magistrate's going to be punished. If you don't do it, the Greyen will." She opened her eyes. "The Greyen that can do what Stella can, they're important. The whole system depends on them."

"Where is she? Was she hurt badly?"

"I don't—I don't think so. She's back at the hut. She hasn't talked to me since it happened."

Jin frowned, grabbed Huyt by his feet and started to drag him out of the sphere. "What will the Greyen do?"

"I don't know," Ruchika said. "I don't think I want to. Do you?"

Jin sighed, shook her head. "No, I guess not," she said. "Do you think—" she began to say, but when she turned back Ruchika was gone, vanished again into the sphere.

Bennett woke with a start, his mind full of images of the pod splintering and falling apart, revealing terrible war engines outside waiting to destroy the compound. A second later, his head began to clear and he realized it was somebody knocking at the door, loudly and insistently. He vaguely heard his name being called from the other side.

He glanced around for his datapad and found it softly pinging on the other side of the room. When he picked it up to check the time, he saw that it had been trying to wake him for twenty minutes. Cursing himself for oversleeping—something that had not been a problem at the House, where Brother Eotes had wandered the halls every morning singing the Song of Dawn—he reached for his robes and began pulling them on.

Just before opening the door, Bennett realized he had put on his robes rather than his new uniform out of reflex. Whoever was outside knocked again, more urgently, and Bennett decided he had no time to change.

"I think this belongs to you," Jin said as Bennett pulled the door fully open. Peter Huyt was on the ground, unconscious, his head leaning against the corridor wall.

"What in the Soul's name—?" Bennett asked.

"You tell me. He's one of yours, isn't he? Not that the Greyen will know the difference."

"What are you talking about?" Bennett knelt and took Huyt's pulse from his remaining wrist. It was weak but regular; some kind of acid had cauterized his wound. "What did this?" he asked.

"Don't you know?" Jin asked. "This vackhead and three of your other friends—including zi Soren—tried to kidnap Stella last night. Seems the ants didn't much care for that."

Rising, Bennett closed his eyes, tried to breathe away some of the pain that was gathering. "So what do the Greyen want?" he asked.

"I don't know, but Ruchika is gathering everyone together so they can agree to hand you over to them."

"All right," he said, rising. "I suppose this has to be answered now. Could you help me get him inside?"

She shrugged, looped her arms under Huyt's shoulders and dragged him into the room. "You really didn't know anything about this?" she asked.

"I hadn't seen either him or Soren at all yesterday, except for briefly in the morning."

"Let's go, then," Jin said. Huyt lay on the bed, breathing shallowly. When they first landed on this planet, she had told Bennett they could not help but be enemies, but she showed no pleasure at what had happened to Huyt. She looked sad, disappointed. "I have a feeling this is going to be something we don't want to be late for."

Liz was not surprised when she heard that Ruchika had appeared in the camp. She knew from experience that failure never went unpunished. She had been washing at the river when word had come to her, and had nearly decided to stay where she was. In the end, though, whatever happened would happen whether she was there or not, and there was nothing to be gained by remaining ignorant. When she got back to the compound, nearly all the convicts were milling around the open area where the xenologist was standing on a discarded cargo crate. Wood's body lay at her feet, wrapped in a blood-spattered cotton sheet.

Ruchika spoke in a strained, artificial voice, as though she were reading from a script. "The Greyen demand that Magistrate Charles Soren and convict Liz Szalwinski be handed over to them, to face justice for criminal acts of war." She blinked and looked around, as though unsure where she was.

"If there is a criminal facing judgment here," Soren said from the back of the crowd, "it is you." His deep, resonant voice was in sharp contrast to the xenologist's rasp. "You interfered with an authorized Fleet operation. Neither you nor the alien have any rights here—as a convict labourer, I should point out, your continued existence is at the sufferance of the Colonization Office." Soren strode to face her, the crowd parting to let him past. He was neither wearing his dark clothes from the night before nor his Colonization Office colours, but a well-tailored Fleet Magistrate's uniform in black and silver.

"You don't even deny it?" Kaur asked. Her voice sounded more her own now. "If the Greyen decide to take action because of this, it's because of you."

"The charge is irrelevant," Soren said. "This entire planet is Fleet property, and none of its residents will be handed over to you."

Jin had waited as long as she could, letting the pieces get themselves into the right positions before she spoke. This was a gambit she could only try once. "The Fleet isn't here yet," she said. "Right now I'm more worried about what the Greyen are going to do if we let them think we approve of what happened last night." Many people were nodding at this. When she went on she spoke just a bit more quietly, forcing the crowd to listen. "On the other hand, the Fleet will get here sooner or later, and when they do they'll want to back zi Soren up, with bombs if necessary. We don't have a jail and we're not going to make any friends by killing them. What we can do, though, is kick them out."

She held up a finger as the crowd broke out in debate over her suggestion. Bennett was trying to be heard over the people around him.

"You set the precedent," she said, pointing her finger at him. "You decided Xiang Kao was a danger to this community and you all agreed to exile her. Well, I say Soren and whoever helped him are all dangerous, and deserve the same."

"This isn't the same thing," Bennett said. "You don't have the right."

"It's all right, zi Bennett," Soren said condescendingly. "I am happy to be exiled from your little community if the terms are as generous as those applied to convict Xiang."

"Wait a second," Ruchika said, stepping off the cargo crate she had been using as a podium. "I don't know if Stella will accept that."

"He's no longer our responsibility," Jin said. "If she wants him she can take him. In fact—" she paused, looked over the crowd. This was it, the checkmate moment every player dreamed of. "I suggest we declare this community neutral territory. Let them fight it out for themselves, without stepping on us."

"You can't talk treason and call it being neutral," Bennett said, and quite a few convicts echoed him. More, though, were still listening, considering her proposal.

"No, wait," Malcolm Smith said. "That makes sense. All either of them could use us for is a battleground anyway."

"He's right—why should we fight for the Magistracy, when it sent us here to die?" asked another convict, a young man whose squint and white skin marked him as being from Setebos, where the miners lived out their whole lives underground.

"You may declare yourselves neutral if you like," Soren said. "Whether or not the aliens respect your status is something I cannot predict."

Jin kept a tight rein on her facial muscles, refusing to smile; better to let everyone forget it had been her idea. Soren was right, of course. Declaring neutrality meant nothing in reality. Where it made a difference was in the minds of the convicts. Soren, for all his medals and his titles, was a tactician, not a strategist. He could not look past the board to the person behind it—and it was clear he still could not imagine a game with more than two players.

Bennett stared at Soren, amazed by his words. What was he doing? Practically the whole colony was being openly disloyal to the Borderless Empire, and he did not care. He opened his mouth but no words came out—what could he say, when Soren had given up?

"I suspect," Soren continued mildly, "that you may find you chafe as much under their yoke as ours. Nevertheless, I will abide by your decision, if only out of a desire to be a good guest. Those who wish to join me may do so—if we begin shortly, we should be able to finish building a shelter by this evening." He turned and began walking away, the crowd parting to let him go. One by one, Leung, Szalwinski, and a few others followed him out to the gate.

"Are you coming, Magistrate?" Soren called to him. Shaken out of his paralysis, he ran after the group with as much dignity as he could manage. Nearing the gate he paused. He had not been part of this plot. Joining Soren in exile, even if it was just to the other side of the fence, meant turning his back on the community and the mission he had come to fulfill. He looked down at the gold stripe on his sky-blue robes. Which is the greater duty, to the Empire or the Emperor, he heard Ande asking.

"Magistrate?"

"I'm sorry, Magistrate," Bennett said, not meeting Soren's gaze. "I have a duty to the people here."

Soren frowned. "Apparently this community is no longer part of the Borderless Empire," he said. "Your duty as Colonial Magistrate is thus discharged."

"I have a prior duty," Bennett said, touching the gold stripe on his robe. "I'm sorry. I'm still at your service, but—I cannot leave my home."

For a moment Soren was utterly still. Finally he gave a curt nod. "Very well, Brother Sims," he said. "Join me when your duties permit." Without waiting for a response he turned and led the others out the gate.

Bennett took a deep breath and grimaced at the smell of the air. He wished that just once he might be faced with something his years at the House had prepared him for.

Sealed in his hut, Father Theou had not heard anything of the meeting at all. He had risen early when Mariela had come to him complaining of nausea, and had spent the last hour giving her a quick exam. He had noticed his medical skills were more in demand than his spiritual duties lately, ever since Xiang Kao had begun speaking for the Greyen. Mariela herself had a guilty look when she arrived—she, too, had gone to hear Kao's words.

He was curious himself. The woman's encounter with the alien had transformed her, from a self-described daughter of Tartaris to someone with an absolute belief in the rightness of her message.

"Well," he said, switching off his implant's infrared scan, "you're pregnant, just about two months along."

"But—but Ken and I aren't—" Mariela protested. "I mean, how could we—"

Father Theou sighed. He had often wished that knowledge about reproduction was not restricted to clergy and Population Control officers. They, of course, liked people to believe that children were born because the Magistracy allowed it. He had met more than a few Distant Worlders who believed that permission from that office was necessary not just to have the antifertility agents taken out of their food but for conception to physically take place.

"It is possible that the treatments in your food that prevent pregnancy were defective, or you may simply not have been getting enough with the cut rations," he said.

There was a knock at the door. "Excuse me," he said. "I'll download a list of activities to avoid onto your 'pad later today. You'll have more constraints the later it gets, but for now there's no reason to do anything but get plenty of food and oxygen."

He walked to the central hall of the four-room hut and pulled the door open, grunting with the effort.

Not pausing to identify herself Jin stepped inside, slamming into a preoccupied Mariela. "Excuse me," she said without politeness.

"Forgive me," Mariela answered, taking a step back.

Jin ignored her, turned to Father Theou. "Where have you been, sleeping late?"

"Why do you ask?"

"Where should I start?"

On the way over to the pod, Jin filled him in on what had happened at the meeting, what she had learned from Soren's files. "That's our last piece in place," she said. "The Greyen can communicate with the ants—the ants understand their colour flashes. There's our test subjects."

He scratched his beard absentmindedly as the airlock closed. "I don't quite follow you. The ants followed Stella's orders?"

"That's what Ruchika said." She bent down to get under the inner door as it opened. "Soren recorded his meeting with Stella and Ruchika—the first one, not the one last night—so we have a few examples of colour flashing where we can be pretty sure we know what they mean. Stella was hard to reach at the best of times, and probably won't let anyone see her after last night—but now we can try the communicator out on the ants."

"What if we signal 'attack me' by mistake?"

"This is your chance to find out if they have souls. Set up a dialogue," she said as she hurried into the comm room. She sat down and hit the OPEN CHANNEL key. "It can't be more than a day or two until the Fleet gets here. If the Greyen ship doesn't come back to wipe us all off the face of the planet today, it definitely will when they arrive. If we're not able to ask them very nicely not to…" She moved her hands together then apart, miming an explosion, and mouthed the word "boom".

Father Theou frowned—something was not quite right here. "Why do you suppose the ants are able to understand Greyen colour-flashes?" he asked. "They reacted when I shone my light at them, but I never saw them using light or colour at all."

"They must have learned," she said, shrugging. "The Greyen came here before us, made contact, taught them their language."

"They haven't made much effort to teach us their language," he said pointedly.

"We haven't joined them yet. According to Soren's files, the ants and the Greyen work together—the ants were using one of the spheres. Or, I don't know—maybe figuring out their language is how we show them we're ready to join."

Father Theou nodded slowly to himself, and settled into the second chair. What concerned him more were the images Jin had related to him of the plain Soren had visited, where wildlife and oxygen were plentiful. There had been no stinktrees there, which supported the idea that they were changing the atmosphere, drawing out oxygen and producing sulphur—but they were so central to the ants' existence, he could not imagine the two species developing independently. He was no xenologist, of course, but he could not help thinking that there was still a piece missing.

He looked up and realized Jin was waiting for him to speak. "I'm sorry?" he said.

"I said, will your implant be able to control four lights at once?"

"Yes, yes," he said. "Why don't you take a nap? Your friend and I can handle the technical end of things."

She shook her head. "The way things have been going lately, I'd sleep through the whole war."

Xiang Kao passed through the sphere in a panic. She felt sick, imagining the scene over and over again in her mind: Stella attacked by Soren and his minions, crying out in vain for help. Her great legs folding, letting her crash to the ground...

The sphere finally opened and she came out next to Stella's hut. There was no outward sign of what had happened, no evidence anything was wrong. She opened the airlock to find Ruchika standing inside; she had been injured, her left eye swollen shut, but had received no life-threatening damage.

"What is it?" Ruchika asked hoarsely.

"I need to see Stella."

Ruchika stood there a minute, gazing at her with her healthy eye, and then stepped aside slowly. "She's just back. Come on in."

Inside, Stella was resting in her sling in the middle of the room. She appeared to be sleeping, her colour spots slowly shifting through a range of blues and greens.

"Was—was she injured?" Kao asked Ruchika carefully, not wanting Stella to hear even though she knew sound meant nothing to her. The xenologist walked stiffly in behind her. "I don't think so. They carried her pretty carefully—I guess she's too valuable to them."

She turned to look at Ruchika, saw her looking back. "She is much more valuable than they know. That is why I have come—I believe she needs protection."

"Protection you can provide, I suppose?"

Kao chose to ignore the other woman's bitter tone. "Yes," she said. "This would not have happened if I had been with her."

"Really." Ruchika moved to adjust Stella's sling, so that she was standing between her and Kao. "Are you sure of that, zi Murderer? Soren isn't one of those fat City Magistrates you spent your life assassinating. If you'd been here, you would have been gassed just like I was."

"Perhaps. Nevertheless, it is certain that he will make more attempts to capture her, and you have shown yourself unable to provide protection." She stepped forward to where Stella was sleeping and put her hand lightly on the Greyen's head, between her broadly spaced eyes. "I see no reason to continue this discussion. It is not you I must convince, but her."

Kao stroked Stella's head gently until she opened her eyes and looked up at her. Stella's colour spots shifted to yellows and reds as she put up a hand tentatively. Kao closed her eyes, opened her mouth, and extended her tongue.

A shudder went through her as Stella made contact. She hated what she had to do, what she had to let her see. She forced herself to become calm and sent Stella the image she was best able to envision the first time they had made contact. The uncertainty and curiosity tied up in that memory were her way of letting Stella know she was asking a question. She called up Magistrate Soren's appearance to make herself entirely clear.

Stella's response was immediate, a vid-perfect recollection of her sudden awakening in the forest, surrounded by Soren and his helpers.

The images moved more quickly as the memory became more intense, coming in sudden flashes:

Confusion, fear. The strange faces of the humans looking down at her, the feel of their hands gripping her skin, bruising it. The smell of one of the preparer-creatures nearby, sudden hope, the pain of rising and calling for its aid. The exhaustion that claimed her as she fell back to the ground, not knowing if she had succeeded. The moment of fear when she reawakened, not wanting to open her eyes for fear the humans were still there. Finally anger, a wave of pure burning dark red, at her powerlessness and humiliation.

Kao received all of this passively, preparing herself for the answer she knew she had to provide. When the flood of images finally subsided, she took a breath and began to imagine herself in her previous life. She remembered the experience of killing a lizard, half as large as she was, on Setebos, not even truly understanding what she was doing. The look on the face of the first man she killed, a cargo crewer who had discovered her stowing away on board the ship to Hesiod. Her early joy at her increasing skill, mixed with the horror that accompanied it. The years of killing, butchering in the service of Junior Magistrate Avon, the unacknowledged ruler of Colicos. The last year of her time with him, when the disease that had claimed most of his body reached his mind and he began seeing plots and conspiracies all around him, ordering executions of all his oldest friends and his own family, until in the end it took a special Fleet squad to restore peace in the streets. The faces of the troops that had been sent to capture her, certain they were going to die. Her decision not to kill them, the knowledge that she had spared them not out of mercy but out of weariness. The memory of killing the ant, the fear she had seen on the faces of the other convicts once they had realized who she was.

Then she tried something she had not done before. She willed herself to imagine a scene that was not a memory, as though she was making a vid. She inserted herself in Stella's memory of Soren, imagined herself killing him and the others with the same ease as she had all the others. She tinged the scene yellow-gold, trying to make it an offering, a gift.

She waited for Stella's response, not even able to breathe. She knew how Stella would react. The sudden revelation of her true self— the self she had tried to forget, tried to keep hidden when they made contact—could have only one response: Stella would turn away in horror. Reject her.

A strange feeling, like a gentle nudge, entered her mind. Acceptance, approval washed over her. She was on the dark coral table while her mother, Stella, beamed at her in pride.

Kao opened her eyes and saw Stella flashing yellow-gold and blue. Tears ran down her own cheek. It was all true: no gifts would be wasted, not even hers.

Stella drew her hand back, breaking contact, and Kao stepped away. She had been so sure that Stella would reject her once she learned her true nature, she had not thought any further than this moment. If she was to guard Stella, how would she have time to spread the news further? It was obviously not safe for Stella to go back to the compound, and impractical to bring too many people to the hut. She would have to share her duties. Just as she had a duty to share what she had learned from Stella, she could share her gift with the others as well. After what had happened the previous night, she was certain there would be more violence to come from Soren—and she owed it to her people to make them able to respond in kind.

Bennett moved over to where Soren was standing, close enough to be heard if he spoke quietly. He had found the small group near the older man's ship, where Soren was supervising the construction of a new structure to house them. He waited until everyone had a task that did not require constant supervision and then he turned to the Fleet Magistrate. "What really happened last night?"

Soren did not turn to look at him. "What you heard. We were missing a crucial piece of intelligence, and we paid for it."

"Paid? Wood is dead."

"Yes." Soren frowned briefly. "'The wise ruler gets into difficulties through placing his trust in others.' He was a bad choice."

"I don't mean to question you, zi Soren," treading carefully, "but are you—are you sure this is the right approach to take? I mean, we hardly know anything about these aliens. I know it sounds insane, but if they really are part of the Allsoul like Father Theou says, killing them would be murder."

"All killing is murder," Soren said, no expression in his voice. "All that matters is how well you justify it. You say—killing beings with souls is wrong—but people can renounce their right to live by becoming criminals. Yes?"

"Of course."

"It's a load of void. Everyone that lives, lives at the Emperor's pleasure. Her convenience. All of your Soft Church business about souls is just a blind to keep people from realizing that."

Bennett found he was too tired to be shocked. "Even if that's true, the Lonely One has a moral duty to do the right thing, just like the rest of us. She may have the power to kill anybody she likes, but not the right."

"That's where you people always fall into error, you know," Soren said, falling into the lecturing tone Bennett had heard so often from Ande. "You believe that the Church is anything other than a tool of the Magistracy. Did you know there used to be many churches, all with their own rules and rights and wrongs? The first Emperor decided that your Church should stay and all the others go because its softness balanced his hardness. Make no mistake, though, in the end the hardness is what counts."

"Why were you so soft on Shi Jin then?" Bennett asked.

"Why not?" the old man answered. "She thinks if she says the planet is neutral, it means something. Let her play her little game if she likes. It won't matter in the end."

"She appeared to feel otherwise."

"Am I responsible for her delusions?" Soren narrowed his eyes, looked over at the compound. "You're right in one thing, though. She was acting as though she had some edge I don't know about. After last night I can't afford to take any more chances—go and see if you can find out what she's planning. Report back to me with what you leaned by sundown."

Bennett nodded noncommittally. He was surprised at how little he shared in Soren's concern. Not long ago the idea of defeating Shi Jin would have pleased him more than anything else. Now, though, he could not help feeling it would be a hollow victory. Looking up at the sky that would soon be full of ships, he wondered if anyone would win anything at all.

Chapter Eleven

Ruchika looked up from the orbital monitor, spat on her palm and rubbed absentmindedly at a spot of blood on her coverall. She was tired, not so much from lack of sleep as from a sense that she had been banging her head against a wall. Everything that Stella had asked of her she had done. She had brought the bodies back to the compound and demanded justice. She had made the group exile Soren and his surviving accomplices, but none of it had made any difference: the Greyen had not permitted her any contact since the kidnapping, except briefly to give orders.

For several days now, since she had first made contact with Xiang Kao, Stella had been reducing the length and intensity of their sessions. It was as though she was...bored with her. Each time Ruchika wanted to go further with their exchange of ideas, information—she still knew so little about what the Greyen homeworld was like, how their culture worked—but Stella was more and more reluctant to let her in past the most surface level.

She turned, gazed at the alien sleeping in her sling. Through technology she did not even begin to understand, the device was able to read all of her vital signs and help her heal minor injuries. It supported her legs, chest, head and the sac of skin on her back, protecting them all from further shocks.

"Why are you keeping me out?" she asked. The Greyen had only the most rudimentary sense of hearing, able to sense vibrations running through the ground but very little else. Emboldened by Stella's lack of response, Ruchika stepped closer, raised her voice. "You promised me," she said. "You promised me you'd show me your home, said you'd take me. It won't be safe here much longer." Feeling drunk, she took another step, close enough to touch.

"What does she see when you talk to her?" she asked. "What do you let her see?" Reaching out, she took Stella's arm in her hands and opened her mouth. She had never initiated contact before, had no idea if it was even possible. Closing her eyes, she touched the slowly waking Greyen's fingers to her tongue.

She felt the now familiar sensations of touching her mind to Stella's, but without the other's guiding thoughts. Instead she dove in, past the surface level of communication into her subconscious. She felt herself fully inside Stella's mind as the Greyen opened her eyes, and saw her own body standing there. It did not look like her own image of herself; instead it looked like Stella but smaller, with only two colour spots and dull grey skin. It was how Stella classified her, dull grey, as she classified herself grey-green—she was a *dulg*. She tried to breathe and felt gills along her throat expand and contract. The small body in front of her was beginning to shake and turn pale. Colour spots on her face flashed red and orange as she tried to cry out. She looked down and saw herself in Stella, the grey-green hand held out to her dying body far away.

Father Theou laid the half-finished machine aside, stretched and yawned loudly. He had nearly finished rigging the small coloured guide lights so they could be wired into his implant. Working with Griffin, he had already completed the software, a program that would modify itself depending on how the ants reacted to each pattern it sent; with luck, after a few hours in the nest they would be able to communicate with the ants and the Greyen as well.

Perhaps, he thought, *it is still possible to avoid this war.* Not just to survive, not just to use one side against the other as Jin so desperately wanted to do, but to show the Borderless Empire that they did not need to fear the Greyen. If he could produce evidence that they too came from the Allsoul, could somehow get it to the Church council, the Magistracy would have to listen. There had always been a rivalry between the two bodies, each seeing the other as a necessary tool towards its own ends. The Church could not afford to defy the Magistracy often, but neither could the Emperor easily overrule the Church council on matters of the soul. And if it could be established that beings other than humans could have souls, then Apomekanidism would not look so heretical.

None of which mattered if he did not complete the communicator. A low rumble from his stomach reminded him that he had not eaten so far that day. The body is the temple of the soul, he had said to many novices who, caught up in the idea of spiritual purity, decided to starve themselves to become more compatible. It was good advice, even if lukewarm soymeat was hardly a fit offering for a temple. He rose, scratched where his implant met his real skin and went out to thread the maze of corridors between him and the mess room.

He returned some minutes later, his stomach full if not precisely satisfied. A few steps before the doorway to the comm room, he froze. There was someone there, opening files on the datapad he had left behind. He stepped closer, trying to be as quiet as he could, and peered into the room. He was not particularly surprised to see that it was Magistrate Soren, copying files onto his own 'pad.

"You won't find anything very useful, I'm afraid," he said, enjoying the small jump the other man made at the sound of his voice. "I'm just doing hardware. Everything interesting is safe up on the ship."

Soren turned, his face not betraying any surprise or worry. He had been trained not to, of course. "That's an interesting definition of 'safe'," he said. "A thin bubble of air about to be surrounded by two hostile fleets would not be my first choice of a vacation spot."

"What do you want?" Father Theou asked, crossing his arms.

"Maybe I should ask you that. You're taking this very calmly." Soren smiled. "If Shi Jin were here, one of us would be dead by now. But you, you're not even breathing hard—because you want to see what you can get out of this little encounter. Maybe some information, maybe a chance to blackmail me. Yes?" The tall man sat down, looking around as though he was perfectly at home.

"I have no intention of making any kind of deal with you," Father Theou said, moving to pick up the equipment he had been working on.

"Tell me to leave, then. Tell me to take my offer away without ever letting you hear it." He paused. "I know how you Soft Church people work. You're natural compromisers, it's drilled into you from day one. Look at you, you're a heretic and all you want is a way to get along with everybody else. Well, I've come to give it to you."

Father Theou stared at him. "All right, then. What's this offer I can't refuse?"

"Show me how to copy the communicator when you're finished with it. Do that, and I'll make your little heresy legal."

※

The body fell away from her hand. Ruchika felt a force pushing her out of Stella's mind but was unable to push back, blown like a leaf back into her own consciousness. She was briefly in total darkness, caught between minds. Then she opened her eyes and found herself in her own body again, lying on the floor in a painful heap. Stella was still hanging in the sling, her eyes open and her colour spots flashing red and black. Ruchika stumbled back. She opened her mouth and edged forward, but the Greyen pulled both her hands up by her side in tiny fists.

She fell back to the control panel and collapsed into the chair, sobbing. A minute later, she felt a touch on her shoulder, turned to see Stella standing there, a hand outstretched. She looked up at her, opened her mouth slowly. The other's fingers brushed her tongue.

"Anger," Stella sent. "Violation."

"Forgiveness: Question?" she sent back weakly.

The Greyen paused. "Forgiveness," she sent at last. "Ignorance. Improvement: Command." She broke contact.

Ruchika watched her turn away, move back to the sling. She reached for her oxygen mask and held it to her face. Shame and triumph warred inside her; she knew what she had done was wrong, but knew just as firmly that it had been worth it. She had done something no other xenologist had ever done. She had seen from inside the mind of an alien.

※

"Well? That's what you want, isn't it?" Soren asked, a practiced look of guilelessness on his face.

"You just want the communicator?"

"If it works. Personally I doubt it will—but I like to cover all the angles."

Father Theou sat down, took a deep breath. It was what he wanted, what he had argued and fought so hard for. Besides, he had no illusions about Jin wanting to prevent a war, knew she wanted to communicate with the Greyen so she could ally herself with them. She would want to be the only link to the aliens so anyone wanting to negotiate with them would have to go through her. If the Fleet had the communicator, though, it would open up a new option—give them the chance to talk rather than rush into fighting. They would not necessarily use it, but if he could talk to them first, convince Bennett that the Greyen had souls, he had some influence now...

"Ekasa te thromo," he whispered, asking for guidance. A second later, he gave Soren a quick nod. "All right. You have your deal."

Soren stood, dusted off his black and silver uniform. For the first time, it occurred to Father Theou that the Magistrate was not exactly dressed for espionage.

"'A virtuous man is as an oasis in the desert'," Soren quoted. "'They are the foundation on which to build an empire.' It's always nice to do business with one, as well."

A painful gurgle passed through Father Theou's stomach. "I think you should leave now," he said, his jaw tight.

"So I should." He stepped out the doorway, paused. "Until next time, Father Theou. Kalaspera."

"Kalaspera," Father Theou answered reflexively. He watched the old man's retreating back until he was gone and shook his head. What had he done? Nothing, not yet. When the time came he could still renege on his deal with Soren, still do the honourable thing. Yes, that was what he would do, tell the Magistrate that he was very sorry but he had changed his mind. He would do that.

When the time came.

Someone was whistling outside the hut, a cheerful sound Liz had not heard since planetfall. She put aside the pail full of pulpcrete and went out the door, saw Soren coming around the curve of the fence.

"Fleet Magistrate?" she said as he came closer.

"Colonial Citizen Szalwinski," Soren said pleasantly. "I have good news: the Fleet is within comm range."

Liz frowned. "I see," she said, not sure what to make of his unusually good mood. Nothing had been said about it, but she could not forget that she had panicked and fled.

"I have to go and meet with them. As you are the sole able-bodied Citizen on planet, I am hereby placing you in command of this colony."

She shook her head. *Didn't he know what she had done?* "But—zi Soren—"

"Take good care of the store while I'm gone," he said, waving off her protests. He fished a datapad out of his pocket and punched in a code sequence with a flourish. Sixty paces away, the ship came alive, the running lights coming on and the cockpit canopy opening. A second later, the thrusters began to burn low, the whole ship humming as the preflight sequence was engaged. Soren waited until the ladder began to descend and took a step toward it.

The ship exploded.

The force of the blast knocked Liz to the ground, making her feel like a portion of soymeat thrown at the wall by an unsatisfied diner. The heat sucked what little oxygen was available out of her mouth, leaving her gasping, trying to pull a puffer out of her beltpouch. She could hear, faintly, the crackle of stinktree wood burning. Someone reached under her shoulders, pulling her up, and she felt a sharp pain in her ribs.

A puffer was forced into her mouth and oxygen flowed down her throat. The sudden rush awakened her.

Their hut was on fire. The fence was on fire. Brother Bennett was holding the puffer up to her face; his mouth was moving, forming words, but no sound came out. The fires, though burning brightly, were silent as well. She opened her mouth to ask a question but it did not emerge, no matter how much she pushed her burning throat.

Bennett repeated his words and this time she could just hear them, as though they were being whispered from a long way away.

"...hear me?"

She nodded. "You're very quiet," she said. "Where's Magistrate Soren?"

"Over there." Bennett was more audible than before but still faint, pointing to where the ship had been. He reached down to open his beltpouch and handed her a vial of burn cream.

Soren was standing still, as though the explosion had not even moved him, looking at the wreck of the ship. She walked over to him and saw the bruises and reddened skin on his face.

"Are you all right?" she asked, not knowing whether she was shouting or whispering.

Soren did not answer, did not turn to look at her.

"Zi Soren?" she prompted cautiously.

Soren turned to face her. The redness in his face was not all from the heat. "All deals are off," he said. "Nobody gets anything until I find out who's responsible for this."

"Zi Soren, I'm sure it was just a mistake," Nick Leung said, sounding very small and far away.

The Magistrate advanced on Leung, making him back away by sheer force of anger. "A mistake? Are you telling me the most valuable ship in the Fleet exploded because of a mistake?"

"I'm—I'm sorry," Leung stuttered, nearly tripping over his heels in his retreat.

"Sorry." Soren shook his head, turned to see a group of convicts running to see what had happened. "The Fleet will be here in two hours," he said, jabbing a finger at them. "If the person responsible for—for this is not turned over to me by then, this entire colony will be deemed a threat to the success of the mission and eliminated. Am I clear?"

The convicts—Liz did not recognize them yet—were stopped short by Soren's tirade. One edged closer to the flaming wreck to get a look at it but froze under the force of Soren's glare.

"Tell the rest," Soren said, waving them away. He turned to Liz and the others. "Tell everyone. I want to find out who did this."

Liz glanced over at the hut and saw that the lack of oxygen had nearly put the fire out already. She supposed she had always known, deep down, that she would never be forgiven—never be allowed back to her former life, never get off this planet. She had lost Soren's trust and the aliens wanted her dead; no matter who won this war, her life was over. All that was left for her was to die here.

Father Theou could not help being disappointed. After only an hour in the nest, he had developed a vocabulary of nearly a hundred "words", a better result than he could have hoped for. His findings so far, however, suggested that while the ants were capable of understanding language, they had no independent wills; all of the words were taken as commands. If that was true, they no more had souls than dogs that came when called—and yet he had been so certain, never before doubting his belief that they were spiritual kin to humanity.

He was quite far into the nest now, at one of the deep inner corridors he had been blocked from entering on his first visit. One of the ever-present guardian ants was barring his way. Deciding to conduct an experiment, he tried to compose the message MOVE ASIDE on the communicator. The lights flashed, red, orange, yellow.

Shocked out of its immobility, the large ant slowly moved aside, its antennae waving at him curiously. Father Theou stepped cautiously into the narrow passage; the air smelled different here, sweeter. He put his hand to the tunnel wall and found it warm and damp. Quickly pulling his hand back, he hurried on, leaving the guardian ant behind.

The passage he was in ended a few tens of paces later in a t-junction, each split curving away into the distance. Choosing the left at random, he soon came to another intersection and then another, realized he was on the outside of a circular maze. He decided to concentrate on trying to reach the centre, choosing the inward passage every time he could.

A few minutes later, he turned a corner and saw one of the black and gold ants, the ones he thought most likely to show intelligence. He closed his eye so he could focus on the communicator and then flashed BRING (SUBJECT) TO CENTRE. The ant's head tilted up as it moved to him, waved its antennae over him carefully and cocked its head to look at him. He repeated the message; the ant took a step back, considering its options, then turned with surprising agility and headed down the corridor.

Following, it occurred to Father Theou that it would be difficult to prove the ants' intelligence with this form of communication. Even though they understood the Greyen colour-flashes, it was not how they spoke to one another. They seemed to talk with a sort of sign language, through the motion of their antennae. If it was a visual language, it might share the same grammar as the colour Greyen flashes, which the ants clearly understood. If he could record how their antennae moved in different contexts, build a vocabulary, his implant might be able to decode their language as well...

Father Theou was jolted out of his speculations by the realization that the tunnel was growing brighter as it widened. The ant leading him slowed, hesitated. Again the certainty gripped him that these were not mere beasts, despite all evidence to the contrary. Something in the being's behaviour told him it was making a judgment, trying to tell right from wrong. Finally the ant moved forward again, bringing him into a huge chamber with a high, translucent ceiling through which yellow light was seeping. Dozens of the black and gold ants were milling around, entering and leaving from tunnel mouths like the one he was in. The ant that had led him there was standing just inside the chamber, watching him carefully.

At the centre of the chamber was an object that looked like a shiny black coffin, about six paces long, suspended in a sling of some material that looked like dark purple pumice. He saw two long antennae coming out of it, waving at a group of three or four ants. He took a step forward, stopped when he saw the ant that had guided him there rear its head. Either this was as far as the Greyen were permitted to go or he was not a fully convincing imitation of one.

He closed his eye and then set him implant to record, turning his head slowly to take in the entire chamber. Xiang Kao's stories would surely pale next to this.

Jin ran into the comm room as incoming message chime rang. She hit OPEN CHANNEL as she sat down and Griffin's face appeared on the screen, streaked with static.

"…about to call you," he said. "Can…read me?"

"Boost your signal," she answered. The static faded slightly. "Can you link me through to the flagship?"

Griffin's eyes narrowed. "I don't have the communicator online yet—I'm still waiting for Father Theou to send the vocab files back up."

"I know," she said grimly. "Link me through anyway."

He paused, nodded. The screen faded to black, with only an audio channel active.

She held her breath for a moment. Time to try a bluff. "Colony to Fleet Command. Come in, Fleet Command." No reply. "Fleet Command, this is Shi Jin. If you want to communicate with the aliens, you're going to have to go through me." She swallowed, closed her eyes. It's just another game, never mind the stakes.

For several long moments, there was silence on the other end. "We will take your offer under advisement, convict," the voice said finally. The channel was closed before she could say another word.

Griffin's face reappeared on the screen. "How did it go?"

"We're still in the game," she said, shrugging. "What's going on up there?"

"Hang on—I'll switch you to external cam." He reached out of the frame to manipulate something and the image cut to the space outside the ship. The Fleet ships were beginning to glow, activating their defences and breaking off to engage the alien ships. There were three of those, with a fourth one now fading into view. Each was as large as the first. Instead of shimmering with colour as that one had, each had a half-dozen spots of bright red that skittered over their hulls. The lights on their hulls moved in response to the Fleet ships' movements—targeting them, probably. The Fleet attack would not begin until all of their forces were in place, but what were the Greyen waiting for?

"Jin?" Griffin asked after a moment. "Jin, what do you want to do?"

She did not want to speak, did not want to admit to him how helpless she felt. How helpless she was.

"Jin?"

CHAPTER TWELVE

The ant that had led him there turned in Father Theou's direction, waved its antennae toward him and began moving toward one of the tunnels.

Guessing that he was expected to follow, Father Theou went after the ant. The tunnel narrowed quickly. It was, he noticed, too small for one of the guardian ants to pass through. After a short stretch where it was barely big enough around for the black and gold ant he was following, where he had to lie on his stomach and snake his way forward, it opened into a small, round chamber with a very high ceiling. Realizing there was light coming from above he looked up and saw that the top of the chamber was made of a translucent material. It was a strange pattern of colours, changing like a prism as he moved his head. There were a half-dozen strong smells, like different types of incense, though their source could not be seen.

The ant looked back at him and waved its antennae over his hands, as if asking his opinion. It struck him suddenly that this was a shrine, some sort of religious activity the black and gold ants did not want the guardians to see. He crawled far enough into the chamber to stand up and look at the ceiling directly. There was no image or pattern he could discern, but this place could have no function but worship. The ant, apparently satisfied, went back into the tunnel.

As he emerged back into the main chamber he checked the time and realized it was much later than he thought. It might take him hours to get back through the tunnels, even with one of the ants guiding him. He turned to the ant, flashed (SUBJECT) LEAVE AREA.

The ant looked at him with what could only be curiosity, its antennae dancing a perfect sine wave, and then followed the arc of the chamber to his right. A glint of shimmering colour caught his attention as his eyes tracked the ant. It was one of the Greyen spheres, set into the far wall.

Father Theou moved over to the object. It had precisely the same dimensions as the one he had seen, the same featureless exterior. He put his hand gingerly on its surface and felt a thrill of electricity that peppered his implant with static, but saw no response. He turned to the ant and flashed GO.

The ant shuffled sideways, unsure. Scrolling through the word list, he selected OPERATE. This time the ant moved in response, ran its antennae along the outside of the sphere. A line of light appeared where it had touched, the sphere's surface parting like a curtain.

Father Theou stepped forward, paused. He had no idea where it would take him: to the compound, to the hut, to the Greyen homeworld for all he knew. No, that was not why he had paused. He knew the communicator worked, now. He had almost hoped it would not, so he would not have to decide whether or not to keep his deal with Soren.

"Ekasa te thromo," he said as he stepped inside. *Guide me.* He closed his eye as the sphere shut. The communicator was active on his implant, the word list still scrolling down as Griffin's program pieced words together. He shut it off, feeling sunlight on his eyelid. When he opened his eye again, he saw the compound in the distance. He stepped out of the sphere and felt the air move behind him as it sealed shut.

He felt a chill as a shadow fell on him. He looked up, expecting to see a cloud, and saw ships instead. Perhaps a hundred warships were moving into orbit, the first wave of the Fleet, parking themselves between the planet and the sun. Many more, smaller ships, fighters probably, were buzzing around them like flies. As he reached the compound gates, the ships began to shine against the darkening sky like stars being born.

What was it Jin had said? Hammer and anvil time. Making a quick Bridge on his forehead, he quickened his pace, running to reach the pod before it was too late.

Bennett had always thought of the Fleet as a benevolent force, something that protected All-the-Stars, especially the Distant Worlds, from raiders and rebels. It was hard to reconcile that image with the shroud of ships hanging over the compound.

The dark ships filling the sky were enough to break Soren out of his trance. He had his datapad in hand and was fiddling with it to expand its transmission range. "Fleet Magistrate Soren to lead ship. Acknowledge. Transmitting recognition codes."

A voice, very faint, came through the speaker. "Your signal is weak, Magistrate. Please link through your ship's transmitter."

"My ship—my ship's transmitter is down," Soren said, his voice just barely cracking. "I cannot rejoin the Fleet at this time. Please advise on status."

"Four enemy craft are in the area. We are moving to engage as per orders." The voice became louder, crackling with static. "Instruments have provided no useful data on the enemy ships so far. We are awaiting your intelligence files before taking further action."

"I'm sending you what I can. Do not take any further action until my word. Have you made comm contact with the enemy?"

"Negative. Broadcasting all frequencies, all languages, no response."

Soren nodded and hit a key on his 'pad. "Understood. Sending files now—make contact when analysis is complete."

"Acknowledged."

Bennett reached out to touch Soren on the shoulder, making the older man spin around in surprise. He put his hands up to show his harmlessness. "I'm sorry, zi Soren. I just—wanted to know how things are going." He glanced over at where Leung, Szalwinski and some others were standing, waiting anxiously for news.

"As well as could be expected," Soren said, keeping one eye on his 'pad screen. He rubbed at his temples with forefinger and thumb. "We still don't know enough about their capabilities, but it'll have to do. All our ships should be in position in a few minutes." The anger in his voice was gone, replaced by a flat tone of resignation.

Bennett frowned. "And then what?"

Turning to look at him, Soren sighed. "And then we fight," he said.

"You mean that's it? They're there, so we're going to fight them?"

Soren gave a small smile. "That's about it. They won't talk to us, and they've brought out a fair-sized war party. We don't have much of a choice—we can't wait for them to hit first, without knowing anything about their weapons."

"But, but if they have souls, this could be murder…"

"This is war," Soren answered, his smile gone. "All that matters is who wins. Once we're convinced that they'll never pose a threat to us again, we can worry about their souls." His voice was still rough from the smoke and fire but had regained its customary tone—that deep note of authority that made him so hard to argue with. The chime on his 'pad sounded, showing an incoming transmission. "Well, this is it," he said, shrugging.

Bennett watched, unable to think of anything to say, as the Fleet Magistrate raised his 'pad to his mouth to speak, thumbed OPEN CHANNEL.

"Soren here."

Jin rose, turned to see Father Theou barrelling down the hall toward her. "Took you long enough," she said sharply, struggling to hide her relief.

He smiled, smoothed himself off. "I took a shortcut. Have you made contact with the Fleet?"

"Yes. I don't think they believe us." She glanced over at the screen. Nearly the full Fleet was now in position, circling the four alien vessels. "How did you do?"

He smiled, reached into his pouch for a length of cable. "Well. I believe we have enough grammar and vocabulary to be heard." He plugged the wire into his implant and the comm and began uploading the files to the ship's computer.

"How long will that take?" she asked, keeping her breath slow and even. There were still a lot of moves left in the game.

"A few minutes."

She pointed at the screen. The Fleet was now fully in position, the lights on the alien ships' hulls dancing to keep them targeted. "I don't think we have that long." She closed her eyes, not wanting to see as everything she had planned fell apart.

She could hear him swallow, hard, from a few paces away. "Have faith, Sister Shi," he said weakly. "We don't know—"

"No, we don't," she interrupted, her eyes snapping open. "They don't know—that we don't know. Do you see what I mean?" He opened his mouth hesitantly, closed it as she went on. "We don't need to know, not yet. Wait—" She put her hand out to the comm console, jabbed OPEN CHANNEL several times.

"Fleet here. We are considering your—" an annoyed voice said through the speaker.

"We have contacted the Greyen and arranged a truce," she said, all in one breath. "If you respect the neutrality of this planet they will do the same. There is no need for a war."

There was a long pause. Neither Jin nor Father Theou dared breathe.

"Stand by," came the voice at last.

"We have a situation here, Magistrate."

Soren frowned, looked over at Bennett, who shrugged. "What do you mean, a situation? How much more of a situation could you have?" he asked, failing to keep the annoyance out of his voice.

"One of the convicts says she's made contact with the enemy. Claims to have negotiated a truce, based on this planet's neutrality."

"Shi Jin?" he asked, though he already knew the answer.

"Yes. What do you advise?"

The voice sounded desperate. *Probably just realized he isn't chasing bandits anymore*, Soren thought. He paused, considering, lowered the 'pad. "What do you think we should do, zi Bennett?"

The young man's eyebrows rose amusingly as he squirmed under the responsibility. "I would—accept the truce, zi Soren. We don't know what we're getting into yet—we're at a disadvantage."

"But then, the longer we wait, the more they find out about us as well, isn't that right?"

Bennett reached up, wiped his long blue sleeve over his face. "Yes. Yes, but, we don't know how much they know already. They may know a lot, while we know that we know almost nothing. So time is more likely to benefit us than them."

Soren thought for a moment and then held his 'pad up to speak into. "If the truce is genuine it should be accepted. But 'in dealing with weeds, firm resolution is necessary'—so get proof."

"Acknowledged. Fleet out."

He hooked his 'pad onto his belt, smiled at Bennett. "Well, Magistrate, is that the answer you were hoping for?"

"Yes," Bennett said, looking shocked. "I didn't think you'd listen."

"I don't believe Shi Jin is telling the truth," he explained. "If she is, we have to assume she's working with the enemy, which means they know a lot more about us than we do about them. In which case we'll need time to gather more information and analyze what we've seen so far."

"You mean you intend to keep the truce?" Bennett asked, uncertain.

"As long as it's useful," Soren answered. "Which is exactly as long as they'll keep it. Think about it: if they know all about us, and they're willing to agree to a truce, they must think we're a threat to them. A truce isn't a ticket to peace, it's a weapon. We need to use it to find out why they're afraid of us, and they're going to try to use it to stop us."

"So it won't save anybody," the younger man said, shaking his head. "It doesn't mean anything at all."

"Of course it does. It means we might win."

Drumming her fingers on the comm console, Jin tried to clear her mind. She had hoped to have more time to talk to the Greyen, more time to convince them to join her. Instead, the Fleet had given her ten minutes to prove that the aliens had agreed to the truce.

Which they hadn't.

As soon as the Fleet's message had finished she told Griffin to signal the Greyen ships using the same frequencies as the broadcast they had intercepted when the first one arrived. She then had him send them the same message she had sent the Fleet, suggesting the planet be considered neutral territory and a truce declared. Several minutes passed as Jin wondered if the communicator had even translated the message correctly. Finally, the ship sent a colour transmission back, which the communicator converted into one word, speaking it in its perfectly even voice:

"No."

She looked at her watch. It continued to run, the seconds passing, adding up to minutes.

Closing her eyes, she saw herself sitting at a game board opposite Lieutenant Wiesen in her home on Garamond. Their pieces were arranged on the board—Wiesen's in what looked like a hopeless situation. His queen, his bishops were gone, his king mostly exposed, while she had almost all of her pieces and control of the centre of the board. Nevertheless he was smiling, trying to hide it. She picked up her queen. What did he have planned? She moved it diagonally, his smile broadening as she did so. Jerking it back with her hand, she moved it along a lateral line instead, was greeted with the same smile. She put the queen back in its original spot, picked up one of her knights and wavered, watching him carefully. He continued to smile. What was he thinking?

Five moves later, her victory no longer looked certain. Ten moves later, she was on the defensive and twelve moves later he had won, all with a bishop, two rooks and a few pawns. She replayed the game over and over again, trying to figure out how he had won.

"I didn't," he said quietly, putting the rough pieces away in his flight bag. "I just gave you the idea that you were going to lose. From there you beat yourself." Smiling again, he faded into nothingness as she opened her eyes.

Reaching down, she jabbed the OPEN CHANNEL button. "Griffin, I want you to send the following message: 'If truce is not agreed to, secret weapon will be deployed. All ships are programmed to self-destruct rather than let secret weapon fall into enemy hands.'"

"Got it," Griffin said, after a pause. "I don't mean to be critical, but that's a pretty old trick."

"For us, maybe," she said, pulling her hand from her mouth as she realized she was chewing her nails. "They haven't attacked yet, there must be some reason for that."

"Transmission coming in," Griffin interrupted. "Running it through."

The seconds ticked away on the clock as she waited for the communicator to process the Greyen message. It had run to 9:25 when the computer said, "Agreed."

"What are the ships doing?" Jin asked. "Tell them we need proof that they accepted."

"We've got it," was his answer. "Take a look." The image wavered, cut to the external view again. Only three Greyen ships were now visible. One of those was in the process of folding in on itself.

"Link me to the Fleet—"

"Already done. Go."

"Fleet, this is Shi Jin. You have your proof. You and your ships have two days to get out of here or the truce will be considered broken, do you understand?" The words came out almost automatically. Part of her was still holding her breath, waiting for the battle to begin.

"Acknowledged," the voice at the other end of the comm said stiffly. "Fleet out."

Jin finally let herself exhale. "We did it," she said in amazement, mostly to herself.

"That we did," Father Theou answered, nodding. He was surprisingly subdued—then again, so was she.

She tried to build up some enthusiasm. "We did it!" still came out halfhearted. She sighed and looked over at Father Theou, who was unhooking his implant from the comm. "We haven't really won anything, have we?" she asked, rubbing at her eyes.

"Not yet." He coiled up the datalink cable, tucked it away in his pouch. "Some time. A reprieve, maybe. A chance to do some good."

She nodded. "I guess we had better use it, then," she said.

"Yes," he answered, sounding unaccountably sad. He took a step toward the door. "I have some business to tend to, but I will see you later. Congratulations, Sister Shi."

"Thank you," she said. "Thank you for your help. You saved a lot of lives today."

He closed his eyes, nodded and hurried out into the hallway. She turned back to the comm and hit OPEN CHANNEL. Griffin was partly outside the frame of the screen, sucking on an ampoule of murky liquid.

"It's too early to celebrate," she said. "We have work to do."

"It can wait." He did a slow backwards roll, winding up back near the screen. "Have you opened all of the coffee I sent you yet?" he asked.

"No," shaking her head.

"Good. The last one's voidfire. You deserve a drink." He raised his ampoule to the screen as if making a toast.

She began to speak, changed her mind. He deserved a small celebration after all his work. It was easy for her to forget how isolated he was up there, how alone. She rummaged around in the bag where she had been keeping her ampoules of coffee, found the one full of voidfire and raised it to the screen.

"*Vi pete*," she said, one of the only bits of Traveller tongue she knew. It was literally a question—"Do you drink?"—but was really an invitation to the other person, an expression of kinship.

"*Vi pete*," Griffin answered, raising his in response and taking a long swallow. She did the same, feeling its heat fill her throat. She closed her eyes briefly as its warmth went through her, and saw a flash of Lieutenant Wiesen's speaking silently. *Play again?*

"What was that?" Griffin asked, spinning lazily on his axis.

He had said, once, that he enjoyed drinking with her because it was the only thing she did completely for its own sake. She had decided never to tell him he was wrong: when she drank she saw and heard all of the ghosts from her past, the people who had died because or in spite of her.

"Nothing," she said, turning away briefly. She reached up to wipe her eyes, keeping her hand out of his sight, and turned back to face him. "Another toast," she said. "To absent friends."

"Sure," he answered slowly, raising his drink.

They each took another pull, sat there in silence. She did not think she had offended him, but she could tell her choice of toast had unsettled him somehow. She drained her ampoule, careful not to drink the bitter sludge at the bottom. "We should get some rest. Signal you later today, okay?"

"Okay," he answered, finishing his drink. He reached out to the screen and it went black.

Rising from her seat, Jin stretched her back and walked out into the hallway, thinking that she had never known Griffin to be the one to end a transmission before. She shrugged. He had been working long hours on the communicator, was probably just feeling weepy from stress, as she was.

A few moments later she was on her bed, not having bothered to take off her coverall or even get into the sleeping bag. The voidfire was making the room spin, leading her to imagine she was on the ship with him, floating in zero-gee. She smiled, let herself fall into a deeper sleep. If she had any dreams that night, she did not remember them.

"We have less of a free hand now, it's true," Soren said to the assembled convicts, "but we can use that to our advantage. The aliens were a mystery before, but now they're just another government—

and we can offer the other convicts a lot more than they can."

Liz put up her hand. Since the ship had exploded, nothing more had been said about her promotion, and she had been hesitant to risk setting Soren off by raising it. "What kind of offer do you have in mind?" she asked.

"Full amnesty," he answered. "This planet will become a full colony, those who have helped us given status as colonial citizens. Those whose loyalty was demonstrated earlier, of course, can expect further rewards."

That was something, at least. Colonial citizens were tied to their colonies; if she was given a higher grade, though, she would be able to leave and start over. But did Soren still feel she had been loyal?

She watched as he worked the crowd, flattering some, frightening others. She could not work up much anger at the Magistrate over the uncharged shocksticks. After all, she had shown he was right not to trust the convicts.

As the crowd began to break up, Soren stepped over to her and leaned in close. "Don't worry," he whispered. "You'll get your chance to redeem yourself."

Jin glanced over the readouts on the comm console. The Fleet had left behind a surveillance satellite Griffin had been able to patch into, so that she could get mass readings and send transmissions without going through the ship. So far, both the Fleet and the Greyen had been as good as their word. Most of the Fleet ships were in the outer reaches of the solar system by now, and the Greyen had not been seen since the truce. They, too, had left something behind, a tiny sphere that had been appearing and disappearing in the planet's orbit.

She had finally gotten Stella to agree to negotiate, using the comm in Ruchika's hut. It was impossible to read any kind of inflection in the translated speech, of course—the translation itself was still fairly rough, though Griffin's program continued to compile grammar and vocabulary—but she could not help sensing resentment in Stella's messages.

"I am proposing an alliance," she said, trying to keep her conversation blunt so as not to confuse the translation program. "I wish to join you against the Magistracy."

"Attack alliance would break truce," the communicator said in its simplified syntax. "Required alliance element,"—a pause—"'secret weapon.'" The last two words were spoken in a recording of her own voice—*the concept must not translate fully*, she thought.

"You don't understand," she said. "I can get you the secret weapon if we form an alliance." *As soon as I decide what it is.*

"Delivery of 'secret weapon' required to join alliance. No other negotiation possible." The Greyen signal cut out abruptly, leaving Jin clenching her fists in frustration. She had meant the secret weapon to be a vague threat, something to convince them they needed her assistance, but they had interpreted it in a very specific way. As Griffin had pointed out, it was an old trick; were they really so cautious as to back off from an unknown threat? Or could there be something the Fleet had that they were genuinely worried about? With their technology it seemed impossible, but still…

One of the displays on the comm channel lit up, granting her release from her questions. It was the satellite's mass alarm, showing several masses moving into the system. Ships.

Standing at the entrance to the ant nest, Soren smiled as he thought of the look on the priest's face when he had handed over his communicator. It was the look of a child lured into doing something he knew was wrong, his mind simultaneously imagining the pleasure and the punishment. There had been no doubt in his mind what Father Theou would finally choose. For all the air of reason and dignity the heretic tried to maintain, he was unable to conceal the strength of his faith, and Soren knew that faith would lead him to violate any other principle he held. He had, after all, been willing to risk his own excommunication and death for his heresy. Betraying Jin—an ally of convenience at best—hardly measured up to that.

He had made a show of defiance, of course, insisting that his observations on the ants had not been part of the deal. Soren had accepted his protests with good humour. Father Theou was not much of a secret-keeper, after all. In his attempts to convince others the ants had souls he had already related everything he had seen to someone or other, and bit by bit all of that had made its way to Soren.

The first chamber, just inside the nest had an antiseptic smell that made his nose sting. Soren held up the communicator to be sure the nearest ant could see it and flashed GO CIRCLE. The ant waved its antennae in his direction briefly and turned a tight, awkward circle.

He smiled, thinking 'the virtuous man obeys his orders without question'. Being a Fleet Magistrate had spoiled him, made him unused to people who had not had obedience drilled into them. In the Fleet, dealing with people was easy: keep your orders clear and your punishments harsh, and you could count on them to obey. It was easy to forget that the rest of All-the-Stars was not always so well conditioned.

That had been Ande's brilliance, all those years ago: he had been the first to realize that while rebels undertook military actions, they did not think in a military way. It was that insight, his ability to think like a rebel, that had allowed him to defeat Shi Jin at Second Tallinn and end the Nine Dragons War.

Soren, in disgrace over his defeat at First Tallinn, had been unable to share in his friend's glory. They had been in the wild together, a bond that was supposed to last a lifetime, and Ande had betrayed that by succeeding where he had failed. Even in exile Ande galled him: Soren was ordered to assume authorship of Ande's book and to teach it to the strategists in the Fleet.

He noticed that the ant was still turning in circles, its legs starting to wobble. He sent a single red flash STOP and moved on further into the nest as the ant staggered the opposite way down the corridor. Following the floor's upward curve, he moved into the inner area. There was one of the guardian ants, filling the corridor with its impressive bulk.

MOVE ASIDE, he flashed. Slowly, the creature stepped forward and to the side. Keeping a close eye on it he passed into the corridor and found his way into the central chamber. At the centre of the room was a black coffin like the one he had seen on his survey mission, the one he had destroyed. Moving as close as the black and gold ants allowed he drew his pistol, set it to beam, and fired.

An intense smell of acid filled the chamber, burning his throat, as the beam cut through the black material. All of the ants looked up and began waving their antennae frantically. The beam sliced through the coffin, splitting it in two. Inside he could see half of a pale, rubbery creature that looked more like a worm or a grub than an ant. It was twitching feebly, dark fluid dripping out of its wounds.

He looked around, saw the ants moving erratically back and forth; some were moving to inspect the wrecked coffin, some them running up the walls or out of the chamber. A group of the black and gold ants surrounded the dying creature, snapping their mandibles at other ants that came near. One of the other ants tried to break the circle, severing a leg of one of the defending ants, and within seconds the entire chamber had erupted into war.

Soren ran for the passageway from which he had come, flashed MOVE ASIDE at the ants that were coming in that way. This time, though, they did not obey: most of them continued heading for the grub thing, but two broke off and approached him. He targeted the nearer of them and fired, slicing through its shell.

By the time he had cut the first ant in half, there were more heading his way, and the power indicator on his pistol was getting dangerously low. He began to run a zigzag and aimed the beam low, slicing along their legs. After he had crippled a half-dozen of them, the others decided he was not worth the effort and broke off, leaving him to find his way outside before the whole nest erupted.

Jin keyed the screen to switch to the satellite's external view, worried that the newly arrived ships were the Fleet returning. The ships that appeared on the screen were not Fleet, however. They were older than the ship that had brought them there, some even older than the Corp War ships she had once salvaged. Many of them looked like two or three ships had been scavenged to put together enough parts for one. They were Traveller ships.

She keyed the comm to Griffin's frequency and hit OPEN CHANNEL. There was, for the first time she could remember, no response. That was why he had not notified her, though the ship's mass alarm had surely sounded when the satellite's had.

She dropped her head into her hands. The Greyen were obviously keeping an eye on the planet, and there was no reason they would see these ships as any different from the Fleet. How could she possibly convince them that this wasn't a Fleet tactic to lay claim to the planet? From what Ruchika had told her about their culture, they might not even understand the idea of separate groups within a single species.

Jin forced herself to breathe slowly and regularly before she hit OPEN CHANNEL again.

This time the light flickered to life; Griffin's face appeared, huge in close up. "Jin," he said. A long pause. "Jin, I'm—"

"Sorry?" she asked, failing to keep the anger out of her voice.

"No," he said, reaching up to rub his eyes. "I just wanted to explain."

She bit her lip, forcing the automatic response to stay inside. "Explain, then," she said instead.

"You don't know what it's like," he said. "You may have lost your home, but I was born without one. My whole people were—any new planet the Magistracy found, they'd colonize. But this one, I thought we'd have twenty years to stake a claim..."

"You sent the second missile, didn't you?" she asked, not listening.

"Yes," he said. "As soon as we had arrived. I knew this was the best shot we would ever have."

"They're going to say this is my fault," she went on. "Soren and Bennett are going to use this to convince people not to listen to me. Do you know how much it costs me, just being friends with you?"

He opened his mouth, about to say something, closed it. A second later he shook his head angrily. "You won't let me forget it. You're proud of your magnificent tolerance, your one Spacer friend, but when a few others come knocking you act just like all the others." The pain of what he had said was visible on his face, tiny drops of water drifting away from his eyes. "I didn't do this to hurt you. I just did it because..." He let the words hang in the air.

"Because it was the right thing to do," she said after a minute. She took a deep breath, nodded. "Have you told your people what they're walking into?"

He shook his head. "Not yet. No sense scaring them right away."

"I'm sorry," she said. "It's just—bad timing, right now."

"I know. But when would it be good timing?"

They looked at one another a minute more, not sure what to say. In all the time she and Griffin had been friends, he had always provided advice, been her conscience, and she had almost forgotten he was a separate person, with a will of his own. She had certainly never imagined him betraying her like this. It was proof that there was always more to learn about every piece in the game.

The floor shook as something hit the side of the pod. "What was that?" he asked.

"I don't know," she said, glad of the distraction. "Check the external—is anything coming down from orbit?"

He glanced over at another screen and shook his head. The pod rumbled again.

"I'd better check this," she said, rising. "I'll—I'll signal you later, okay?"

He smiled weakly, nodded. "Sure. Jin?"

"Yes?" she stopped, turned back to face the screen.

"I am sorry. Not for what I did, but for not telling you."

She looked at him, studying his face. For all his skill in strategy, he had to be the most guileless person she had ever known. It must have gone completely against his nature to keep something from her. Or maybe she did not understand his nature as well as she thought she did.

"Thank you," she said simply, watching with pleasure as his smile deepened. No, she had not been wrong—there was simply more to him than she had known. She gave him a smile back, touched her hand to his cheek on the screen. "Later," she said, hit CLOSE CHANNEL.

She took a few deep breaths as another shudder went through the floor. She grabbed her bag of puffers and she walked quickly to the airlock, waited for it to cycle open. Stepping out impatiently, she narrowly avoided being sliced in half as an ant snapped its jaws at her.

Griffin floated nervously in front of the main airlock, waiting for the docking light to flash green. He had known, even before the mass alarm had sounded, which ship would be the first to arrive—the Griffin, the ship he had grown up on. They would have been the first to believe his message, the first to trust. The others were the ones they had convinced.

At last the two ships were aligned, each one's airlock hissing open. There was a lone figure floating there, his shipcousin Perun. Griffin remembered him as a sour, prematurely balding young man, whose constant sweating had filled the air with drops of smelly water.

"Hello, Perun," he said carefully, his tongue unused to Traveller talk. "You look well."

"You don't." The bald man looked around. "Are you alone here?" he asked.

"Yes. How are you doing?"

Perun shrugged. "Added a few stars to the sky. Vasili died just a few kilhours after you left, Lada about twenty k ago." He paused. "Elena is still alive. She and I are Eldest now."

Griffin nodded, watched for any trace of expression on the other's face. "Thank you for coming," he said.

"Thank you for calling us." He paused, looked around once more. "Tell me, Vyslav. What have you gotten us into?"

"Just what I told you. Neither the Empire nor the aliens have a clear claim here—it's as close to a home as we'll ever find."

"I'm not sure a battlefield is a good place to build a home," Perun said, furrowing his thick brow. "It seems to me we'll have twice as many landsiders telling us to go to Void."

Griffin's patience was starting to wear thin. "Did you come all this way just to argue with me again?" he asked.

"No." Perun smiled and shook his head. "Now that I'm Eldest, I don't have the luxury of needling you for fun—just for the good of the Ship. I came to see if your message was true."

"Did you think I was lying?"

"I thought you might be wrong." Perun gave the bulkhead a kick and floated past Griffin, into the ship. "Every time some ship has found a planet they thought nobody wanted, the Magistracy came along and claimed it. Why should this be different?"

"The aliens will keep the Empire away. They've already been and gone."

"Maybe. Or maybe they'll come back with a bigger fleet." Griffin tried not to let his anger show as his shipcousin watched him closely. "Still," Perun said after a moment, "we might as well give it a try. I suppose we can at least fill our tanks before we go."

Griffin rolled his eyes. "Don't do me any favours," he said.

"Oh, I'm not," Perun said innocently. "Elena and I made our decision before I came aboard. I just wanted one more chance to annoy you."

Gritting his teeth, Griffin suppressed the urge to strangle the bald man and instead pushed away from the bulkhead, into the other ship. It had been at least a hundred kilhours since he had seen any of his shipcousins; at least a hundred kilhours since he had heard the old songs sung, or joined the Dance. That was something Perun could not take away from him.

Two black and gold ants were fighting one another, each trying to seize the other's head and slam it into the pod. Every time one succeeded they hit the pod with surprising force, making it quiver.

Jin jumped out of the way and looked around. There were probably a dozen ants within the compound. They were not paying any attention to the convicts, except to treat them as obstacles if they got in the way. Glancing over at the main cluster of huts, she saw one of the convicts lying on the ground, bleeding from a long cut in his side.

Jin crouched low and took a long, circular path to where the man was lying. Jumping aside as one of the ants was flipped over onto its back, she sprinted to his side. He was still breathing, the cut not bleeding too much. She hoisted him up by his armpits and began to drag him to the pod that held Bennett's quarters, thankful the ground had been cleared of bladegrass.

Before she could reach the airlock, one of the ants nearby made a deep stab in its opponent, causing some kind of bodily fluid to spurt out of its shell. Drops of the liquid fell on Jin and the victorious ant turned in her direction, waving its antennae. The ant paused over its victim's body, dripping a thick white liquid from its mouth, and then advanced slowly towards her.

Jin shook the injured man, keeping her eyes on the ant. "Hey, are you awake? Can you walk?"

The man lifted his head slightly. "I—I'm not sure."

She helped him onto his hands and knees. "Get into the pod and find Brother Bennett. Do you understand?"

He did not reply, or if he did she did not hear it; her attention was fixed on the ant that was moving towards her, twitching its antennae and snapping its mandibles open and shut. The ant took another step forward and then turned its head. Jin followed its gaze and saw Xiang Kao at the gate stabbing one of the ants with her spear, flipping it over. Nearby, Kenneth Fujitu and Malcolm Smith were doing the same, more awkwardly. The ant near her had turned to face Kao and the dozen or so spear-wielding convicts that were behind her.

Jin turned and saw Bennett walking out of the pod. He was wearing his robes again, not the ill-fitting Colonial Magistrate's uniform

Soren had given him.

"Bennett!" she called. "Someone got hurt."

Bennett nodded. "He'll be all right," he said. "How did this happen?"

"The ants have gone crazy or something, attacking each other. We just got stuck in the middle."

Not far away, Xiang Kao was driving a spear through a fallen ant's eye; Jin shuddered in sympathy as the point went in. When she turned back to Bennett, he had begun to walk away, towards one of the other huts. "Where are you going?" she asked.

"To get some answers."

Father Theou heard a knock on the door and rose, slinging his pouch over his right shoulder. "Come in," he said, glancing around the hut to make sure he had gotten everything.

The door opened and Bennett leaned in, looking sheepish. "Father Theou," he said, sounding uncertain. "I'm surprised you're here. Haven't you heard what's—"

"Yes," he said, nodding slowly. "I know what is happening. And I know whose fault it is."

Bennett stepped inside, a look of surprise on his face. "Whose?" he asked.

"Mine."

The younger man paused momentarily, scratched the back of his neck. "We're talking about the ants, right? Do you think it's because you were in their nest…?"

"No, that isn't it—not precisely." Father Theou looked away. "I found a way to communicate with them, and I traded it to Soren for…future considerations."

"So Soren…" Bennett said, frowning.

"Yes. I believe so." He closed his eye, refusing to let the tears emerge. "I gave him the way to get into the nest. Somehow he started this—started them killing one another…"

"But why?"

Father Theou sighed. "You tell me. I suppose he feels they'll be less of a threat if they're killing one another, or that this will turn the convicts against the Greyen."

"And if they kill a few people in the process?"

"All the more convincing."

Bennett nodded. "You couldn't have known what Soren would do," he said.

"I could have guessed. I could have assumed that whatever it was would be something I'd want no part in. But I let myself—" He trailed off, shook his head sadly.

"So what are you going to do about it?" Bennett asked after a moment's silence.

Father Theou took a deep breath "I am going to end the war." He saw the sceptical look on Bennett's face and laughed. "After all the times I made peace between you and Shi Jin, this ought to be child's play."

"They're not obeying the colours anymore," Bennett said. "They came right into the compound."

"I'm not going to give them orders. I'm going to ask them questions." He reached up and tapped his implant's camera lens. "Now I can listen, as well as speak. Or at least, I believe I can. I have to find out how this war started, why their behaviour has changed so much. I have to find out if they can choose to stop fighting—if I can repair the damage I've done."

Bennett opened his mouth, closed it. "Soul be with you," he said, reaching out to make a Bridge of blessing on the other's forehead.

"Thank you," Father Theou answered. "And with you."

They each stood still for a second, looking at one another. Father Theou held up a hand, returned Bennett's gesture. "Kalaspera, Brother," he said, walked out the door.

Malcolm grabbed hold of his end of the ant, and lifted the same time Kao did. He was glad to have the tail end; the head, half-smashed, was dripping white goo on the ground. Kao did not seem to mind.

"Do you have a good grip?" she asked. He realized his end of the ant had been slipping, heaved it higher.

"Yeah, I got it," he answered. "You okay?"

"I will be all right." Goo from the ant head had smeared all over her front, and it seemed to be sticking to her. "Wait for a moment."

He nodded, lowered his end of the ant. They were about halfway between the field and the spot outside the wall where they had piled the dead ants for burning. He pulled a stalk of bladegrass out of the ground and handed it to her to wipe the goo off with.

"Malcolm," she said, not looking at him, "I need to know something from you."

"Sure," he said. "What is it?"

"Why are you with us? I only ask because—" She looked up at him. "Because you, of all of us, need the Greyen the least. You fit into society. Brother Sims and Shi Jin both value you, and Magistrate Soren surely would forgive your crime if you were to join him. You do not need to believe, the way the rest of us do. Why are you with us?"

He thought for a moment. "Why are you asking? Why now?" he asked.

"I have never had people follow me before—never even listen to me, really. I am not sure I like it?"

"The responsibility?"

"Yes." She scraped off the last of the mess and tossed the stick away. "I would not hesitate to risk my own life for our cause, but I do not know if I can risk yours."

"You're not," he said. He looked right in her eyes, held her gaze. "I am—and I'm doing it because I want to. Not just because I believe in 'the cause,' but because I believe in you."

"I—" She looked away. "Thank you."

He nodded. "Ready to go now?"

She took her end of the ant, lifted. "Yes."

"All right then."

The wind brought a whiff of smoke from the ants' pyre, and he smiled at the smell: rich and dark, like—

—like the meat Stella had given them. Like ant meat.

Father Theou slowly edged his way into the nest, unsure precisely how he might avoid being detected by the ants. The means by which humans tried to move in stealth would hardly be relevant to creatures who did not much use their sight or hearing, but he could not overcome a lifetime's worth of instincts that were telling him to tip-toe.

Not that he had needed to, so far. The guardian ants had not been at their usual stations and the ants he had seen had not been interested in him. He had hoped to find one of the black and gold ants—the ones he thought were most likely of an intelligence comparable to humans—without going into the tunnels, but had seen none so far.

Staying close to the wall of the corridor, he edged inside the first large chamber. The usual frenzy of activity, the constant bark-chewing and acid-spitting, was absent and the broad pools full of stinkpaste had been allowed to harden.

Finally he reached the corridor that led to the innermost chamber. Within was a mess, strewn with the maimed bodies of black and gold ants. At the centre of the chamber lay the coffinlike object, cut in half by what had undoubtedly been a pistol blast. Whatever had been inside was beyond recognition. The entire room was filled was an acidic stench.

As he stepped toward the middle of the large chamber one of the black and gold ants stirred, struggling to raise itself on its legs.

Father Theou crouched down to get closer to the injured ant and focused his implant on its feebly waving antennae.

"Bring controller?" the computer translated for the ant.

He blinked, not quite believing he had succeeded, wondering if he had perhaps unconsciously programmed the translator to say what he wanted to hear. NO, he flashed.

"Not like other light-talkers. Smell is different."

Chewing his lip nervously, Father Theou decided to try letting the machine translate his own speech for the creature. If this entire conversation was actually happening, the ant was even more intelligent than he had hoped, and was "speaking" in the same grammar as the Greyen. Though it was using a different medium to communicate, the difference was like that between speaking and writing—separate ways of communicating meaning, but the same rules and norms. "I am from a different species," he said carefully, letting the communicator translate it into colour flashes.

"Yes. You are like the other, who destroyed the controller."

If he had needed any more evidence about Soren's—and his own—responsibility, he had it now. "Did that start the fighting?" he asked.

"We do not all agree to follow the controller, but it makes smells that make us obey. We have no choice."

"The controller is one of you?"

"No. The light-talkers bring the controller. They came many thirty-sixes of hatchings ago, when we could follow our own will. Then we lived in the soft earth and built domes of colour <no equivalent word> for our hatchings. They brought the controller and the others, made us live in the rock."

"Others?" he asked, his mouth wide in surprise. "You mean the other ants?" The ant's antennae made questioning waves. Apparently "ants" did not translate fully. "The others like you, of different sizes and colours."

"Yes," the ant said after a second. "They were stupid. The light-talkers made the controllers tell us what to do and made us tell the others, to dig in the rock and to spread the trees and grass."

"But you can speak to the—the light-talkers?"

"We are taught to see their orders. The controller is stupid. It can only make us obey, not give us orders."

"And—when the controller was killed?"

There was a pause, as the ant was apparently considering its response. "Controllers have died before. The light-talkers soon bring us another. Never before has one been killed by a light-talker, or with jaws."

"But why did you start fighting?" He fought to keep his voice level, so the communicator would translate it correctly.

"Some felt we should continue to follow the orders of the light-talkers, the rest felt we should not. We were unused to having our own wills, had forgotten how we used to decide what to do, in the hatchings when we lived in the soft earth. The only way we knew to decide was by jaws."

Father Theou blinked, checked his implant to make sure it was recording. He had always suspected the Greyen were using the ants somehow—the sphere in the chamber was proof of that—but had never imagined it was so totalitarian. It was certainly not much like the ideal partnership Xiang Kao had described to divert an entire species' evolution and make them serve only one purpose.

One purpose…That was it, the missing piece he had felt was there, between the ants, the Greyen and the stinktrees. That was why this world was so different from what the survey had shown. He had to tell Jin, before she made any more. "I must go now," he said.

"Be cautious. If those that still follow the light-talkers know they did not kill me, they will return. They will kill you if they smell that you are not a light-talker."

Father Theou took a step away and paused. "Are there many that believe you should still work for the light-talkers?" he asked.

The ant's antennae waved erratically. "Yes. It has been so many hatchings since we had our own will, many have forgotten. Many believe that this was the way we were meant to be."

He sighed deeply, took a breath from his puffer. He knew he ought to feel vindicated—that sort of disagreement was the proof that they had not only minds but souls. He was certain, now, that this was the ministry he had been meant for. These creatures needed him, even more than the convicts in the compound below.

Father Theou heard the sound of chitinous legs against the rock and looked up. Two more of the black and gold ants were entering the chamber, waving their antennae in his direction.

There was not much time to find out whether or not these ants were hostile—and no more time to react if they were. He had seen how quickly they could move on their six legs. Trying desperately to control his breathing, he activated the sound recorder on his implant.

"If you are hearing this message, it means that I am no longer able to give it to you myself…" he began.

Chapter Thirteen

"Why didn't you tell me?"

Bennett waited for Soren to turn and face him. The Fleet Magistrate was sitting in a simple stinkwood chair in the new hut, reading over files on his datapad, and showed no signs of having heard him.

"I asked you a question, Magistrate Soren," Bennett said, for once not caring if he sounded insubordinate.

Soren took a swallow from his flask. "I heard you," the old man said, not turning his head. "I am not required to consult you on command decisions. 'The wise ruler gets into difficulties through placing his trust in others.'"

"The ants have gone crazy. Whatever it was you destroyed was the only thing keeping them from attacking us."

Soren finally turned to face him and spoke in that slow, reasonable voice that was more persuasive than anything he might say. "The security of this colony is no longer a priority, Magistrate. Getting accurate information about the enemy is, and the ants were an obstacle." He paused, cocked an eyebrow. "This is a lot of fuss about a bunch of bugs. Don't tell me you're inclining towards Father Theou's heresy."

Bennett took an involuntary step back. "Of course not," he said.

Soren sighed deeply. "It's my fault, really. 'A piece of wood must be steamed before it is made straight;' I'm afraid the Church may have already steamed you to their shape."

"My duty is to this community, whether I serve the Church or the Magistracy. There's no contradiction there."

The Fleet Magistrate cocked his head, contemplating Bennett's words. "I suppose you're right. After all, my choices are limited. 'If a state cannot do without potters, how much less can it do without virtuous men?'"

Suddenly Bennett understood what Ande had meant that first time they had spoken, when he had refused to take part in running the colony. The authority they carried, the simple way they spoke were enough to make the people around them slaves just as much as the ants had been. How much of that before you start seeing them that way, before they become just pieces on a board? Bennett mumbled his apologies and slipped out of the hut. What could he do? All those who had listened to him before were unlikely to be turned against Soren, now that he had offered them citizenship. For that matter, what alternative could he give them? He was alone, without anything to offer.

He shook off a chill from the evening air and looked around, wondering if anyone had seen him crying. The last rays from the sun had somehow turned everything golden, even the air itself. The bladegrass field was a thousand gilded candles, glowing with light, the pods in the distance as majestic as the domes of the Great House on Avalon. He shook his head. How many days had he been here and not seen this? How could this planet have hidden it for so long?

A moment later it was gone in twilight, the landscape once more dull and dangerous. When Bennett stood, though, he found he felt light, and his feet already knew the way home.

Ruchika watched silently as Stella made her way over to the comm panel. The sac of skin hanging from the Greyen's shoulders had grown larger, interfering with her balance. Her delicate hands operated the machine's controls expertly, signalling to the satellite and from there to Jin's communicator. That would have been Ruchika's job, before; handling machinery was not something Greyen normally did themselves. Ever since Ruchika had forced contact, though, Stella had been avoiding her as much as possible.

That was fine with Ruchika. She did not really want Stella to know that she had seen how the Greyen saw her—or to realize that she could now understand Stella's colour flashes.

The comm screen lit up as the signal was accepted at the other end. Jin's face appeared with a caption of four colour squares at the base of the image. "What can I do for you?" the small woman asked, the colour squares below translating it into language the alien could understand.

Stella flashed her colour spots into the comm camera. "You have stated the ships in orbit now are allied with you," she said.

. "Yes. You don't have to worry about them."

"Do these ships possess the 'secret weapon'?"

There was a pause at the other end. "Yes," Jin said guardedly. "Yes—yes, they do."

She's lying, Ruchika thought. *Or bluffing.* Stella would not know, of course, lacked the ability to read the tone of Jin's voice. There was nothing the Fleet could have that the Greyen did not, and certainly Jin would have no such secret weapon. She knew she ought to tell Stella, show herself to be useful, but she decided to wait. That information might be more valuable later.

Stella flashed back at the screen, her lesser spots revealing shades of pink and orange that Ruchika knew to be excitement. "Delivery of one ship with 'secret weapon' will permit alliance," Stella said.

On the screen, Jin took a breath and nodded. Stella reached out to the comm panel, closed the channel and then keyed a quick, jagged pattern and the screen lit up again. It now showed a room with curved walls of luminous pearl, flashes of colour appearing and disappearing at random. Only not random: just as she could now understand Stella's flashes without translation, Ruchika now recognized the meaning of the colour, speed and location of the flashes—this one meant 'select a destination', that one 'open a hole.'

A Greyen stood facing the screen. Behind it stood two smaller, dull-grey creatures which Ruchika recognized from Stella's mind as *dulgs*. They had only two colour spots each, only enough to show anger, fear, or submission. That, she realized, was how Stella saw her.

"They will deliver the lightswimmer," Stella flashed.

The senior Greyen's outer spots coloured a dark, satisfied red. "Good," she said. "Remain and await further instructions."

Scattered spots of pink and yellow betrayed Stella's concern. "This location is not safe," she said. "The delivery will take place in orbit. I could return—"

"Remain," the other flashed. Behind her a monkey-rat scuttled by, its clever hands gripping invisible handholds on the wall. "Your service is still required."

"I give of my labour," Stella answered in meek shades, shrinking into herself defensively. Ruchika leaned in closer, hoping to get a better look if another monkey-rat entered the room.

"One of the creatures is watching," the other Greyen said, flashing red with alarm.

"There is no danger. They are motherless," Stella said.

The other flashed a wary green, seeming to accept Stella's answer. "How much longer can you serve?" she asked.

"A tide or two, no more. Will I be able to leave then?"

"If possible," the elder said, and then cut transmission abruptly. Ruchika stepped behind Stella, seeing the shock of betrayal register in pinks and greens in her face, and slipped her arms under the Greyen's shoulders to help her to the sling. Before she could reach it there was a knock on the airlock. Showing the dark orange that signalled annoyance, Stella turned to Ruchika—the first time she had even acknowledged her presence in hours—and flashed her the dark blue and harsh yellow that meant *deal with it*. Relieved, Ruchika went into the 'lock as Stella climbed into her sling.

Ruchika peered out the 'keyhole' she had made in the airlock seal. To her surprise, she saw no one waiting in the twilight. Since Soren's attack she had hacked the airlock so that it would only open a few fingers' width at first; she still saw nothing at eye level, but on looking down found a black and gold ant, its antennae waving questioningly in her direction.

That was strange: Stella had not been in recent contact with the creatures, and Ruchika had never known one of the ants to come to the station on its own initiative before. Even stranger, it was carrying a piece of metal in its inner mandibles. She looked closer and saw it was part of a cerebral implant.

She stepped outside, watching the ant. Its two rows of eyes followed her carefully as it tilted its head up, offering the machinery to her. She reached out to take it, hastily pulling her hand back as soon as the creature released the machinery. It was only a small part of an implant, just a few data storage wafers, a speaker, and a tiny battery. The ant watched her as closely as she was watching it; its antennae were still, pointing at the machine in her hand.

Ruchika looked the machine over and found the connection between the data wafers and the battery, where a tiny gold wire had been carefully unwound. She moved the wire back into contact with the battery terminal. A small, tinny voice, faint but unmistakably that of Father Theou, came out of the speaker.

"If you are hearing this message, it means that I am no longer able to give it to you myself…" it began.

She gave the machine back to the ant, which took it from her gently and scuttled away. The message was no more than two or three minutes long, but what it told her about the relationship between the ants and the Greyen—combined with what she had overheard between Stella and her superior—were enough to fill in the last parts of the puzzle. She now understood what the 'secret weapon' was, why the Greyen were afraid, and she was sure that Shi Jin did not. Jin would not be able to continue her bluff for long, and sooner or later she would hand the secret weapon over without knowing what she was doing. When that happened, the Greyen would have nothing to fear—and Stella would have no use for her at all.

Pulling her fingers out of her mouth—she had only just noticed she was chewing her nails—she stepped quietly back into the hut. Stella was still in her sling, sleeping. Trying to keep herself calm, she sat down at the comm and began to compose a message poem.

Jin sat frozen at the comm panel, nibbling on the carrots she had dug that morning. All she had left to do was find a Traveller ship to give to the Greyen and they would join her. If the Greyen had scared the Magistracy before, she could only imagine how frightening they would be with her planning their strategy. A good half of the Fleet would probably refuse to fight when they heard, she thought. Of those, half might come over to her side. Not that they would be needed. She had nearly broken the Borderless Empire with nine salvaged battleships; with the Greyen on her side, she would be unbeatable.

The INCOMING SIGNAL light snapped her out of her fantasy. She hit the OPEN CHANNEL key eagerly, expecting to see Griffin; instead it was a memorial poem, filling up the screen from right to left with perfect computer calligraphy. It said:

> The Greyen were here first
> To colonize this planet
> With ants and trees and grass
> They fear the TSARINA
> Your secret weapon.

Jin shook her head. This did not make sense. The Greyen could appear and disappear at will—how could they not have the TSA-RINA? For that matter, why would they need it? Soren might have sent the message, trying to keep her from closing the deal. This was not his style, though. For one thing, she was sure he could write better poetry. Besides, he had not believed she had brokered the truce, and definitely would not believe she could convince the Greyen to form an alliance with her.

The INCOMING SIGNAL light flashed. She hit OPEN CHAN-NEL again, and this time Griffin's face appeared on the screen. "We have a ship," he said. He did not look directly at her. "The Dragonet, a small ship whose crew is going to come live here. It wasn't easy to talk them into this."

She closed her eyes, rubbed at them with her thumb and forefinger. "I just got a message—text, no source address. It said the TSARINA is what they want from us."

Griffin scratched his beard, nodded. "It makes sense. The secret weapon had to be something they'd seen in action."

"I'm sure they just want to know what the Fleet is capable of. It can't be anything they don't have already."

"No?" He began to rotate slowly, always a sign something was on his mind. "What if they don't, though?"

She threw up her hands, exasperated at his stubbornness. "They must. They're hundreds of years ahead of us, and we've had it since before the Borderless Empire was founded. It can't be anything new to them."

"Suppose it is. Suppose the way their ships move is based on a completely different idea. Tactically speaking, what would it mean if they didn't have the TSARINA?"

"All right, teacher," she said, sighing. "Well. It would mean, probably, that they couldn't go somewhere they didn't already know existed. Assuming they really do disappear from one place and reappear in another, they need to know where they're going before they can do that." She paused, nodded to herself. "That makes sense, actually. That sphere can't take you everywhere, just places where there's another sphere. So—that means that to get to somewhere new, they have to go through normal space. Without the TSARINA, even if they go at near-lightspeed, it would take them years to get from system to system." Her mouth opened slightly as the implications of what she had just said became clear to her. "Their ships are knights and ours are rooks. They'd be more manoeuvrable in their own territory—places they already know—but we can cover new territory a lot faster."

"That explains why we never encountered them before," Griffin said. "If their ships can't travel past lightspeed, it's natural that first contact would come from us moving into their space." He took a deep breath. "So—assuming this is all true—what are we going to do?"

She found herself momentarily speechless and took a deep breath. A harsh cry filled the air as Yertle soared into the room. He was the proof of what the message had said—an animal that could not possibly have evolved on the planet as it was now: the ants and trees were their own technique for terraforming the planet—Greyenforming it—to make it suitable for colonization.

"Hand it over," she said at last. "We don't want the Fleet to have any kind of edge over us. If we're going to win this one—"

"What are 'we' going to win?" Griffin said. "If you give them the only weapon they're afraid of, do you think they're just going to go home once the Magistracy's defeated?"

"Worry about that later," Jin said. "If we attack with a strong force, a lot of the Fleet will defect to our side. Then when we need to deal with the Greyen, we'll have the power to do it." She watched her friend's eyes and saw that he was not convinced. "Give them the ship."

He paused, watching her. "No," he said quietly.

Soren looked up from his 'pad when he heard the door open and saw Peter Huyt, looking more red in the face than usual.

"What is it?" Soren asked, unable to conceal his annoyance at the interruption. Huyt opened his mouth and made noise, but was unable to put any actual words together. "Slow down. What is the problem?"

"Outside," Huyt said. "You have to see."

Sighing, Soren rose, put down his flask, hooked his 'pad onto his belt. He was not happy at having been left behind on this Soulforsaken planet, nor with the epidemic of insubordination that had now spread to Bennett, of all people. Not to mention Ande. The truce had been a mistake, he realized. It made the Magistracy look weak, and the appearance of strength was more important than strength itself. Shaking his head, he followed Huyt out into the night, shivering at the cold, to where the man was pointing excitedly at the sky.

$$\frac{4}{5}$$

Jin swallowed the shout that was in her throat. Yertle, as though answering her unheard yell, squawked loudly. "I'm not kidding."

"Neither am I. I won't tell them to do it." He had stopped spinning and was looking right at her.

"This is our last chance—" she began. She felt like crying with the frustration. Every time she took a step closer to her goal, something got in her way.

"Not our last chance. Yours," he said. "You want to win, to beat the Magistracy, and you don't care what happens after that."

"That isn't true."

"Then why are you about to give an alien species that we know nothing about the one weapon they need to conquer the universe?" He sighed, looked away. "I'm on your side, Jin. If you don't believe that, I don't know what would convince you. But I've got a lot of people depending on me now, and so do you. This isn't good for any of us."

She closed her eyes, resting her head in her hands. Not knowing what to say she took a bite of carrot and chewed slowly. She had been surprised, when she ate her first one, to find that they were utterly unlike the carrot bits in the food the ships brought, unlike anything else she had ever tasted, but good. She heard Lieutenant Wiesen's voice inside her mind, saying it doesn't matter how many pieces you take if you're playing for the wrong goal…

"What do we do, then?" she asked. "Just lose?"

"I don't know," Griffin said, scratching his beard. "Maybe, maybe we don't have to win. In that game you taught me, what was it called when neither side could win?"

"A draw, or a stalemate. I always hated those."

"The Magistracy would hate it, too."

She narrowed her eyes, not knowing what he was getting at. "What do you mean?"

He began talking more quickly, excitement coming into his voice. "People believe in the Borderless Empire because they have no alternative. But if it made a truce, gave up even one planet it had claimed…"

"It wouldn't be borderless anymore," she said, nodding slowly. "It wouldn't be All-the-Stars. So if we could keep the truce going, not join the Greyen or the Empire—"

"We'd be a finger in their eye," Griffin said.

She smiled. The image was appealing. "The problem is, I've already told the Greyen we're going to hand over the TSARINA. It's only a stalemate so long as they're afraid of the Empire and vice-versa."

"Tell them you've changed your mind. Tell them you're considering your options."

She shook her head. "They aren't going to like that."

"What have you got to lose?" he asked.

"My head, but what else is new? Patch me through to Stella."

He smiled, nodded. "Sure. Jin?"

"Yes?"

He took a deep breath. "You remember when we met, on the Hanzi waystation, and you needed a ride back to Garamond to find out what had happened there?"

She shrugged. "Of course. Why?"

"Did I ever tell you why I agreed to take you?"

She thought for a moment. "No. No, I don't think you ever did."

"It was because when I said no, you didn't offer more money, or threaten me, like any other landsider would have. You tried to convince me you were right—and you were." He smiled, though the memory was painful for them both. "I'm glad you haven't changed."

"I'm glad you haven't, either," she said. "You're still keeping me honest."

He blinked as his smile broadened, and several small drops of water went flying away from his eyes. "I'll put you through," he said.

She swallowed hard, waiting for the channel to open. "This is Shi Jin," she said. "I can't give you what you want right now. I'll be in contact again later."

She took a deep breath, hit CLOSE CHANNEL and waited for Stella's angry reply. After a few seconds, she was able to breathe again. That had gone better than she had expected—the Greyen must be in a reasonable mood. She leaned back, exhaled heavily. Yertle hopped up on her lap and gave a small trill.

She nearly fell out of her chair when the mass alarm sounded. She leaned forward, sending the bird flying, and called up the mass display on the screen.

A dozen huge Greyen spheres had appeared in low orbit, surrounding the tiny Traveller ships.

"So much for the stalemate," she said.

"It is time," Xiang Kao said. Her followers, her friends, were gaping in wonder at the white discs appearing in the dark sky.

She looked the group over as they stood in the clearing outside their complex of huts. The wind had picked up, blowing cold air through her cloak of leaves. Many of the convicts had now joined her, were ready to fight and die for the vision she had given them. They would still be outnumbered by Soren's forces, but she had no doubt the odds were in their favour. Those following the Fleet Magistrate did so largely out of fear. Her people were fighting for a dream.

"There can be no compromise," she said, looking from one face to the other, reading their resolve. "At the end of this night, they will lie dead or we will. The dream we share will be made reality—or it will be nothing but ashes, forgotten as though it had never been. Which end will come depends on us."

She raised her spear and shook it. The others held theirs high, passed ahead into the sphere and on to the battle, to whatever world they would end up making. She was about to follow when she saw that Ande had emerged from his hut, was watching her.

"Are you coming?" she asked. He had hardly spoken to her since she had started to organize her people for war, spending all of his time in his hut.

He surprised her by considering it briefly. "I don't think so," he finally said, walking up beside her. He was having some difficulty breathing, she noticed. His time spent in the hut, where the oxygen supply was constant, had made him unused to the air outside.

"Why are you here, then?" she asked. "Have you come to tell me you disapprove of what I am doing?"

"Do you need me to?"

She paused, watching his eyes. He did not look angry, just tired. "No. I wish that you could see the worth of what I am doing, but I do not need you to."

"And you? Do you approve of what I'm doing?"

"You are not doing anything."

"Precisely."

She glanced over at the sphere, where Malcolm, the last to enter, was waiting for her. "I do not approve, then. If you truly disapprove of what I am doing, you should convince me not to—or convince the others. I have no doubt you could if you wanted to."

"Yes. Yes, I probably could." He nodded. "But who am I to say I'm right? Who am I to tell other people what to do?"

"This is not the same thing," she said, suddenly angry. How could he not understand? "We are not forcing what we want on anybody. We are merely protecting our dream."

"And if your dream has to be built on the bodies of your people?"

She turned away from his eyes. "Then it will be. Everything has a price." Not looking back at him, she went to join Malcolm at the shell.

Jason stood feeling the weight of the spear haft in his hand, running his finger along the edge of the knife. He would not have believed the soft wood of the trees could become so hard, so deadly. It seemed none could live on this planet without being transformed. Even the sky had changed. The night before it had been moonless, but now the Greyen ships were hanging in the dark sky, the Fleet ships comets circling around them.

Nor had he escaped change. When Anna died, he had written the last three lines of Zheng He's mourning poem, over and over:

> I thought I was strong
> But when I lift my pen
> I find my sleeves are wet with tears

But he had never cried. Once she was gone, she seemed hardly real, her face a poem with smudged characters, stamped before the ink had dried.

Last night, though, Stella had touched him, helped him to dream his way past the grief and find her again, let him see Anna's face again at last. He had been afraid the memory would disappear, like it had every other time he had dreamed of her, but when he woke up it was still there. He had tried to fill the house with pictures of her, right after, but they had been nothing but shells. This memory was really her, and the moment he dreamed it he knew there was nothing the Greyen could ask him he would not do.

"No."

Jin had done everything she could to break through the interference the Greyen ships were generating and open a channel to the ship. Even her satellite link was down now, the mass detector blank. There could be a hundred or a thousand ships up there now, for all she knew. She had been fighting the urge to run outside and look up to find out.

"...problem here..." Griffin's voice came faintly out of the speaker, disappeared in a crackle of static. She ran her finger along the frequency control, guessing that he was doing the same thing she was. So long as they were both moving targets they would never find one another, she thought. She nudged the control up to the top of its range, pushed signal strength to maximum. No point in conserving power now. "Griffin, come in. Come in, Griffin," she said, over and over.

"...you, Jin?" she heard through a storm of pops and hisses.

"Griffin? Stick to this frequency," she shouted, knowing that how loud her voice was would make no difference.

"Hang...to link with...ships...signal," he said. The speaker was silent for a moment as she sat rigid, listening intently. "Can you hear me?" he finally said, only a slight crackle of static in the background.

"Yes," she said quickly. "What's happened? Are they gone?"

"No—I just linked my comm to the other ships. By all sending the same signal, we can just barely get through." She heard him exhale heavily. "I've been trying to contact the Greyen, but nothing so far. We know they can understand us now, so—"

"So they don't want to listen," Jin said. "I think they've decided not to wait for us to give them the TSARINA."

"I...not," Griffin said over the rising interference. "...power, Jin. What should we do?"

She opened her mouth to speak, found no words inside. She had been outplayed, was as helpless now as she had been the day Ande Linden detonated the decoy ships to win the battle of Second Tallinn and end her war.

She had replayed that day thousands of times in her mind over the years, wondering if there had been any way she could have anticipated his plans, countered them. From the moment he became Fleet Magistrate, though, he had taken her off guard, just as the Greyen had now done. She had had to guess his limits, the rules he played by, and so had been thrown on the defensive. It was the same with the Greyen—she had no idea what they might or might not do to get the TSARINA.

There was no way around it. She had lost.

The shockstick felt cold when Soren pressed it into Liz's palm, favouring her with a look that said *I know I can count on you*. She had been given command of one of the three squads; Peter Huyt, too, had been rewarded, given a squad of his own and allowed play the part of the wounded hero to the hilt.

But then that was what they were all here for, wasn't it? Kill a rebel, get a war wound, get a medal and a pardon and get sent back to civilization. It was that or face whatever punishment the Greyen had in store for her.

"Shouldn't we...wouldn't it be tactically wiser to have some pistols?" Nick Leung asked.

"Even if we had them, we couldn't risk them falling into the rebels' hands," Soren said. "These will have to do."

"We love the hammer when we need it," a voice said quietly in her ear. "Then it goes back in the toolbox." Liz turned to see Magistrate Sims standing behind her, wearing his blue and gold robes.

"Magistrate?" she asked.

"Not any more." He brushed some dirt off his robe. "I was told awhile ago that a pistol has no choice in whether or not it kills, and so bears no guilt. But I have a choice."

"But this is war," she whispered, looking over at Soren nervously. If he had noticed Bennett's arrival he showed no sign.

"Why is it war? Because we are right and they are wrong? Or because we are angry and afraid?" He gave a small smile, then turned and walked off toward the compound.

She watched him go, confused. Why had he come, just to walk away? Why had he chosen to talk to her?

She noticed a commotion around her, realized Soren had finished arming the troops and Huyt and Soren's squads were already moving out. Her people were looking at her expectantly, no doubt wondering what Bennett had said to her. She paused, looking from face to face. Few of them looked like criminals. None of them looked like soldiers.

"Let's move out," she said, gave them a minute to fall in line behind her then set off after the others.

Shi Jin's left hand clenched into a fist, knocking against her forehead as if it could knock an idea free. It was hopeless. After all the replays, she had finally decided there was no way she could have beaten Linden from her position. The only way she could have won was to be in his place and not hers.

"Griffin, listen," Jin said quickly. Ande Linden had won the war by learning from her; maybe now it was her turn to learn from him. "Tamper with the TSARINAs. All of them, all the ships."

There was a pause. "Jin, I don't know if I can convince them. A lot weren't sure about coming here to begin with."

"They won't get away. It'd take the fastest of them nearly a day to get out of the system." Her fist began to knock rhythmically against the comm panel in a mix of fear and excitement. "I know what I'm asking. What is it your people say? Nothing's free."

Seconds passed in silence, making Jin check to make sure the channel was still open. Finally Griffin said, "All right, I'll try. I just hope this doesn't annoy the Greyen even more."

"So do I." She hit CLOSE CHANNEL, settled down to wait, drumming her fingers against the panel. Yertle, agitated by the excitement, gave a cry and soared out into the hallway. Closing her eyes, she tried to slow her breathing, suppress the adrenaline rushing through her veins. She only hoped Stella would not destroy the crippled Traveller ships out of spite.

Stella. She had forgotten the alien was still at the station, still vulnerable. If she was hurt now, there would be no way to stop the Greyen wiping out everyone on the planet. She was out of her chair and out the airlock within seconds, hoping she was not too late.

As soon as he was out of sight of Soren's people, Bennett broke into a run toward the pods, nearly colliding with Jin as she came out of the airlock.

"Get out of my way," she said, pushing him aside. "I've got to protect Stella."

"It's too late," he said. "Soren's got thirty, forty people headed for the hut. We have to warn Stella they're coming."

She shook her head. "There's too much interference from the ships. They're blocking transmission—and they're not listening anyway."

"Maybe—maybe the others will protect her," he said.

"With Xiang Kao in charge? It'll be a slaughter. We'll be lucky if there are ten people alive on this planet by morning."

He covered his face with his hands. "That's it, then," he said. "There's nothing we can do." He paused, lowered his hands, and looked at her. "Wait a minute. There is somebody even Soren and Xiang Kao will listen to—Ande Linden."

"He wouldn't help either of us before."

"You asked him for help?" Bennett asked, looking at her in surprise. He shrugged. "Never mind. If we ask him together, both of us—that has to convince him. Doesn't it?" His last words were spoken in desperation, but he believed he was right. Ande had not just been being stubborn—he was waiting for someone to give him the right reason to take action.

She considered a moment. "Okay," she said. "Let's give it a try. If we use the sphere it'll give us a chance to catch up."

Without waiting for his answer, she ran off toward the gate. He took another breath from his puffer and pushed himself to follow, praying that the Soul did not want to bring any of its children home that day.

引

The convicts in Liz's squad straggled behind her as they made their way out of the valley. Almost none of them had been this far up in the hills before, and few realized how long a march it was.

Up ahead, Soren stopped, turned, and held up a hand. Liz held a finger up to her mouth, relaying the command, and a second later the whole forest was still. She listened carefully, heard voices murmuring in the distance. There were people waiting for them, Xiang Kao's group. *This is it*, she thought. There could be no quarter, no mercy:

she imagined the Greyen would have something worse than death in store for her if she were captured.

Soren gave the signal and Liz held up her hand to her group, waving them forward in silence. Their job was to guard against an ambush by flanking the enemy, finding one hut where the back wall had decayed enough to get her people through and prepare an ambush of their own.

They moved through the woods until they found a hole just big enough to squeeze through. She squeezed herself into the hut and then brought her people through one at a time, moved to where the 'lock had once been and peered out.

Two dozen convicts, Xiang Kao among them, were standing in front of the alien ship, each holding long stinkwood spears. Liz looked to her left, wondering when Soren would make his attack.

Suddenly Xiang Kao's people snapped to attention and moved forward. Xiang Kao held out a hand, stopping them. Liz followed her gaze and saw Soren walking down the path, alone. She tensed, ready to attack and held up a finger to signal her troops to do the same. Soren walked closer to the rebels until finally he stopped, no more than ten paces from Xiang Kao.

"I have come for the alien," he said.

"She is under my protection," Xiang Kao answered, watching him carefully.

"Are you refusing a direct order, convict?" he asked. She did not answer. "Very well, then. By the authority of the Emperor, I am—"

"Wait!" A voice came from within the alien sphere standing opposite the hut. Ande Linden walked out. "This battle will do no good to any of you," the old man said. He had a voice like Soren's, deep and calm. "There is no sense in wasting our blood on this soil."

"This is a military operation," Soren answered. He sounded uncertain, caught off guard by Ande's sudden appearance.

"Is it? Then where is the Fleet? Is the Lonely One so helpless she needs us to do her dirty work?" Ande moved to stand between Soren and Xiang Kao, looked from one to the other.

"The Empire needs every hand that can hold a sword," Soren said. He sounded shaky, took a step back as Ande approached.

"It is the Emperor's duty to protect the people. To defeat our enemies. Are you so certain that you would claim the right to start this war?"

"Stay out of this!" Soren shouted. He looked around at his followers, many of whom had followed down the path to see what was going on. "Don't listen to him. This war is our duty. We can't let them get away with—"

"Don't condemn us all to death because you want to die a hero," Ande said, taking a step toward him. "You don't have anything to make up for."

"He's right," Bennett said as he stepped from the sphere into the clearing. "This is our last chance to turn back."

Jin followed behind him. "How many of you really believe you'll be allowed to live here, even if they do win the war? As soon as the aliens aren't a threat anymore, the Empire won't have any more use for you," she said.

"Come on, Charlie," Ande said, taking a step closer to Soren.

The Fleet Magistrate looked like a cornered animal, turning his head from side to side. Liz could see the convicts watching him carefully, wondering how he would react. Soren took a step closer to Ande.

"Come home," Ande said, reaching to take the other's hand. The Fleet Magistrate nodded, looking as though he was sleepwalking.

"No," Xiang Kao said quietly. Before anyone could move, her spear was deep into Soren's stomach.

The tall man stumbled forward, his eyes still locked with his friend's. "Ande?" he asked, falling.

Everyone froze. Xiang Kao held her dagger in front of her, warding off anyone who would challenge her. "He had to pay for what he did. Stella said so."

Liz looked on in shock. The alien—the alien had ordered Soren killed. She was next, she knew it.

"Get them!" she shouted, running out of the hut. Jason Barr moved to block him, but she brought her stick down on the man's head, shocking him into unconsciousness. Swinging wildly, she moved on toward the alien ship. Behind her she could hear the others charging their shocksticks and attacking Xiang Kao's people. *This is it, then,* she thought. *It's war.*

CHAPTER FOURTEEN

Jin took an involuntary step back from the battle. It was a mess. Xiang Kao's people were holding their own against their attackers but were on the defensive. The rules of the game were against them: they had to rout all of Soren's people to win, while the others only had to get inside the hut.

"I'm sorry," Ande said. The old man was crouched over Soren's body, cradling his head in his hands, and she could not tell whether he had been speaking to her or the corpse.

"You almost convinced them," Bennett said.

"He always thought it was his fault," Ande said, not turning to look at them. "The worst defeat in the Borderless Empire's history. He spent the rest of his life looking for a glorious death to make up for it."

"He got half of what he wanted." She did not understand how Ande could feel sympathy for the man, whatever their history. Then again, she could not have imagined feeling sympathy for Ande until that moment. "We can't just stand here. I've got to—"

"Too late," Bennett said, sounding stunned by the violence in front of him. Two of Soren's people, Nick Leung and Liz Szalwinski, had managed to fight their way through to the station's door. Szalwinski turned to face Xiang Kao's followers, warding them off with her shockstick, while Leung worked at opening the door.

"Got it!" he shouted, and moved inside. Szalwinski followed him while the remaining convicts on their side redoubled their efforts to get by Kao's people. Jin looked over at Kao and saw her kneeling on a convict's chest, drawing her bloody knife out of his heart. She looked surprisingly unconcerned.

"Go back through the sphere," Jin said to Bennett.

"Why should I go back to the compound?"

She kept her voice quiet. "I don't think it'll take you back to the compound. It'll take you wherever Stella went."

He frowned. "What makes you think—?"

"They tricked us!" Leung shouted from inside the hut.

"That," Jin said. "Now go, and tell her what I told you." She looked at the convicts, who had stopped fighting momentarily. "I'll try to handle things here."

Bennett nodded and stepped into the sphere. It closed behind him, once more as smooth and featureless as a pearl. Ande was still kneeling by Soren's body, his eyes closed. She wished she could let him do this, but knew he was somewhere else. It was up to her. She took a step forward, smelling the rusty odour of blood in the air.

Bennett had only ever gone through a Greyen sphere once before, moments ago, and had found it disorienting. Or rather, he found it not disorienting enough—he was familiar enough with the sense of dislocation involved in regular travel that moving from place to place so easily felt deeply wrong.

The sphere opened on a cave, lit only by a few emergency lights off in a corner. It was not large, no more than twenty paces long and slightly less across, with a ceiling low enough that Bennett had to stoop once he stepped out of the sphere. So far as he could tell the sphere was the only entrance or exit to the chamber except for a small passageway that was choked with stones. There was a thick, musty smell in the air, distinct from the dank of the cave.

In the middle of the chamber, Stella was lying on her stomach on a block of some porous dark purple stone. He had only seen her once before, briefly, and was surprised at how much larger the sac of skin on its shoulders had grown. It was almost as large as the alien's head now, looked like a swollen thumb. Ruchika was standing over the alien, stroking the sac gently; as he stepped out of the sphere she turned and saw him.

"What are you doing here?" she shouted. At the same time he heard another voice, straight into his mind without going through his ears. *They've found us*, it said. The voice was unmistakably Ruchika's, though it came at the same time as she was speaking.

Shaking his head to clear it, Bennett said, "Shi Jin sent me. With a message."

"Get out of here!" *Don't worry, I'll get rid of him*, the second voice said, though he did not think it was directed at him.

Bennett took a step closer to the xenologist and her alien patient. "What's going on?" he asked.

"Nothing. Go away." *Stella, I don't know what to do.*

"Something's wrong, isn't it? Does it…does she need medical help?" He reached out to touch the taut sac of skin hanging between the alien's shoulders, then withdrew his hand at Ruchika's look. The alien's colour spots were flashing wildly, frantic reds and yellows.

"There's nothing you can do," Ruchika said. *What do I do? It won't come.* She was starting to look panicked, hyperventilating.

Bennett adopted the calm, reassuring tone he had learned from Ande and Soren. "She's hurt, isn't she?" he asked.

Ruchika looked up in surprise—not when he spoke, but a second later. "You really want to help?"

"What?"

"You said you really want to help. With your mind, not your voice." She closed her eyes, continuing to stroke the alien's back. *Like this,* the other voice said. *It's because of her.*

"The mind-talking," he said.

"Yes," she said aloud, echoing it in his mind. "They do it to teach their children, while they're still in the pouch. That's why they can only do it when they're pregnant—their planet's so dangerous you need to know how to survive before you're even born. When they give birth, they spray the chemicals all over the area, so all the other Greyen nearby can touch the baby's mind and make her part of the community."

"She's pregnant?" he asked, trying to hide his repulsion.

"She won't let it come," Ruchika said, casting him a glance that told him he had failed. "The pouch is ready to burst," —*that's why you can hear me like this*—"but if it comes out now, it'll contact our minds, not other Greyen. In their eyes, it won't even be a person."

He nodded, stepped closer to examine the alien's pouch. There was no doubt that it was about to burst. A few small lesions had already appeared, from which mucous was dripping, and he could feel a wet mist hissing out as well.

Putting his hand on the pouch, to try to guess at the baby's position, he felt a wave of pure fear and anger crash against him. He took two steps back before rallying against the emotional pressure. The quality of the "voice" was different from what he had been hearing before: this was Stella, not Ruchika.

He paused, briefly, to marvel at the fact that he was in contact with an alien's mind, and then got his attention back to his work. He pushed against the emotions and colours that were coming at him from the alien and concentrated on just his hand, letting it fall gently on Stella's pouch.

"It's ready," he said, feeling a sudden kick strike the pouch wall and his palm. "If she doesn't let it out soon it's going to break out. Or die, I think."

Ruchika swallowed. "I know. They were supposed to pick her up but something happened—the ships are all busy." He "heard" her direct a thought to Stella. *I'm sorry. You just have to let it come.* Below that he heard a quieter, more furtive voice, one he thought she was trying to hide: *She won't be able to leave me now. We'll be connected.*

The Greyen's colour spots turned a dark, angry red—the equivalent of a scream, Bennett guessed from the pain that came with it. Now he was in closer contact, able to feel the muscles of her pouch straining to keep the baby in. Through that he felt a smaller voice, like Stella's but different, sending out primitive flashes of panic.

It had a soul. He had never paid much attention to the debate of when unborn children gained souls, but there was no doubt this being had one, was alive and ready to enter the world.

"The strain's too much," he said to Ruchika, forcing himself back into his own mind. "They'll both die if she doesn't let it go."

"Are you mad?" Perun's bald, sweaty face filled the screen. "You call us to come live in the middle of a firefight, and now you want us to destroy our only chance of changing our minds?"

Griffin sighed. He knew he could persuade the other ships to tamper with their TSARINAs, making them self-destruct, if he could convince Perun. He also knew that convincing Perun was about as likely as getting air for free. "Listen, have you seen those ships out there? You couldn't get away now if you wanted to."

"And that is supposed to convince me?" The bald man spat a piece of algae gum away from the screen. "All the more reason to get out of here now."

"Do that, and they'll just seize the ship. I'm sorry to have gotten you into this, but it's the only way out now."

Perun scowled. "And what do we do then? How are we supposed to be Travellers, if we don't travel? Do you want your own ship to be stuck in a single system, not even able to make it to lightspeed?"

"The whole point is that we're not going to be Travellers anymore. We can stay here, take as much air and water as we need—have a home. That's why you came, isn't it?"

"Peh. It was a foolish idea to begin with."

"Is that why all those ships came, because it was a foolish idea? You know the rules—you don't get something for nothing. If you want to stay, you give up the power to leave."

"Not much of a deal," Perun said. He was chewing more vigorously on his remaining gum, though, a sure sign that he was thinking it over.

"It's the only one on the table," Griffin said.

"Da." Perun nodded, spat. "All right, we'll do it. But Vyslav, if this doesn't work out, you scrape algae from the tanks for the rest of your life, you understand?"

Griffin breathed a sigh of relief, smiled. "That's not too bad. I figured you'd kill me if it didn't work out."

The other man returned his smile, revealing a mouth full of rotted but wickedly sharp teeth. "I didn't say how long the rest of your life would be," he said.

"She won't let go," Ruchika said.

"What do you want me to do?" Bennett asked. "I have a scalpel in my pouch, for emergencies. Do you want me to…?"

She nodded and looked down at Stella. *I'm sorry*, he heard her send. There was no response, just the burning red pain of keeping the pouch closed.

Making a quick Bridge on his forehead—*ekasa te thromo*, he said, knowing that it was not only aliens that could read minds—he opened his beltpouch and drew out the small scalpel. He hit the red button on the base, to sterilize the blade, and opened it. He ran his hand over the pouch, trying to feel out where he could cut without doing harm to the baby, and found a ring of muscle that was being clenched tightly. The feelings of anger he was receiving intensified when he touched it and he paused, suddenly unsure. He tried to clear his mind, order his thoughts into simple messages. *It will die*, he sent. *I can't let you do this, but you can still let it go.*

The sensation he got in response was one not of defiance but of panic. The muscle he was touching twitched tighter and he realized that she was spasming, no longer able to control whether it opened or closed. There was no more time. He tried to convince himself that he had heard her decide to let the pouch open, before the choice had been taken away from her, and began to cut.

It took only a few seconds for the scalpel to sever the muscle, cauterizing the grey-green flesh behind it. Once he was done, it twitched again, unable to pull against anything now that the ring was broken, and began to disgorge a thin black liquid. The musty smell grew stronger as the tiny alien tried to fight its way from the sac with its powerful legs. Using the scalpel as carefully as he could he cut away at the now loose skin, giving the baby an opportunity to escape.

Free, it tumbled along its mother's back, slippery with the black liquid, finally landing on the stone block. It was much paler than Stella, its skin nearly translucent and all of its colour spots a dark red. Its body was more squat as well, mostly legs and head, with a small tail.

Bennett felt himself being drawn outside of his mind as the alien baby opened its mouth, felt tiny gills opening in her throat, drawing in air, as she surveyed the creatures around her with eye and mind. He felt herself lying on the warm stone, nearly unconscious, feeling the lack of the connection that had been so close for months, afraid of what would happen to her child. He lived simultaneously as himself, as Ruchika and as Stella; he felt afraid, wondering how Stella would punish her for making this happen, at the same time as the warm, perfect peace of the pouch filled his mind. Memories of being raised by geneworkers on Apogee played side by side with having her life's path chosen for her as a pouchling.

We need to accept the baby, Ruchika's mind-voice was saying to him. *It needs something to replace the love it's been getting in the pouch, or it won't grow properly.*

Bennett looked down at the newborn alien. Accepting it was ridiculous, loving it impossible. Its mind recoiled from his at that thought, the alien itself twitching and squirming. He remembered the first contact he had made with it, minutes before, when he had become convinced it had a soul. *All who have souls can be compatible.* He closed his eyes, looked into its mind, and saw its soul. *We are all one,* he thought, sent, believed.

He could sense Ruchika's agreement as she sent the child the feeling she had first had on seeing Stella: *I am not alone. You are not alone.* Stella was sending an emotion that was beyond words, the perfect acceptance she had herself once received. The child absorbed all of these, sent them back twice as intensely.

"The child should be all right now," he forced himself to say out loud. "You can take him back whenever it's safe."

We cannot go back, Bennett heard in his mind. It was not Ruchika's voice; he could sense the xenologist's astonishment at Stella's using words. *She is tainted by you. The others would not touch her now.*

He opened his eyes, looked over at Ruchika. "You don't have to go home," he said. "That was the message I was supposed to bring. The only way to keep the planet safe is to keep the truce going indefinitely. To do that, we'll need some of your people to stay."

So I should stay here, impregnate myself and bear dulg after dulg so I can speak to you? Or worse yet, be impregnated by my child? The sense of revulsion along with that thought was overpowering. *No. Death would be less humiliating.*

"You don't have to," Ruchika said. "There's the translator, remember? And—" She paused. "I can understand you now, your normal speech. I can interpret for you and for your child, when she's old enough."

He could feel Stella considering Ruchika's words. *She is strong,* Stella sent. *From touching alien minds. Much stronger than I am, or any other of us. She would be too useful to them—they would make her carry pouchlings all her life, talk to aliens as I do, never let her have warmsun.* That last was not a word, but a sense-image, the touch of sun on Greyen skin—their definition of pleasure. It made him feel almost drunk. *We will stay.*

He nodded and smiled. It was the same decision he had made. Stella had taken the child in her fragile arms and was holding her close. He could feel the contact between their minds fading away as the chemicals in the air evaporated. *What are you going to call her?* he sent while he still could.

Stella answered in colour flashes, the connection between them gone.

"I didn't get that," Bennett asked. He could no longer feel her presence in his mind, or Stella's. "What's the baby called?"

"Born in the light of foreign stars," Ruchika answered. "Exile."

Jin took another step closer to the crowd, raised her voice. If she was going to do anything, now was the time.

"Everyone stop right now!" A few people paused, looking up. "I said stop!" she yelled, feeling her voice become hoarse. "There's nothing to fight about. Stella is gone and Soren is dead."

"And they killed him," Liz Szalwinski said.

"You were going to kill Stella," Malcolm Smith answered. He had a long, wicked slash across his forehead, dripping blood into his eyes, but looked otherwise unhurt. In the dim light reflected from the Greyen ships above, Jin could see that most of the people there were wounded in some way, about a dozen unconscious or dead.

"Shut up, all of you," Jin said. She wanted to use every trick she had learned at the Academy to make them stop. Even if it worked, though, it wouldn't be for any longer than the last truce had lasted. She had to do what she had done with Griffin, so many years before—not bribe them, or threaten them, but convince them she was right. "This is just what they want—the Greyen and the Magistracy—to get us to fight each other for them. We have a chance here to—" She paused, took a breath from her puffer, and turned to face Xiang Kao. "Right now the Greyen are up there trying to take what we wouldn't give them. They're using us just as much as the Empire is—but that doesn't mean your dream can't happen."

Xiang Kao listened impassively to Jin, watching the mental target dancing over her chest as she spoke. "You are wrong," Kao said when she had finished. "Or you are lying. The Greyen will not harm us."

"It's true," Ande Linden said, looking up at her. "Shi Jin explained it to me and it's true."

"No." Kao looked around at her followers, saw them watching her nervously. They had killed, died for her and her dream. "Ande, it's not—"

"I'm sorry," Ande said.

He could not lie to her. He had been the only one who believed she was anything but a monster, until the Greyen came—but if he was right then she was a monster, in service to a greater monster. She looked at the ground, away from his eyes, and saw the bloodstained knife in her hand. "If what you say is true, my dream is nothing. Everything we have fought for is nothing."

"It isn't," Jin said. "Your dream can be real, but we'll make it real, not the Greyen. This planet is ours if we want it—we can make the truce permanent, use the Empire to scare off the Greyen and the Greyen to scare off the Empire."

"The Greyen won't be scared of—" Kenneth Fujitu began.

"They will," Jin said. "They are. I can't tell you why, but believe me, that's why they're here."

"And what about us?" Liz asked, wincing at her dislocated shoulder. "I suppose you'll hand me over to the Greyen to seal your truce?"

Jin shook her head. "Whatever's happened up to now, it's in the past," she said. She turned back to Kao. "This has to be a fresh start—for all of us. This is our planet."

"Our planet?" Liz asked.

"That's right. And we're all full citizens of—Soul, it needs a proper name, doesn't it?"

"Call it...Exile," Liz said.

Jin furrowed her brow and then nodded. "Yes," she said, glancing up at the sky. "For everyone who doesn't have a home, this is home now."

Our own planet, Liz thought to herself. *We'll probably all starve and be blown out of space, wiped out by the Fleet and the Greyen both. But at least—at least...*

Liz shrugged, moved to join the ragged column heading back to the compound.

There had been, it turned out, one more death than anyone knew about. Bennett learned of it when he had remarked to Ruchika that Father Theou would love to hear about Stella's labour. She told him he was dead—killed by the ants, she thought. She had only learned what he had found out because one of them had brought her his findings.

The next morning Bennett set out for the nest. Jin had pleaded with him to stay, saying he was needed to preserve the truce between Soren's and Xiang Kao's people, but he knew he had a duty to perform. He had not given Father Theou enough credit when he was alive, and was determined not to make the same mistake now; the Soul rarely offered second chances. Father Theou had been right about the Greyen having souls, and if he had been equally right about the ants Bennett needed to know it.

The nest was very quiet, almost deserted. In Father Theou's stories it had always been full of activity. Now what few ants he saw were wandering almost aimlessly. The great guardian ants that had done so much damage to the compound were nowhere to be seen.

Suddenly he came face to face with one of the black and gold ants. He froze and extended a hand cautiously. The creature moved closer, waving its antennae over his hand. After a moment, it turned and scuttled away.

Not sure what to make of that, he continued, moving further into the nest, until he saw another of the black and gold ants heading toward him. He saw that it was carrying a piece of machinery in its mandibles. The machinery was part of a cerebral implant—Father Theou's implant.

Sweat began to trickle down the back of his neck as the creature approached. Was this the one that had killed Father Theou? Somehow he had managed to make himself forget that he was going into the midst of the beings that were responsible for the priest's death, but that fact filled his mind now. The ant came closer, waving its antennae at him. He was unable to move.

The ant lowered its mandibles and dropped the implant to the ground. A tinny voice came from the machine as the ant waved its antennae in a curious pattern. "You are a light-talker," the ant said. "Light-talk."

Bennett knelt down and picked up the implant parts it had dropped. They were a battery, a tiny microphone, a mini-camera, a speaker and a bank of four coloured guidelights. He spoke into the microphone. "You—have you seen others like me?" he asked, watching the response come out as colour flashes from the guidelights.

The ant wove a pattern in the air with its antennae, making the implant speak again. "Yes," it said. "One spoke to us, destroyed the controller. When it was dead, we knew no way to decide what to do except for jaws." It snapped its large mandibles together for emphasis. "The other listened to us, told us we could decide for ourselves."

"The controller made you do what the light-talkers said?"

"Yes. We are afraid they will bring another controller. If they do, we cannot keep from doing what they say. The other said the trees will kill your people but we cannot say no when the controller is here."

Bennett took a breath from his puffer. It was astonishing what Father Theou had done, finding a way to communicate with beings so alien. The fact that such a brilliant mind had been wasted in the Borderless Empire convinced him he was doing the right thing, supporting Jin's truce. "We can keep them from bringing another controller," he said slowly. "If you tear out the trees. Not all of them, but some."

The ant looked like it was thinking it over. "We will do that," it said. "If we can."

"Thank you," he said, not sure if it could be translated. "The other—the one who helped you to stop fighting—what happened to him?"

The ant's antennae drooped slightly. "The ones that did not want to be free killed him," it said. "They are few now, but then we could not stop them."

It was true, then. "I'm sorry," he said. "I'd better go now."

"Do not let your people come here," the ant said to him as he turned away. "It will take many hatchings for us to learn how to decide things for ourselves, without jaws. It will not be safe until then."

"Don't worry," he said. "We'll have enough to do by ourselves for a while."

Once the sound of the footsteps had subsided the ant reached down, took the dropped machinery in its mandibles and brought it back to the one that had given it.

"You will stay?" it asked, trusting the machinery it wore to make noises the light-talker would understand.

The light-talker took the machinery from its jaws and fitted it back into place in its head. "Yes. They won't come looking for me again."

"The other said it will keep another controller from coming. You will help us learn how to decide things for ourselves, without jaws?"

"Yes."

Father Theou watched the ant wave its antennae in the pattern he now recognized as pleasure and scurry off to carry his answer to the others. He made the Bridge on his forehead, not as a plea but as thanks to the Soul for bringing him to this point. This was the ministry he had been meant for—bringing the Word to thousands of beings that had only just discovered they had a soul.

It was about the last thing Jin could have ever imagined herself doing, but here she was, attending Magistrate Soren's funeral. She had thought the Fleet would send a ship to pick up his body, but Ande had just shaken his head.

"I'm the closest thing to family he had," he said. "And this is the closest we'll ever get to a home."

Ande was talking now at the gravesite, telling a story from their childhoods on Cicero. "Every planet has some customs the others don't," he said. "Where we come from, you're supposed to spend your sixteenth year out in the wild—the Werewolf year, they call it. Charlie and I were the same age, and we were friends, but you're not allowed to live with any help, even from another boy. We each made it through fall, all right, but when winter came we found out just how flimsy the shelters we had made were." Many in the crowd nodded at this, their own experience building shelters recent in their minds. "Each of us was too scared to suggest we get together, share our warmth. Or too proud, maybe, because each of us came from good families, and it would be a terrible shame to admit you needed help. So there we were, each freezing in our little huts, when Charlie came up with the perfect answer: he burnt his own hut down.

"He said it was an accident, of course, and maybe it was. But with his hut gone and winter there, nobody could begrudge us sharing my hut, so it worked out well for us. Still, I think he always resented it, a little—that I hadn't volunteered to burn my hut down first."

The crowd suddenly went silent, and Jin blinked in surprise when she saw why. Stella was there, wearing a version of Father Theou's communicator. Ruchika stood behind her, looking uncomfortable.

The Greyen stood still for a moment and then began flashing colours at the translator. "It is easy to do wrong, telling yourself you are serving your people," the machine said. "The result does not change the intent. I will not forgive the damage he did to me, the danger he put my pouchling in. But I will understand." Without waiting for a response, the alien turned and left, Ruchika trailing behind.

That night a celebration was arranged, a tradition Ande had called a wake. This time Jin felt compelled to participate. For one thing, she finally felt she had something to celebrate; she had been working with Bennett and Ande to draft a truce agreement that would satisfy both the Greyen and the Magistracy. Each had a single ship in orbit to negotiate—a hopeful sign, or so Ande had said.

So there she was, sharing smoke and voidfire with people who would likely as not have wanted to kill each other just a week before. Those feelings weren't going to dissolve overnight, but for now they seemed to be driving people to dance and sing that much harder.

The formal dances she had learned at the Academy did not suit Jason Barr's voice, his incomprehensible songs, so she was trying to just let the music move her. It made her feel weightless, as though each step threatened to send her up into the sky. The feeling frightened her at first, but she was reassured to see Bennett was making an even bigger fool of himself, flailing his limbs around without regard for rhythm or tune. She laughed and moved to join him.

Much later, Barr's voice dropped low, raspy with smoke. The others became quiet as he sang a song for those that had died:

> I'll cry for you
> When the stars go out
> When the sun burns dark
> And cold
> I'll laugh with you
> When we meet again

When you're young and I
Am old.

Blinking away the smoke that had filled her eyes, Jin rose and crept back into the pod. Careful not to wake any of the revellers that had already retired to their bunks, she went into the comm room and checked to see if the Magistracy's reply had come in yet. Seeing that it had not, she sat down to wait. Seconds later she was asleep, her chorus singing Barr's song in her dreams.

Jin awoke to a hand on her shoulder, shaking her gently. She opened her eyes and saw Bennett and Ande Linden standing silhouetted in the doorway.

"What is it?" she asked.

"They said no," Bennett said. "The Magistracy. They won't accept it."

"They're crazy." Jin felt herself start to shake, on the verge of tears. "They already accepted the idea of the truce. They know they can't win a war. Would they rather kill themselves than let us go? What do they want?"

The question hung in the air for what felt like several lifetimes. Finally Ande spoke, slowly, quietly. "It's you," he said.

Jin looked up at him, not understanding. "What do you mean?"

"You did more than beat the Magistracy at First Tallinn, you humiliated them. They can let this planet go, they can let the worst murderer in the universe go—but they can't let you go."

"So, I guess I don't get to harvest my carrots," she said, not quite taking it all in.

"No, we can't accept this," Bennett said. "You worked too hard for this. You knew we couldn't trust either side from the beginning. We'll call their bluff."

"Don't be so sure what I knew," Jin said. "And don't be sure they're bluffing."

Ande shook his head sadly. "They're not," he said. "I should know, I wrote the book they're using."

"Then we take cover," Bennett said. "In the ant nest—bring as many puffers as we can, hope it's all over before—"

"No." Jin stood as straight as she could. She took a breath and let it out slowly. She thought of her last game with Lieutenant Wiesen, where she had found a way to checkmate him by sacrificing her queen. She had had it all worked out; there was no way he could have avoided losing.

Except, she realized, he had. The game was still set up in her room, still going, though they would surely never finish it. He had kept from losing by taking the only move left to him, a move that wasn't even on the board. "Tell them I'm not going to be on the planet," she said.

"If they take you back with them—" Bennett protested.

"Just tell them."

No one spoke as Bennett keyed in the message and sent it. They all watched the satellite images intently, waiting to see if the Fleet would break off. Finally the INCOMING MESSAGE light went on. Biting his lip, Bennett hit OPEN CHANNEL.

"Message received. We will take your offer under advisement." the voice on the other end said.

"That's it," Ande said, nodding. "They'll accept it now."

"What are you going to do?" Bennett asked. "Maybe—maybe the Greyen would take you—"

"I have one more move left," she said.

Jin's heart was in her throat as she waited for the airlock to open, and not just from the ascent to orbit. She reached up for a tether hook to steady her as the air hissed in, the door sliding aside.

Griffin was standing on the other side. "Hi," he said.

"Hi." Yertle launched himself off from her shoulder; less certain, she paused, propelled herself forward. It was not the ship they had come on, but Griffin's ship, the one she had taken passage on so many years ago. Behind him, two of his shipcousins were watching her. She recognized them as Elena and Perun, both of whom had been on the ship when she had last been there. Elena was old, older than any landsider; her face was almost nothing but lines, her nearly translucent hair forming a halo around her skull. She was looking Jin over carefully.

"Eta maya padruga," Griffin said to Elena. He turned to Jin. "She understands Earthlang, but she won't speak it."

"I know. I'll learn."

The Eldest smiled and took an ampoule of dark liquid from Perun. "Vi pete?" she asked.

Jin nodded. "Da." Moving awkwardly forward, she took the offered ampoule, drank deeply and handed it back. Her head, already swimming from the loss of gravity, felt like it had just floated off of her shoulders. Elena put the ampoule to her lips and squeezed it hard until all the liquid was gone.

Griffin reached out to take Jin's hand. "Come on. There's something I want you to see."

"Shouldn't I start learning how to earn my keep?"

"After. You'll want to see this."

Letting Griffin tow her weightless body behind him, Jin drifted into a long corridor in the ship's outer ring. He dragged his foot along the hull to kill their velocity, coming to rest at a porthole. The planet's night side filled the view outside.

"What am I supposed to be seeing?" she asked.

"Wait."

A few minutes later, she saw an arc of light emerge on the planet's right side. It began to slowly spread across the curve of the world until she could see green and blue peek out through yellow clouds.

"That's what you gave them," he said. "That's what you won."

She smiled, bit her lip. He meant well, she knew, but this only reminded her that she could never set foot on that planet, or any other, ever again—at least not as long as the Borderless Empire stood.

Or maybe that was how he wanted her to feel. Maybe he was saying it was time to stop running, stop looking for the next victory around every corner. She turned away from the planet below and saw his gentle smile. *Everything has a price*, the Travellers said. Lieutenant Wiesen had told her the same thing—you have to give up a few pieces in order to win. She had not lost so much, compared to some. She could watch the world she had won grow, though she could not touch it. She was alive. Reaching up to touch his cheek she gave him a half-smile, the best she had to offer.

She was home.

〃 〃

Matthew Johnson has been reading, writing and watching science fiction since the day his mother put him down to watch *Star Trek* when decent folk were going to church. His fiction has appeared in places like *Asimov's Science Fiction*, *Tesseracts Ten* and *Fantasy Magazine*. Stories of his have been reprinted and received honourable mentions in a variety of year's best anthologies, as well as being translated into Czech, Russian and Danish. His story "Public Safety" was nominated for the Sidewise Award for Alternate History.

He lives with his wife Megan and son Leo, in Ottawa, Ontario, where he writes the Talk Media blog for Media Awareness Network as well as developing media education resources such as the Internet literacy tutorial *Passport to the Internet*, which has been adopted in schools in Canada, the US and around the world. His personal blog is www.zatrikion.blogspot.com. *Fall From Earth* is his first novel.